Shadow
of the
Zeppelin

BERNARD ASHLEY

ORCHARD

'Oh, my God!'

Alone in his Royal Flying Corps BE12, Second Lieutenant George Simmonds had never seen anything this big in the sky, menacing above him like something from another world – a huge silvery monster, long, fat, with three gondolas hanging beneath her. She dwarfed him as he banked sharply to try to come up and get a line on her belly, thumb ready on the trigger, planning where he would dive to avoid the beast when she was hit and burst into flames. But as he came out of his banking she was suddenly gone, lost in cloud, and fly and search as he might he didn't get another sighting. Disappointed, his fuel running dangerously low, he had to set his course for base. And when his heart had stopped its racing he shook his fist up at the sky and swore an oath. 'Another time, Menace – another time!'

Shadow of the Zeppelin

ORCHARD BOOKS

338 Euston Road, London NW1 3BH

Orchard Books Australia

Level 17/207 Kent Street, Sydney, NSW 2000

First published in the UK in 2014 by Orchard Books

ISBN 978 1 40832 727 2

Text © Bernard Ashley 2014

The right of Bernard Ashley to be identified as the author of this
work has been asserted by him in accordance with the
Copyright, Designs and Patents Act, 1988.

A CIP catalogue record for this book is available
from the British Library.

1 3 5 7 9 8 6 4 2

Printed in Great Britain

Orchard Books is a division of Hachette Children's Books,
an Hachette UK company.

www.hachette.co.uk

1

There wasn't a moon and there weren't any searchlights but there was a bit of light in the sky, and whether Freddie had heard bombs or not he couldn't remember – but something made him get up from his bed and look out, and there it was! Big, and ghostly, he could hear its engines, like some flying devil from another world. Being May it wasn't warm at night, and the sight of that thing shivered him like winter, up and down his back and round his legs. He dived into bed, pulled up the blankets and lay there scared and angry. The swines! The cowardly Huns!

They'd made life different now. Going to school was the same, so was his mother's job as a midwife, but shopping for her these days meant standing in long queues for food, and in Woolwich there was always the sight of men marching off into the army and the girls going to work in the Arsenal to make bombs and bullets. Houses and pubs were being knocked down and people were being killed and injured, although the bombs weren't dropping around their way. The papers weren't allowed to print where they fell, but up to now they didn't seem to be on this side of the river.

He knew he wasn't old enough yet, but he couldn't wait to leave school. He was on the tall side and his voice was breaking, so quite soon he could tell lies about his age. And his dad had been a boy soldier so why couldn't he be one too? Living close to the Royal Artillery at Woolwich where the gunners trained with horses and field guns, it was soldiers all around him. And if he could get to wear the khaki, wouldn't that put a firecracker up the backside of his big brother? When he wasn't at work, all Will wanted was his boater and his blazer, his lady friend, his gramophone and nights at the music hall. What he didn't want was to go to the war like loads of other boys' brothers. Now excuses for Will were running out, and it made Freddie look like a coward himself when all he wanted to do was get at those bully Germans – and get Wally Quinnell off his own back.

And the Germans needed stopping – dropping their cowardly bombs from airships onto houses and pubs and office buildings. Zeppelins, these monsters were called, and some other sort. His dad worked in the Woolwich Arsenal making shells and bullets, but when he'd been brought home ill from work his mum had packed him off over the water to Poplar to stay with a midwife friend – 'Just for a couple of days, Freddie, while I look to Dad'. The sight of that Zeppelin had scared the fly-buttons off him – and he was dead set on making his brother go and fight the Germans, stop them flying over – or his name wasn't Freddie Castle…

* * *

Ernst Stender sat on his bunk at the Petty Officer's end of the crew hut and read again the letter from his wife. Rachel's words were the most loving she'd written since he'd been called-up – and nothing could ever match the thrill of what she'd kept for the end of her letter.

'By the way, the doctor says we will have a new mouth to feed in the summer. Yes, you are going to be a papa. Imagine our child with your dark hair and my blue eyes! From now on I shall get fatter and fatter, but you will still love me, won't you?

I send you all my love –
Mama-to-be Rachel xxx'

He looked around the hut hoping no one had seen the look on his face. He was going to be a father! He and Rachel had been waiting for this news for some time, but his call-up had left him hoping rather than knowing. The conscription officer had persuaded him to volunteer for this coastal posting where everyone was a fighting man – no longer a boyfriend, or a husband, or a son, or a father – more a sort-of brother to everyone else in the hut. But Rachel's happy letter united him with home and it took his mind to that peaceful place: a quiet district of Berlin where he and Rachel would raise their child in tranquillity when this war was over.

Other crewmen on their bunks were reading, one of

them riffling the pages of his Bible, another deep into a thriller; one was darning a sock, while around the stove – a social centre even when it wasn't lit – a game of cards came and went in noisy bursts. But tonight everyone here would be part of the same operation, and the atmosphere was tense. He concentrated on Rachel's words as he shut out the hut to hear her voice in his head say, 'You're going to be a papa!'

He needed the courage she gave him because he was scared. But now he would be fighting for his child-to-be, too, and he'd have to be brave. What he was going to do that night was going to be done for that special person's future. Germany was at war, and he was assigned to the naval air force, rewarded with the in-between rank of Petty Officer: but why had he let himself be talked into it? Why couldn't he have been a soldier, or a real sailor on a ship? A wounded soldier with his battalion beaten would at least stand a chance of staying alive, he could lie low in a crater or a ditch; and a sailor could try to keep afloat on the wreckage of his ship. But a shot-down flying man was doomed. No parachutes were ever issued so the choice would be to jump or to crash and burn – and what sort of choice was that?

He folded his letter away as his superior Josef Porath came into the hut. The Chief Petty Officer steersman had him and Karl Klee in his team and he'd taken them both under his wing. He sat on the bed beside Ernst, the pair of them leaning forwards, heads bowed like a pair of old friends chatting: Josef bigger and tanned, Ernst pale and wiry with the build of a runner rather than a wrestler.

'I've been to a briefing,' Josef confided. 'The army Schütte-Lanz airships flew last night, tonight it's our turn.' He was a regular serviceman, a northerner with a border-country accent, who took pride in the naval service doing better than the army.

'Where are we going?' Ernst guessed it would be another sortie over the trenches of France, or an attack on a shipping lane in the North Sea.

'London.'

'*What?* We're bombing London?'

'Got to be done, got to be done – carrying more than six tons of TNT and incendiaries.' Despite the noise of the card game the hut suddenly seemed a quiet place to Ernst.

'Docks, and ordnance targets?'

'I'm not allowed to say until we're airborne.'

Ernst understood that. But his only sorties so far had been over France and the sea; he was new to the airship service but they'd picked him for compass steering because his civilian surveyor's job involved calculating distances and angles.

The naval maps showed the munitions factories at Enfield and Woolwich, as well as the string of London docks along the River Thames, so they'd find them all right. The difficulty in this humid weather was targeting any part of southern England in the midst of summer air currents and electric storms off the coast. And what had smacked everyone in the face was the crash of Zeppelin LZ10. It had frozen the blood in Ernst.

The problem had sounded almost routine at first: trouble with an engine. The telegraph operator had received a message to say the airship had fuel-supply difficulties and she wouldn't make her Nordholz base but was heading here to Hage. At this everyone was out, looking into the sky – and he'd thought he'd seen her to the north-east, hovering under a dark storm cloud. But what came next wasn't the LZ10 on a controlled approach. It was a sudden violent flash of flame and an explosion like ten racks of bombs going up.

A Zeppelin in flames was every flier's worst nightmare, and after a long wait the first eye-witness messages came in. LZ10 had been struck by lightning, a jagged flame bursting from the hull as fire engulfed her and sent her into an eighty-degree nose-dive – piling up on the tidal flats and burning to a twisted skeleton. The entire crew was lost – Lieutenant Karl Hirsch and nineteen men – but only eleven charred corpses were found in the wreckage; so the question everyone asked was, had the rest made that other terrible choice and jumped – their bodies lost at sea?

That accident had paralysed his nerve; but Josef had fallen in next to him, walking the flat grass of Hage. 'Put it away, put it away; of course accidents happen.'

'I thought they said fire can't spread inside a Zeppelin skin. It's not as if it's one big hydrogen balloon.' Ernst had counted the sixteen separate cells in their own airship and he knew that if one cell got hit the gas would disperse in the outer envelope. 'That's what they say, isn't it?'

Josef took longer strides than he did and he'd got ahead; now he stopped and lit them both a cigarette. 'Pressure height, Ernst, that's what did it for them, that's where Hirsch was unlucky. His ship got above pressure height, and all her cells started valving gas into the envelope – just as the lightning struck.' Josef put his fingers to his small moustache as if he were adjusting it. 'But with the help of the Lord God, Mathy won't make a mistake like that.'

What Josef had said was like a good friend's arm around his shoulder. A captain with Lieutenant Mathy's reputation would surely keep his airship under the pressure height, wouldn't he? Although that wasn't the only thing that could affect them. They were also in the hands of the weather, and the physics of flight, and of luck, too, as it struck both sides. But one thing was clear in Ernst's mind: help from Josef's Lord God didn't come into things. War on earth was made and its winners were decided by what men did.

2

'Blooming awful time of it, Freddie.'

With a thud his mother put her midwifery bag on the kitchen table. She looked worn out. She could usually call up something of a smile, but right now she looked too done-in to try.

'The baby?' Freddie knew she always felt sad when a baby died – but also how it really got to her when the mother went too. And her face was telling him that was what had happened.

She hung up her coat on the back-door hook. 'Zeppelin! Coward Zeppelin! Wonder you never heard it. One God-Almighty bang a street away, the poor girl was shocked rigid; and the baby, too...'

'Over this side? Zepps over this way?' The nearest a German airship had dropped its bombs up to now was on the other side of the river. Apart from the shopping, living here in Eltham wasn't a lot different from peacetime, unless you were worrying about someone fighting over in France; and thanks to weedy Will that worry hadn't hit their family yet.

'Bomb fell near the Dockside station, just yards away. Wallop! Everything shook like a fairground cake-walk, ceiling down all over the bed...and that poor girl...' His mum turned her face away. She was crying, and she didn't cry. He put his arm around her.

'Poor little blighter. Killed by the war before he even got to have his bum slapped... And the girl went into spasms.'

But was she crying over the mother and the baby, or was it the shock of that Zeppelin? He knew how he'd felt just seeing one.

'Don't you dwell on it, Freddie. They won't dare come over here no more; 'cos if they do we'll have our guns ready this time. Royal Artillery's only up the road, an' you don't get much better protection than that.'

Yes, and Will ought to be up there training with them, sticking up for his country and his family.

She dried her tears and washed her hands, ran an eye over him. 'You had a flannel round your neck?' He nodded and scowled: he was too old to get asked questions like that. 'Then go and get yourself dressed for school.' She put a kettle on the hob. 'How's your dad?' – the question catching him as he was going out of the door.

He didn't know how his dad was. Waking up hungry he'd come straight downstairs to cut himself a slice of bread. But he'd heard him coughing, so he had to be awake.

'I'll see if he wants a cuppa...' Slide out from under a hard question, always the best way; and before his mother could say any more he hurried up the stairs.

His dad was in the big bedroom with the curtains still closed, and at first it was hard to see his face.

'That you, Alice?'

'It's me. Freddie.'

'Oh. Mum not back yet?'

'Just got in.'

'What time…is…it?' Everything his dad said these days was interrupted by wheezes like an old Puffing Billy.

He looked away as his dad was racked with a deep cough.

'About a quarter to eight.'

The cough would end with a big spit into the pot on the far side of the bed, which always made him want to fetch-up himself. To get away from the sounds of it he went over to the window and opened the curtains. 'Cup of tea, Dad?'

'I want free of this devil's dust, that's what.' His dad had been working in the Arsenal on a new sort of ammunition when a train had derailed and hit the corner of the building, covering him in brick dust and choking him with asbestos as the ceiling came down.

Freddie heard him thumping his chest, but weakly. Not wanting to watch, he kept his head turned away, looked out over the gardens at the back.

The coughing had stopped but the voice was hoarse. 'Did Will get off all right?'

Freddie came back to the bed and stood by it. He

wouldn't sit on the edge because his dad said it made him feel 'entombed'.

'Think so. Didn't hear him go.'

Apart from the open spaces for going out to play on this new estate for Arsenal workers, the best thing about the house after moving from Woolwich was that he and Will didn't have to share a bedroom. It had once been fun both in together but up here Freddie was pleased to have a room of his own. Will had turned into someone else who'd lost his 'go' after his new girl friend had come along. He worked at Pryce's the printers in Woolwich; but going by the way their dad looked at Will when he started on about the ink staining his hands, the man must have thought the same way as he did – it was a soft sort of job when there was a war going on.

'Nice and sweet, Freddie, the tea – there's a taste in my mouth I wouldn't wish on my brother Len.'

Freddie frowned. When his uncle's name came up it was never in a nice family way, and mention of him always got a 'Shush!' from his mum.

'You'd wish it on the Kaiser.' He did sit on the bed. 'A Zepp's dropped a bomb right near Mum's work.'

'What? God, she's all right, is she?'

'She's put the kettle on, anyhow.' He'd say nothing about her crying.

'Get her to come up, will you? Have you…put a flannel round your face?'

Not him too! He was too grown up for this. 'Yes, I have.'

'Give us a kiss.'

He leant towards the pale face, seeing the difference in his dad's eyes; they'd gone from being sharp enough to skewer a rat to dull like a milky marble. 'I'll see you at dinnertime.' He kissed his bristly cheek.

'Come in quiet. Mum'll be asleep in your room.'

That was the routine when she was on nights. She'd leave him some sandwiches to eat in the kitchen and go up onto his bed in the back room.

'Ta-ta, then.' He went to the door.

'Get her up here. Didn't think the blighters'd start this side. Blown off course, probably.'

That might be true – blown off course – or that Zepp could have been aiming for the Arsenal, or the barracks up the road. Both a bit close, whichever one it was…

Freddie walked through the estate to Grangehill Road School. It was built like his old Woolwich school – the Babies, the Girls, the Boys – one department on top of the other.

He didn't pick up with any old Woolwich friends on the walk there – he'd missed his mate from two doors down, Don Brewster. It was only a few days since the end of the summer holidays and it still felt strange, coming to school every morning instead of going out for a game on the grass or up the woods. Still, as long as he beat the bell and missed a caning he never minded a walk on his own: there were a lot of things to think about. There was his dad's illness for a start – his mum sent-for to bring him home from the Arsenal one Friday afternoon, just about managing to get him to the tram. Then there was Will's lady friend. He didn't know how Will had met her, but she was a bit older than him and she worked in Cuff's Emporium not far from Pryce's printers. She was pretty but a bit toffee-nosed, and when he'd seen her and Will and some friends going into the Hippodrome as he was going swimming she'd almost led Will away from him, as if Freddie Castle wasn't fit to be known by the likes of them. And Will had definitely changed, he wasn't fun any more, no crazy cartoons of people they knew, and his paint brushes were as dry as dust in a jam jar on his window sill. But the worst thing of all was him still being around. He should have been off fighting the Germans.

Then – and never out of his head for long – there was Wally Quinnell. Quinnell hated him. He lived in Grangehill Road, and with a lot of the others from that side of the school he'd got a bug in his bed about the Arsenal kids from the new houses. He'd got a head like a mallet and had a hard punch on him for anyone who pulled a face at his tangly old jersey; and if he kicked you with his clod-hopping boots you'd feel it for a fortnight.

Big as he was himself, a fight with Quinnell would hurt – hurt badly. And he knew only too well why he'd got it in for him. It was because Quinnell's brother was in the army over in France, and he knew where Will worked in Woolwich – that he hadn't volunteered.

He went through the boys' gate and looked around. He wasn't deliberately dodging Quinnell, but his spirits still took a dive when the boy ran across the playground and stuck his face at him.

''Ere, Castle – heard about the Zepp over Woolwich?'

'Yeah.' And he bet Quinnell's mother hadn't been as close to its bomb as his own mum. But he kept his mouth shut.

'That's why we're walloping Fritz over there, see, to stop all that sort of thing.' The way it sounded, Quinnell's brother was fighting the Germans on his own.

'An' that's why my dad's been making the bullets an' shells to shoot the rotten Zepps down.'

'Not the same, is it?' Quinnell's face was twisted up.

'What's not the same?' The school bell had just stopped ringing, which gave them about thirty seconds to get into their classroom.

'Not the same as being brave – doing what the posters say.'

Freddie knew very well what the posters said – and so did his brother Will, because Pryce's had printed some of them.

Your Chums are Fighting – Why aren't YOU?

WOMEN of BRITAIN SAY – "GO!"

and Lord Kitchener with his big moustache pointing his finger at everyone:

YOU – JOIN YOUR COUNTRY'S ARMY!

'Us Castles are as brave as the Quinnells any old day of the week!'

'Get off! Your brother's gotta be all lily if 'e looks like you – with your floppy hair an' your toffee nose.'

'Least it's not dirty!' *Toffee nose?* Just because it wasn't as squashed as an old spud. And that was all there was time for because the boys' door would shut any moment and then they'd both get the 'late' stick. So he'd had the last word. But what went on churning him was the truth of it – Quinnell was in the right. Will ought to go. With Zepps dropping bombs near their mother's work it was his duty to volunteer. It could only be Miss Amy Margerison who was stopping him. He'd gone all soft on her and he wanted to please her, because if not it meant his brother Will really was a coward, and he didn't like the sound of that word.

3

Freddie was out on the green with his bat and stumps when Will came home from work. Indoors, their mother was getting their tea; later she'd pull her Sunbeam bike out of the shed and ride off to Wood Street. He hated her doing night duty at the maternity hospital, not being at home in the evening, but she had to take her turn.

His dad upstairs would knock on the floor and call for something, and it was him who'd go every time: Will never seemed to hear. Worse, when she was out, Will treated the downstairs as if it was his gentleman's lodgings. Amy Margerison would come round, and they'd want the parlour to themselves to play Will's gramophone – leaving him to sit up at the kitchen table drawing, or to get out the solitaire marbles, or read his *Boys' Own Omnibus* – anything to keep out of their way.

No, Will definitely wasn't the same sort of brother he'd been before. Sharing the bedroom in the old place, he'd been funny, told him things he wasn't supposed to know about men and women and babies, and made him laugh with the cartoons he drew. He was a good artist – it was why old Pryce had taken him on straight from school, because as well as setting type and operating the press Will could design cards and posters – and their mum was proud of that. But these days he left all that behind at work: since he'd met this Amy his pencils were blunt and his secrets went into her ear, not his.

And he shouldn't have still been at home, anyway.

What Freddie enjoyed these days were the summer evenings, a real treat out here. The estate had open spaces in front of some of the houses – which looked more country than London – and the one outside theirs was larger than most, meant to be like a little village green. He and Don and the others bowled at one other, or played hockey with walking sticks, although they mostly stuck to the old games: last-man-in and rough riders where everyone ended up in a heap. But Will coming home from work was always the end of all that. It was wash hands and sit up to tea, and listen to his brother showing off about some latest craze, or telling them who was on next week at the Empire because he'd printed the posters.

But tonight Will was going to the Woolwich Hippodrome – 'The first house, won't be late—' And a good job too, because after what Quinnell did that day Freddie knew he might say something nasty if Will was sitting there smoking and laughing in the parlour. It had been rotten. Quinnell had gone on again about his own brother over in France who he reckoned would probably get a medal from the King – while waving around a pigeon's feather he'd found in the playground and sticking it down the collar of his shirt.

'Pass it on to someone you know. Tell 'im it oughta be white.'

Freddie knew about white feathers, and the women who sometimes dished them out to men who should have been soldiers. Being given a white feather meant being called a coward. And although he'd snapped the feather, thrown it back at Quinnell and walked off – in his heart of hearts he agreed with it. Instead of old Pryce's printing ink Will needed to get a few drops of German blood on his hands; and he might just say so tonight.

Tea was over and he'd done most of the washing-up, while Will went upstairs to cut his inky fingernails and change his shirt. His mother went off to Wood Street and he sat and chatted with his dad about the Arsenal football team, soon to start the new season in the wartime league at Highbury. They'd used to play in Plumstead and it had been good, walking there from Woolwich to go to see a match, shouting for his dad's favourite player, Charlie Lewis. The only trouble was, the ground was near to his grandad's and Uncle Len's house, so they always walked the long way round. They didn't get on, his dad and Len, something from when they'd been young. Grandad and Uncle Len ran a log-selling business, delivering round the houses and pubs, where his dad said Uncle Len was known for getting paid part of their money in ale and sometimes turned nasty.

'Couldn't get me a paper could you, Freddie…? Find out who they're playing Saturday.'

Of course he could – so long as Will could spare himself from the mirror and answer any knocks on the floor while he chased the newsboy round the streets. With a penny in his hand he went to the front door – and, bad luck, it was just as Amy Margerison was lifting the latch on the gate: with a stupid polly-parrot look about her with her flowery hat and flouncy look, just as if she could wave the nasty war away with her fancy gloves.

'Going out on the town, Fred?'

'Getting a paper for Dad.' That was about her level – theatres, music halls and flicks.

'Don't hurry back, will you?' She laughed like a little chirpy bird, pretending she didn't mean it – but he knew she did. And there was something about that stupid hat on the side of her head. What a soppy thing to wear! His mum had gone to do a night's work over at Wood Street and this one was going out on the town. Something welled up inside him like bubbling blood. This polly parrot had taken away a not-bad, funny brother and turned him into a pretend toff who said more to the looking glass than he did to anyone in the house. Wally Quinnell was as proud as punch of his brother; and he was as ashamed as the devil of his.

His head had gone all swimmy, and with a voice

coming out like someone else's he heard himself say it. 'Will's not in yet. He's gone up the Artillery to put his name down for the army.'

'*What?*' A wispy thing on Amy's hat shook like a little leaf.

He started marching on the spot, singing:

'Fall in an' follow me, fall in an' follow me!
You do as I do an' you'll do all right,
Fall in an' follow me!'

He knew he looked stupid, and straight away he wanted her to know it had only been a joke. 'See your face!' But it hadn't been a joke, and definitely not a funny one. And didn't it make *him* the coward for getting at Will through her? He should have said things to his brother straight, man to man.

'Is he in or isn't he?'

'He's in.'

'Then why did you say he'd gone up the Artillery to put his name down? Why should he volunteer? You're too young to know, but this is a stupid war.' She stood on the doorstep poking at him. 'We're only in it because we're friends with France, and France is only in it because they're friends with Russia. Our argument isn't with the Germans at all…'

'Oh, the dear ol' Germans! Well, it bloomin' is when

26

they're dropping bombs near my mum!'

'Will agrees with me, why put lives on the line for the sake of governments? He certainly won't go unless they conscript him, and I'll back him all the way to Timbuktu.'

She didn't sound so soppy now. But he wasn't stupid, either. 'What about when German soldiers come marching down your street?' He'd heard his mum and dad talking about the Kaiser's men invading across the sea, or troops dropping down from Zeppelins on ropes. 'What about then?'

'*Oi!*'

He twisted round. Will was at the parlour window. 'What's going on out there?'

'Your little brother. Has he told you? He wants you up at the barracks, volunteering…'

Hell-'n'-hailstones! Why couldn't he take back what he'd said? Now her stupid hat and lah-di-dah ways had got him into hot water, a lot hotter than if he'd come out with things straight.

'Oh, yes?' Will pushed the window open wider. 'And what's it to you what I do?' His face was suddenly swollen, his eyes staring. 'Are you getting at me, Fred Castle?'

If only he'd ignored Amy coming here looking stupid and just run off for his dad's paper. Now there'd be a war indoors. Amy was shaking her head at the cheek of him, that wispy thing on her hat quivering again – and he could see what it was: a small, thin feather. *A feather*.

And, no, he wasn't running off just yet. 'I got given one of them for you today!' He pointed at Amy's hat.

'A lady's hat? What's this? You got given a lady's hat for me?' Will's voice squeaked like a bat's.

'Not a hat, a *feather*. Not a white one, but it was meant to be. A boy at school gave me a white feather to give to you.' There. He'd said it. Will had to know the truth. It was only a shame about the stupid joke with Amy Margerison.

Will slammed the window shut. Amy turned to close the gate and stood waiting to be let through the front door. And he ran off to find the paperboy – deciding that he'd walk home very slowly, and hope the two of them had gone out by the time he got back. Then he'd go to bed early and try to be asleep by the time Will's key went into the lock. He might feel ashamed of his brother – but he hadn't been very clever about dealing with it, had he?

4

Three weeks and four missions later, Ernst had learned an important lesson. Today he had drunk nothing for a couple of hours. He didn't want to have to climb the ladder from the control gondola to the latrines if he could help it. It was a chancy business getting up into the hull when they were fifteen kilometres above the ground in the dark: the canvas chute around the ladder gave no real protection from the cold, and frozen hands and thick gloves made holding-on hazardous, so with the airship dodging the searchlights at over fifty knots there was a real danger of falling back onto the gondola hatch. Besides, how did you tell your commander to hold off aiming the bombs while his helmsman had a pee?

The ground crew pulled Naval Zeppelin L13 from her shed, facing her into the prevailing wind for the ascent. From his commanding position in the gondola, Lieutenant Mathy was overseeing the pre-flight checks on the airship's systems while the Executive Officer controlled the manoeuvring of the craft on the ground. Together the airship's two gondolas carried sixteen men – seven including him and Josef and Karl Klee in the control cabin, with him on the wheel for compass steering and Karl on the elevator wheel. At various times men would climb up into the hull, then on up the internal ladder or along the walkways inside the vast outer skin – the sail-maker to repair a tear in the canvas, or spare ballast crew to man the machine guns on the roof platform. But over the trenches the previous week the airship had been flying at an extreme height to get out of range of the French big guns, and in the thin air the hull had got so cold and the breathing so difficult that a man from their hut had fallen exhausted from the ladder and broken his neck. Thanks to God, Ernst's steering job kept him down in the gondola – until he needed a pee…

What everyone knew was that for the first time tonight they were carrying a three-hundred-kilo bomb with 'Love Gift' chalked on its girth, Mathy's name for it. Ernst could only imagine the sudden lift of the airship when that monster was let-go; unless they were all holding on tight in the gondolas it would be like someone tipping up a box of toy soldiers. Zeppelins and their bombs were all about size – and about fear. Looking at the huge L13 made his head go swimmy. A hundred and fifty metres long and nearly fifteen metres wide, she was like a creature out of some mad scientist's imagination.

Josef put his arms around both him and Karl. 'The army say they had a good night last night. London, north and south. Today they're crowing all over the wires – but be very sure, boys, we're going to finish what they started.'

'We hope.' Karl looked away. 'We hope.' He acted a

30

bit superior sometimes, as if he knew things that others didn't.

'We'll do more than they ever could – we're going to hit London in the market district and at St Paul's. Deny their stomachs and kill their souls!' He took his arms off their shoulders and adjusted his small moustache. 'Got to be done, got to be done. What the army only scratches at, the navy destroys.'

But Ernst wasn't worried about Josef's army-navy rivalry; it was their target that night that troubled him. London. When he'd volunteered for airships Zepps were bombing military and naval targets only – the Kaiser had forbidden air attacks on the British capital, but now he was ordering its destruction. And Josef could say what he liked about hitting stomachs and souls; if they bombed London it would mean killing ordinary people like Rachel back in their quiet quarter of Berlin.

Away with those dark thoughts! Such thinking wasn't good for a brave man who wanted to help to win the war.

By 16:30 the L13 was lifting off. The Executive Officer had given the order and the tethering ropes were released. The hydrogen cells inside the hull would be expanding as the ship rose clear of the mooring tower, her engines already spinning their propellers to take her up and out over the coast, dipping and yawing as the elevator men up in the hull worked the ballast to steady her, he and Karl holding their ships' wheels, him for direction, Karl for elevation. After hours of planning and preparation they were heading for their target.

Word on the radio said that L11 and L14 were lifting off from Nordholz, the three of them heading south-west towards England's east coast, climbing steadily with men posted up top on their machine-gun platforms on the look-out for enemy fighters. Maybe bullets couldn't blow up the hydrogen cells, but Royal Flying Corps planes could still strafe the gondolas or the engines and leave an airship to drift off who-knows-where. But Ernst took heart from his memories of children's fairground balloons rising above everything; in minutes L13 could climb to heights the British aeroplanes would take an hour to reach.

By 20:35 they were over the Norfolk coast at Wells-next-the-Sea. In his thick under-clothing, his flying suit, helmet and gloves – but still shivering in the cold – he stared down through the mica window at the seaport below, its street lights glowing in the dusk.

'Cut engines to a third!' Mathy's command was relayed to the engine machinists. 'Keep her steady into the wind. We'll hold off for an hour till dark.'

'Lieutenant.'

Such clever thinking. So far they'd not been attacked, but they would certainly have been seen, and likely inland targets would have been warned that they were coming. But when darkness fell the ship would be invisible unless a searchlight found her. It wasn't so much the enemy defences that scared Ernst, though. Holding their Zepp off the coast was a good tactic against artillery – but what he'd be looking and listening for were sounds of thunder and flashes of lightning – any sign of a coastal summer storm. Carrying no parachutes saved weight, to carry a few more bombs and to allow more lift in getting out of danger – but if they were hit the crew had that terrible choice: to jump or to burn, this death or that – and no one would ever forget what had happened to the men of L10.

There was a sudden clatter of feet and a knocking on the gondola hatch. A look-out from the machine-gun platform came clambering down. 'Information to report, sir. L14 has turned three-sixty degrees, heading north-east. And we're icing up ourselves.'

Mathy's face didn't change. 'Thank you. Return to your post.'

So there were problems. L14 had turned for home. Ice could damage any airship; it came off all their hulls in the freezing high altitude temperatures, and shards were known to spear engines and rudders.

Mathy stuck out his chin. 'So we shall do the work of two!'

And now, damn it, Ernst wanted to pee.

At last Mathy gave the order to proceed south-west, and by 21:45 they were cruising over King's Lynn, following the Bedford Canal, which was clear on the maps and easy to follow by the lights of small villages. Ernst pictured what it might be like down there: a warm September evening with a few farmhands in one of those English taverns drinking beer. But snap out of that! Peace-time for them and for everyone else was a long way back…

'Ha!' Mathy was pointing to the south, an incredulous look on his face. Cruising over Cambridge at 2,600 metres, there on the southern horizon they could see the glow of London, ninety kilometres away. 'Look at the English – still too stupid to black-out their lights!'

The moon was a new sliver but there was just enough light in the sky for them to pick up the London road from Buntingford to Ware, at which point Mathy ordered a change of course to give them a north-westerly approach, dropping five small bombs over the countryside to check the accuracy of the bombsight. So far, so good. But that was the end of a quiet approach. As they came in over the north London suburbs there was a sudden flashing of guns from the ground – shells exploding low and harmless – but in his head Ernst saw a monster gun down there to combat Mathy's 'love gift' bomb, some huge thing that could make the height, hit the hull, explode the hydrogen, and send them diving down to their deaths...

Knuckle-head! Such an imagination. Why had he been born with it? Better the sort of cold knowledge Mathy had.

'There – Regent's Park.'

His eyes followed the lieutenant's arm and picked out its broad spread. But now he was in crisis. He'd wanted to pee for over an hour; and just as the bombing action was hotting up he was almost wetting his trousers. Could it have come at a worse time? So, what to do? Speak up and feel a schnook in front of Klee and his commander, or disgrace himself all over the gondola floor?

'Sir, I need to go above.' The lieutenant's scorn would be better than steering the airship standing in his own wet.

'Be quick, then! Klee, take over.'

Karl left his elevator wheel and took the helm as Ernst opened the hatch and started to climb the ladder to the hull, reaching up into the canvas chute. Mathy had reduced speed to thirty knots ready for bombing but even so the slipstream tore at the protection as he gripped tight for his life. Slowly he climbed the rungs, just these two trembling hands in their thick gloves keeping him from falling.

And suddenly the chute went. A shard of ice must have torn the canvas, and in the speed and bluster it was giving way, the wind tearing into it, ripping it off like tissue paper from a toy kite. Within seconds the canvas was flapping behind the ladder – just as a blinding white searchlight pinned him in its beam. 'Help!' Clinging there like a paralysed moth his stomach turned, his head went light and his body froze. Below him the engines kicked and the airship lifted nose-first as she surged for the cover of cloud above. But in the jolt his left hand lost its hold and he had to fight with everything he had to hang on, his body twisting him inside out. Both feet had lost the rungs and as the ship climbed higher and faster he dangled there in the emptiness, kicking to find some sort of support. If not, he was going to lose it – he was going to fall…

But his right foot found a rung, and then his left, and as he hung on hooking an arm through the ladder he realised what he'd done; he'd wet himself. The warm stream got through to his skin – and now there was no need to climb into the hull. He clung on as the ship found cloud, levelled off and cut her speed, and before his hands froze too much for him to hang on any longer, he clambered down the ladder.

They may have been surprised inside the gondola to ever see him again, but no one said anything other than shake their heads at news of the chute splitting. Mathy was too intent on turning to the attack; and if Karl or Josef noticed his wet trousers they were too decent to say anything about it.

Turning back and coming in from the north-west, Mathy dropped their explosive bombs – the first to be aimed at central London, a string of them as he headed the airship west. Josef called out locations from the map of London – Farringdon, Aldersgate, Moorgate, Holborn – the sight of railway lines making it clear that Mathy was aiming at the transport network.

But the big moment was when Mathy suddenly gave the order for the dropping of his 'love gift' over this busy part of London – the bomb so heavy that as it was released the nose shot upwards, just as Ernst had foreseen.

He gripped hard at his wheel and looked out. The three-hundred-kilo bomb teetered, fins already screeching, righting itself quickly and falling in a vertical to explode among the built-up streets below. There was a booming flash, flames lit up the sky, and before thick smoke could veil the destruction he saw the buildings that were no more, sockets on the ground; and he knew that what he couldn't see were the people they had killed and maimed, ordinary Londoners out and about like Berliners on a Friday night.

A sudden dazzle of searchlights hit the ship. The blast from a bursting shell buffeted the gondola, but Mathy held their course and made sure that his final four bombs were aimed at Liverpool Street station. And only now did they turn north for home, climbing fast so they could hide in cloud.

Ernst kept a firm grip on his wheel, but those shells had been too close, his chest hurt and he had trouble breathing – and he hoped to heaven that no one could see his shaking hands, and that they wouldn't know it wasn't his legs being wet that was troubling him but the way they'd gone to straw. He never wanted to have to climb that ladder again. He never wanted to fly again. He wanted this war over as quickly as possible – the Germans victorious, of course – but now he was firm in his mind: whoever had to suffer in England, whether they were soldiers at their guns or old men in their beds, or families like his in their suburbs, for a quick surrender by the British he would help Mathy drop hundreds of 'love gifts' on them. All stupid feelings of humanity had to be banished from his head. This war had got to be won at all costs – right? Of course right!

5

Freddie went out after tea with Don and a few others. Will was going out again with Amy, the Holborn Empire tonight, second house, but it was what happened before he went that drove Freddie out. He was in his bedroom sorting some Firefly comics, his door slightly open.

Their mother was saying cheerio to their dad before going off to Wood Street, and their bedroom door wasn't quite closed as Will dived in and out of the bathroom, combing his glossy hair and cleaning his teeth. And in one of his dad's rare loud moments he could clearly be heard.

'I wish I was a younger man, Alice – and rid of all this...' He coughed, and his voice went quieter. 'Because I wouldn't be lying here and I wouldn't be working on new-fangled bullets in the Arsenal, I'd be shooting them.'

'Our boys need all the bullets they can get, Sam – and you'll be back making them before you can say cheese. You've done your country's soldiering bit.'

Freddie wanted to creep to his door and close it. It upset him to hear his dad feeling sorry for himself.

'I was a lad with a fighting spirit in my day... An' that's what they...need at the Front right now. Lads with fighting spirit in their hearts... I'd bloomin' go if I could.'

The bathroom door shut with a great bang; and now Freddie did get across to shut his own. His dad might have meant to be heard, or he might not; but Will had definitely got the message – which boiled down to what his dad thought of him, the first time he'd come out with it – and at the first chance Freddie nipped down the stairs and took himself off.

From behind a tree he watched Will come out and go hurrying up to the tram stop, looking every bit the lah-di-dah, off to a show. He copied the way the toffs went about, nose in the air, saying the sayings, whistling the tunes, his fair hair all floppy. He seemed to fancy himself on the Holborn Empire stage himself. And Freddie wondered what it must feel like to know your dad thought you weren't up to being the man he was. And it wasn't nice. It wasn't nice at all.

Will knew he was being quiet, but there was plenty of buzz on the Waterloo tram, filled with people heading into London for a good night out – and thank heavens for that: Amy seemed quite content listening to what was going on around her while he had a think. The kerfuffle with Fred the other day had been upsetting, but what his dad had said tonight was worse – and he needed time to get over it, try to get himself back in the mood for their treat at the Holborn Empire – complimentary tickets from Mr Pryce in good seats for a top show.

Some people just didn't understand. Amy was right about this war, even though men were rushing to go off. It wasn't Britain's to fight. Germany had attacked Belgium and then France, but Britain didn't need to be involved, did it? He'd got a good job, a lovely lady friend, and with nights like this he liked the life he led. Why would anyone with two-ha'p'orths of common sense want to go and get killed over there to help one foreign country kick back at another? All right, the Germans had sent some Zeppelins over England to frighten people, but when all was said and done they didn't amount to much. Tons more houses got burnt down by accident with boilers or gas pipes than got hit by any bombs. It wasn't as if Fritz was marching down Woolwich High Street, or flying his colours from the flagpole on Buckingham Palace.

He looked around the tram, and no one would think there was a war going on. Most people were in their best clothes, talking loudly, with someone whistling a tune that wasn't 'Tipperary' but 'When You Wore a Tulip' – and that was the way it should be, no matter what Fred or their dad or anyone else thought. What were they all doing? Just running to the bugle call, too fired up to think. He patted Amy's hand and they smiled at each other. What a beautiful face. What a princess she was – and she gave him the heart to do what he was doing, keeping him firm in their stand against the war-mongers.

She kept telling him how brave it was *not* to volunteer and to stand up to the sneers of people who thought he should. And, as she said, there was more than one sort of bravery in this world, wasn't there – like sticking to your principles?

Mark Sheridan – on stage in his top hat, frock coat and flared trousers – had the audience where he wanted it as he sang his famous song:

> *'Oh! I do like to be beside the seaside*
> *I do like to be beside the sea!*
> *I do like to stroll upon the Prom, Prom, Prom!*
> *Where the brass bands play:*
> *"Tiddely-om-pom-pom!"…'*

In the grand circle Will and Amy squeezed hands. Sheridan was a top music hall performer, and here he was right in front of them. Two complimentary tickets sitting in the dressy second-house audience.

> *'So just let me be beside the seaside*
> *I'll be beside myself with glee*
> *And there's lots of girls beside,*
> *I should like to be beside*
> *Beside the seaside!*
> *Beside the sea!'*

'Not for me!' he whispered. "Long as I'm beside you!'
He took a look at Amy in her smart straw boater and
high-necked lace blouse. No one would know they'd
come from Woolwich on a tram and not in a hackney
carriage.

Sheridan closed the first half of his new 'Winkles'
revue with a hilarious song and dance to '*Sur le Pont
d'Avignon*', where he was something different in every
verse – a '*monsieur*', a '*belle dame*', a '*militaire*', and a
'*musicien*' on a miniature violin. At the end of each take-
off everyone joined in the well-known chorus:

> '*Sur le pont d'Avignon*
> *L'on y danse, l'on y danse*
> *Sur le pont d'Avignon*
> *L'on y danse tous en rond.*'

'Fancy a glass of lemonade?' As they got their breath
back Will jingled some change in his pocket.

'Only lemonade.'

'Of course.'

He led her to the lounge bar at the rear of the grand
circle. The whole theatre was lush, with deep carpets and
silk wall panels, and everyone knew the grand circle
lounge bar at the Holborn Empire was the place to be
seen. Amy was elegant and beautiful, and he felt proud
as he went forward for their drinks.

But he didn't get to order them. A tall woman in black suddenly came across the lounge to stand between him and the bar.

'Young man, are you a soldier on leave and out of uniform?' She had a loud voice that went into him.

'Excuse me, please.' He tried to move forward around her. Not another one! Not here, tonight.

'Do you have a "King and Country" badge somewhere on your lapel, or a card to say you're waiting for the call?'

He hadn't. His job at Pryce's didn't qualify for the war-worker badge his father carried from the Arsenal, nor had he volunteered and was only waiting to be called up. 'Please stand aside, madam.'

The lounge had gone very quiet now, even the bar staff had stopped serving while everyone watched to see how this would end. His stomach rolled, these demonstrations were always difficult – but he'd got to summon up Amy's resolve and keep his head high.

'Instead of gallivanting at the music hall you should be serving your king and your country over in France. And I therefore present you with this!' With a flourish the woman brought up her hand and showed what she'd kept hidden in the folds of her skirt. What he'd expected – a white feather. As if holding a fan that she might snap open she presented it in front of his face. 'Take it.'

'No thank you.' He turned back to Amy.

Amy pulled him away. 'Come on! Leave the lady to her pantomime.' And she led him out of the lounge.

'You're a coward, young man!'

They went towards the auditorium but he stopped short of the doors. 'Do you want to go home?' It was quite late and trams would be scarce when the second house ended. 'At least we've seen Sheridan in the flesh...'

Amy straightened her boater. 'I think so. If he sings his "Kaiser and the Belgians" song they'll all break their necks to look at you.'

They turned from the grand circle and walked to the foyer, Amy following him slowly in her hobble skirt. But he was just about to grasp the handles on the glass doors when a great rush of air hit him and a huge explosion suddenly rocked the theatre. He felt his legs fly from under him as the blast threw him back to collide with Amy – who took the full force of the glass doors in her face. She fell screaming as people ran in panic from the grand circle, him fighting them to get to her, desperate to drag her to one side as she lay clutching at herself.

'You're all right! You're all right! Let me look.' It was bad, he knew it was bad.

She went on screaming, reaching out with hands that smeared the silk wall with blood. And he stared. Her beautiful face was one mess of blood and cuts and splinters of glass; her eyes were closed – but had she shut them in time? People trampled past as he slid down the wall beside her and nursed her, coaxed her, quietened her, telling her over and over that she was going to be all right.

'Don't try to open your eyes. Wait for help.' He looked around where some people were actually queueing for their coats from the cloakroom – just as a second explosion rocked the place again, and another, and another. Coats were left where they were. People didn't know whether to run in or run out of the building.

'Hold her, please! I'm getting help.' He gave Amy over to an usher and ran through the foyer into the street, it was all he could do; what else? He'd got to get help from somewhere. Outside it was all screams and shouts and artillery fire, everywhere was mayhem, people running, chasing cabs – all looking up to the shell bursts and searchlights in the sky; and there, caught in two beams was a sight that dropped his stomach: a Zeppelin, garish yellow in the glare, hovering up there like a monster from hell, its black shadow projected up across a cloud.

A street-accident ambulance came weaving through the blast damage. The bomb must have fallen a street away, but here slates and glass and bits of balustrade were everywhere. He waved at it but it wouldn't stop. He looked around frantically. There were no police in sight so he ran back into the theatre – where Amy was sitting on the floor with her back to the wall being attended to by a woman in black.

'Open them gently, see if you can open your eyes.' The woman dabbed at Amy's cuts with her handkerchief. 'We must leave the glass where it is, not pull at it; it will require tweezers, and patience.' She stroked Amy's brow.

Amy was whimpering but she had quietened down, seemed all screamed-out.

'If you can't open your eyes I shall bandage them for your comfort.' The woman took a black silk stole from around her shoulders.

He bent to Amy, her eyes still closed; he held her hand.

'It's Will.'

'Will…'

'See if you can open your eyes for me. See if you can…'

He knew the moment was critical, which the woman in black seemed to understand.

'The reflex would be to shut them,' she said, 'and there are cuts on the lids. So with any luck…'

Slowly, fluttering her hands as if she was hardly daring to do it, Amy opened her eyes. Both eyes.

'Good girl. Can you see me?' He put his face in front of hers.

Almost imperceptibly Amy nodded.

'How many heads have I got?'

'Just the one.'

The woman in black stood up. 'Then we must thank God for that. I shall call my carriage and have you taken to a hospital.' Now she looked at him.

Of course, he knew who she was. Only a few minutes before, she'd tried to give him a white feather.

'Thank you very much…'

'Mrs Brillington.'

'We're very grateful, Mrs Brillington.'

She lifted her chin at him. 'And you are…?'

'William Castle.' There was a long silence, the two of them looking at one other, then down at Amy. He bent to lift her to her feet. 'William Castle,' he went on, slightly raising his voice, 'of the Royal Artillery.'

'The Royal Artillery? I'm so very sorry.' Mrs Brillington's face showed how embarrassed she was.

He had got Amy to her feet, was holding her beneath an arm as Mrs Brillington took her other side.

'You should have said, William. I didn't know…'

'I didn't know either.' And he hadn't – up to that moment. The three of them edged towards the foyer doors. 'I'll be in the Royal Artillery by tomorrow, or whenever they'll take me. Forget all the right and wrong arguments, no one does this to my girl without me doing something about it.'

They went out of the theatre for Mrs Brillington to call up her carriage.

'Then God go with you, William.' She pulled a small gospel from her handbag and gave it to him. 'May the devil take them – this is a very dirty way to fight a war.'

They spent two hours in the Charing Cross Hospital, Amy having the glass taken from her face. They told her she was one of the lucky ones; her eyes had been spared, while five people had been brought in dead, three of them children. They dabbed her with iodine and let him take her home in a cab, while others in the hospital would be there for a very long time.

And he knew that this certainly *was* their war. They were under attack, just like the Belgians and the French – and he wasn't being patriotic for Mrs Brillington. Tomorrow he was going to put himself forward to start fighting back.

Freddie went with Will to Woolwich Town Hall that Saturday morning, up the steps and into the marble entrance where a statue of Queen Victoria stared through them.

'Crikey, she's got the grumps! You wouldn't think I've come to volunteer.'

A town hall attendant nodded his head at Will and pointed to a table at the side where a soldier was sitting, a big man with medals on his chest and an inkpot and paper in front of him.

'Have ye come to enlist, laddie?'

'Yes, sir.'

'Sar'nt. Wha's your name?'

'William Castle.'

'Castle, William.' The sergeant dipped his pen into the inkpot and wrote carefully on an official form, blotting every word of Will's name, address, next-of-kin and civilian job as he went. Will was taking little glances around the town hall as if he was looking for a quick way out.

'This is ye're attestation form. I've signed it here, and ye'll sign it there.' The sergeant swivelled the form around for Will to read and sign, dipping the pen in the ink for him. 'Then ye'll tek yeself through yon door to see the medic...' He pointed to a door with 'Medical Room' pinned on it. 'An' then ye'll march back here to me.'

'Yes, sir.'

'*Sarn't!* Ye'll need to learn a lot faster if you want to serve in the Royal Artillery, laddie.'

'I'm sorry. Sergeant.' Will straightened up from signing and went across the marble floor, knocking on the medic's door and being let in.

The Royal Artillery sergeant was a fierce-looking man, a man of action with fingers that made his pen look like a matchstick.

'Come out fra' behind that pillar, laddie, an' I'll tell ye what's what.'

Freddie came out. The man wasn't busy; it didn't seem as if there was much volunteering going on, Will was the only recruit in there.

'Don' fret, you won't be goin' home alone, he's a way off bein' a soldier yet. If he passes fit he'll get the King's Shilling an' he'll await his joining instructions and travel warrant. Then ye can say your adieus.'

'What's a travel warrant?' He thought he should know, for passing on to Will.

'An army railway ticket.'

'Won't he just go up to the barracks?' He cocked his head in the direction of the Royal Artillery buildings at the top of the road.

'He'll be put where we need replacements.' The sergeant grinned. 'Filling some dead man's boots.'

He didn't like the sound of that. The *Kentish Independent* newspaper had pictures every week of local dead and alive soldiers, with bits about what they'd done – won medals or gone missing, or been taken prisoner, or 'laid down their lives for their country', sounding as if they were knives and forks.

The sergeant suddenly stood up, twisted himself inside his uniform, pulled down his tunic, and made his strapping creak. 'It's a good career, the army. Regular pay, regular food, regular comrades…'

And regular getting killed. But that didn't stop Freddie wanting to go himself.

'… Something to think on when ye're a bit older.'

Definitely. Half a chance and he'd be in here like a shot. His dad had been a soldier, and now his brother was ready to fight the enemy, who were dropping bombs on London and killing his mum's mothers and babies. The Hun needed fighting and getting beaten, and he wanted to be one of those who did it.

The door to the medical room opened and Will came out, adjusting his starched collar. He put a thumb up to Freddie and walked smartly over to the sergeant to give him a slip of paper.

'"Fit for service", laddie. Your attestation form will be countersigned by a Justice of the Peace this afternoon.' The sergeant bent to a drawer and took out a silver coin. 'And here's your King's Shilling, Castle.'

The coin was handed over, which Will dropped into his blazer pocket. It seemed a bit ordinary, like being given change in a shop; at least a bugle and a drum ought to be part of the King's Shilling business.

'Up straight, soldier! About…turn!'

Will turned smartly about. They did this sort of drill in school so Freddie did the same, a few paces behind him, bringing his boot down with a nice loud crack on the marble floor.

'March off and await your joining instructions.'

'Yes, Sergeant.'

Will marched down the hall towards the street, Freddie behind muttering, 'Left, right; left, right; left, right...' But he knew this wasn't any boys' game – Will seemed like a soldier already: his shoulders pulled back, his arms swinging straight, and his chin pushed forward as if he couldn't wait to get into battle. If he was nervous about joining the army he wasn't showing it, and Freddie tingled with pride. From this moment on their family's life would be different. It wouldn't be 'The Sunshine Girl' on the gramophone in the parlour, it would be Will's bedroom lying empty and them waiting for news from the Front. His brother might not have a uniform or a regiment yet; but he'd taken the King's Shilling so he was a soldier now; and there was no going back on that.

6

Ernst felt grateful. If Josef knew about him wetting himself on the ladder he made nothing of it; he was a good friend, the difference in rank between them was something that showed itself only on duty; while Karl was probably too superior to say anything vulgar. His right eyebrow was permanently raised as if he'd just had a slight surprise – it put Ernst in mind of a man who wore a monocle but had left it on his dressing table. Besides, everyone knew how danger and fear could make men shame themselves in much more disgusting ways; and the worst way of all would be to go into a funk and pretend to be ill. Instead, he took deep breaths and great pride in being a regular crew member of Zeppelin L13, serving under a brilliant man like Lieutenant Mathy. That 'love gift' raid on London had made the man a hero in all the German newspapers, and Petty Officer Ernst Stender had been part of it, serving under him in the same gondola. When the war was won he'd tell his son or his daughter about it; and who knew, if raids went on like that, perhaps he'd get an Iron Cross for the child to play with.

'London again tonight,' they all said. Rumour ran through the huts quickly. The attack would involve the crews of three airships. Ernst took himself off to a quiet corner of the mess hall and wrote a letter to Rachel and his unborn child, leaving it prominent in his locker. And always in his head was that old, scary question. *Jump or burn?* What would he do if the ship was hit and the gas exploded? It would incinerate the hull, the Zepp would nose-dive, and there'd be no chance of anyone surviving unless they were close to the ground. So, what *would* he do if it came to it?

Jumping would be quicker and less painful than burning to death, and at least there'd be an identifiable body to be buried; while in a hydrogen fire the heat would turn a dog tag to a molten lump, and one day Rachel might stand weeping at the wrong grave altogether. But there was another thing he had to think hard about. Jumping to his death would be suicide, even if it was the enemy's action that made him do it. It would be his choice. And he knew what some sects of his religion said about that. Some stricter religious leaders said that a suicide should be buried in a special part of the cemetery – which meant that for all time he might not be allowed to lie near his parents nor next to his dear Rachel.

Just then Josef walked into the mess hall, saw Ernst and came over to him. 'There's a face on you, Ernst! You're not dead yet, you know.'

Could Josef read minds now?

'"Jump or burn?" Josef. "Jump or burn?" I was

thinking about what I would do...'

Josef looked quite decided about it. 'There's no question, Ernst – depending on the height of the airship, mind. If we're kilometres high, you jump: it's quicker, and there's no pain until you hit the ground, when you're probably unconscious anyway...'

That would be consoling for anyone allowed to jump, Ernst thought.

'...But if we're close to the ground you could hang on and take your chances. So, you wait and see...'

But it didn't really address Ernst's problem. 'Even if I wait, and I jump at the last second, it's still committing suicide, isn't it?'

Josef shrugged. 'So? You're dead anyway.'

Ernst was frowning, though, and Josef sat them both in chairs at a mess table. 'What is it, then? We all think about "jump or burn", but what's especially bothering you?'

Ernst faced him, cleared his throat. 'Some people of my religion believe that if you commit suicide you aren't entitled to be buried in the same part of the cemetery as people who die in other ways. It's an eternal sin...'

Josef adjusted his moustache.

'...Not everyone thinks like that,' he went on, 'some think it's nonsense, that there's no problem; as far as I can tell it all depends where you worship, but I believe that's what would happen to me.' He looked into Josef's kindly eyes. 'I believe that if I were to jump I would not be entitled to be laid to rest in the same grave as my Rachel.'

Josef had a quick answer. 'Perhaps she could choose to be with you instead, on your side of the wall. If it's got to be done, it's got to be done.' He patted Ernst on the shoulder, made to get up. 'But this is all morbid talk. It won't happen, anyway; don't bother your head with it. Or bother your head when the time comes and leave it for now.' He got up but bent his face towards him. 'Life's too short.'

Which sounded entirely the wrong thing to say.

'What religion believes that, anyway? I've never heard of it.'

'My religion.'

'And what denomination are you? I've never seen where you go. I know you don't come with me to Padre's Hour.'

Ernst stood up, too, and lifted his head. 'I'm Jewish, Josef. I don't make anything of it, I don't wear the skull cap or the shawl; in here I choose my food without making a fuss; I'm not very orthodox – but I belong to the synagogue at Fasanen Street in West Berlin – and I do know that the rabbi would segregate a suicide.'

'Ah, well, then. Do what you have to do when the time comes.' Josef smiled a big smile. 'But it won't come, Erno, it won't come. Believe me.'

And that cheered Ernst, because Josef had never called him Erno before.

He changed the subject. 'London again, then?'

'You've heard right – London. But I don't like the look of the weather.' Josef adjusted his moustache. 'Storms forecast over the sea…'

'Damn.' He feared lightning more than shells, but he wouldn't let Josef know that.

'No problem, we're with the redoubtable Mathy. With the help of God he'll steer us clear of trouble.'

And it would be Ernst's own hands on the wheel to obey the hero's orders. He knew his pride was a weak foe in facing up to his fears, though, and he spent the next hours sweating about not being shown-up for a coward that night.

As darkness began to fall, Second Lieutenant George Simmonds of No. 39 Squadron, Royal Flying Corps, was in the pilot's seat of his BE2 at the end of the Sutton's Farm runway, east of London. His observer, Sergeant Philip Scott, was in the seat in front of him, and with them in the biplane were six carcass bombs, twelve grenades, one hundred and fifty Ranken darts and five powder bombs. They were ready for take-off because radio intelligence had picked up a Zeppelin heading for the south of England – probably targeting London again – and Simmonds' plane was ready to take off and climb to meet her. But Simmonds knew the BE2 would only just make the eight to ten thousand feet the airships flew at, so carrying most of that ammunition was probably a waste of fuel – bombs and darts had to be dropped onto the tops of airships if they were going to set their hydrogen alight, which meant the planes had to get higher than they were; while the Hale grenades, shot from a rifle by Scott, would mean flying well within the range of the raider's machine guns. In any case, the rate of the BE2's climb meant it took fifty minutes to reach ten thousand feet, so the best chance of a kill was to catch the blighters flying home and stop them from ever coming back.

They both knew the danger they were in. It was only twelve years since the Wright brothers had first lifted the Flyer off the ground at Kitty Hawk, and while engines and designs had changed, the world hadn't. It still got dark at night; and while going up was fairly straightforward, coming safely down again was never easy.

A flash lamp from the flight hut told him that 'opps' had cleared him to take off. He opened the throttle of his V-8 engine, got the thumbs up from his observer, and heading west he bumped the BE2 along the runway until it rose into the air and he could set about climbing in spirals to get to his fighting height. There was hardly any moon so he was hoping the boys on the searchlights would find what he was looking for. But he knew that unless the Zepp came in low to get its bearings the chances of a kill were pretty slim. His next priority after that would be to land his BE2 in darkness; and that wouldn't be a walk in the park.

Seeing the storm ahead, Ernst wished he was on one of the other airships. They'd been flying to port and starboard of L13, slightly aft; but not any more. The sight of flashing in the dark clouds must have made them play for safety, and they were turning about and heading for home. So would Mathy do the same? No such luck. He gave no orders to change course, and the jut of his jaw could have spoken for him.

'Sou'-sou'-west-two-two-three.'

'Lieutenant.' From the compass he could see how this would take them clear of the worst of the forked lightning, but sheet lightning flashed anywhere, and right now it was turning the night sky to daylight. There was no time to climb above the storm clouds, either. The trouble was, the glint in Mathy's eyes said their mission was to bomb London, and that was what they were going to do.

Flying under the leading edge of the storm felt like walking beneath swarming bees in a tree: any second, any second, any second...and with his eyes fixed on the compass Ernst still couldn't get that terrifying question out of his head: *'jump, or burn?'* It seemed it would never go away. If he stuck to his religious belief, would he have the guts to suffer the agony of burning alive?

To put some distance between themselves and the worst of the lightning he found himself steering almost blind over the North Sea, the storm wrapped around the ship like a black tent, with sudden currents of charged air buffeting her this way and that, first lifting then dropping her nose, or catching her amidships and slewing her. His main focus was on the compass bearing and he knew Karl's was on the altimeter. From tales they'd heard, in the frictions of a storm an airship could be sent plummeting before the ballast could stabilize her; and if the engines faltered she'd be at the mercy of the winds. And right now he was fighting the wheel to hold the direction he wanted, knowing that in the dipping and yawing each sudden change of angle could mean the hydrogen had been struck and they were only seconds from disaster.

'Careful, helm! Keep your course.' In the last dip and sway they'd veered off the sou'-sou'-west reading – which he corrected with a firm hand. And now the cloud around them began to thin, and he could hear the fabric of the hull cracking its creases out and the sounds of the engines. They were coming out of the storm, and Mathy was coolly looking at his charts as if he was on a training exercise.

'We'll lose some height to get a fix on the English coast.'

'Got to be done, Lieutenant, got to be done.' Josef was helping work out a new compass-bearing to put them back on course. 'Nor'-nor'-east-twenty.'

'Nor'-nor'-east-twenty.' Ernst swung the helm to line up with the new reading as Karl at the elevator wheel began the descent.

'Level off at two-and-a-half thousand metres – just below the cloud base.' There wasn't a hint of doubt in Mathy's voice.

Ernst relaxed just a fraction. With that storm behind them, surely they'd come through the worst of things...

The BE2 was tried and tested, well known for its stability. But as Simmonds put it to Scott, any aeroplane's disadvantage was that a Zeppelin could hover above a cloud base with her engines off and listen for the sound of an aircraft, while they wouldn't hear a thing until the rattle of a machine gun hit them.

The Observation Corps had briefed him on the various approaches the Zeppelins took to get to London; they mainly came in over the Norfolk coast and headed south-west via Cambridgeshire and Hertfordshire into the northern suburbs; and once they'd spotted the Thames – not difficult except on the darkest of nights – they could use their charts to put them above their targets. Now Scott set them on a course that had a decent chance of finding an airship that was following the favourite pattern.

'North-east forty degrees.'

'Bravo! We're on it already.'

'Level off at seven-thousand feet, sir. Count Zepp could well be coming in under the cloud for bearings, which'd give us a few hundred feet of air space.'

'Seven-thousand it shall be. If we're lucky we can rid ourselves of some of this damned munition.' Simmonds attained his height, and at sixty knots the BE2 was well north of the Suffolk/Norfolk border; and checking below them Scott marked their progress over the River Orwell and pointed out the flickering lights of Norwich.

'Much further and we'll say how-do to the Zepp over the sea – or the blighter isn't coming.' And it was a moment later when Scott's head was down over his chart that Simmonds suddenly shouted.

Looming through cloud above them was what looked like the hull of a giant transatlantic liner – ominous, ghostly and terrible.

'She's at eight thousand feet. I'll get aft of her and climb.'

Scott was looking for flashes from the airship which would say they'd been seen and were being fired at. 'Cut engine and dive, sir. Get out of their hearing – make up our height from behind. Hit them from above.'

Simmonds swore. 'If we had the ammo we need we could fly at 'em right now, lay into her from underneath.' He needed incendiary bullets, explosive rounds he could fire flying directly at the Zepp – nitro-glycerine ammunition that would ignite an airship's hydrogen gas. But those bullets were still at the testing stage – and all he could hope to do right now was to out-climb the airship and drop on her from above. He feathered his engine, held the plane on a shallow dive, and dipped his port wing to get round behind the target when suddenly they were rocked off balance, bucking in the air with wings fluttering and struts screaming. He took them into a steep dive to restart the engine, both their helmets almost ripped off their faces.

What had hit them? Were they on fire? Would the controls respond? Forget fighting the enemy – they'd got their own lives to save.

Zeppelin L13 went in over the Norfolk coast at Mundesley. At top speed and with a light following wind coming in off the sea she'd be over London in just under two hours.

'Plot a course to take us east near Dartford. We'll find the Thames and hit the Royal Arsenal at Woolwich.'

Josef spread a new chart and the Executive Officer set a compass on it. Mathy rubbed his hands. 'We'll demolish what they're making to throw at us.'

Ernst nodded as if Mathy had been speaking especially to him. He'd been scared and ashamed of himself when he'd wet his trousers, and he'd wanted to kill every Englishman necessary to win the war. But in his heart of hearts he was happier when they were hitting military targets – and everyone knew the Royal Arsenal at Woolwich was as big a danger as a fighting division.

'Sou'-sou'-west-two-one-zero.'

He turned two degrees to port – to be frozen by a banshee shrieking. His feet went from under him and a splintering crash from above said they'd taken a hit.

'Damn and blast!' He pulled himself up and looked out to see the flashes from guns on the ground – followed by a barrage of shells whistling past.

'We've taken one!'

'Lucky pot-shot!'

'Full speed and climb!' Mathy was on his own feet and back in command. 'What word from above? What damage?'

The Observation Officer pressed his headphones tighter, shook his head. 'No contact, Lieutenant. The set's dead.'

'Steady us up, helm! Steady us up!'

'Lieutenant.' Ernst was wrestling with his wheel as the airship spiralled in the sky; but slowly, compass point by compass point, he brought her under control.

Mathy was up the interior ladder and at the gondola

hatch. From the helm Ernst could see that the chute had gone again and there was a large hole where they'd been hit in the keel – but there was no fire: the shell must have passed right through.

'I want a man up there to report on the damage.' Mathy looked down at them all. 'The ladder's half gone. I want a volunteer. Anyone?'

A volunteer! The task was so dangerous that no order had been given; but a brave man was being invited to step forward. Should it be him? Ernst knew only too well how hazardous ladder-climbing was when the thing was intact – and half-gone it meant someone pulling himself up like a gymnast on a rope, kilometres above the ground.

He swallowed, as quietly as he could, because now the ship was holding steady. With Josef in the gondola either he or Karl could be spared.

But he would soon have a child to care for, wouldn't he, and Karl wasn't married… He wanted to look around at Karl, imagined him intent on his elevator wheel.

'I'll go, Lieutenant. Got to be done, got to be done.' Josef was handing his charts to the Observation Officer. 'Needs an experienced man.' Quickly taking Mathy's place in the hatch, and with just a pause as if to plan his way up the shattered ladder, Josef pulled himself out of sight.

Ernst kept his eyes fixed on his compass, kept himself

facing ahead, shoulders hunched away from everyone; he didn't want to have to look eye-to-eye at any officer or man aboard. He muttered, 'Two-one-zero' as if keeping that course had delayed him volunteering. But he knew very well what had happened. His courage had been tested, and it had failed him.

Suddenly the struts stopped screaming as the BE2's engine kicked in. Simmonds looked at his altimeter and levelled off at four thousand feet, dipped a wing, tested his controls, which seemed to be responding, and went into a tight U-turn for a look at the Zeppelin. Quick action had saved their lives, but now he and Scott needed to take stock of the situation. What he saw pleased him, the airship's outer envelope was sucking in and then out again as she tried to climb. The guns at North Waltham had just missed the plane, but they'd scored a hit on the airship, because after keeping her course for a mile or so she made a lumbering turn to starboard which told him she was running for home. The question now was, did they chase her? How much fuel had they got left?

And then Scott told him. 'Cross strut severed, sir, starboard wing.'

Simmonds looked out along it. The broken strut was flapping between the upper and lower wings, flight controls all right for the time being, but the damage would be putting more strain on the port wing structure;

and if that wing crumpled they'd sycamore down to earth – with no parachutes to give them a ghost of a chance. Chasing the Zeppelin was out of the question.

'Give me a heading for home.' But already he was delicately dipping the port wing to turn towards Sutton's Farm.

Taking things slowly he got them back around midnight. Flares were being lit along the runway, but he still used his favourite method of night landing. 'Belt and braces,' he told Scott. He made a pass over the runway at two hundred feet and ordered a parachute flare to be dropped, which he flew beneath, and by the light of what seemed like a full moon floating down above him, he lined up for his final approach and landed the BE2 all in one piece.

'We'll get the blighter another time,' he told Scott.

'You bet, sir.'

'And please God we'll soon have the proper ammo to shoot at her.'

Mathy also ran for home. With vital information from Josef about a fuel line punctured and a port engine hit, he nursed the airship back to Hage. He dumped their bomb load and as much fuel as they could spare, avoided the storm clouds flashing to the north-east, and called for maximum power from the remaining engines.

'Helm, east one-ten south.'

'East one-ten south, Lieutenant.' Holding the airship on course with an engine down left no time for dwelling on what Ernst had or hadn't done that night. A sagging airship was hard to manoeuvre – he'd got his hands full.

At last he saw the sheds at Hage, the dawn light rising above them. He nosed L13 at the tower; and they landed hard on the concrete, a sudden crash that threw them about again – one broken leg and a badly cut head, with the gondola struts fractured, the propeller shafts split, and the leading girders buckled up in the hull. But they were down, and, apart from one man they could all walk away from the airship. It was at a cost, but they were back on the ground.

Ernst fell out of step with Karl and walked alongside Josef, patted him on the shoulder. 'To life, Josef!'

'Got to be done, got to be done.'

But he knew what he'd be carrying away from tonight. It was this heavy feeling of guilt that told him he had failed himself. He should be ashamed. He might not have been chosen, but he should have volunteered. Josef hadn't been *that* quick to step forward; he could easily have got his own word in first. But he had frozen at the wheel. He'd ducked a test, and he was very clear in his own mind that, unlike Josef Porath and Lieutenant Mathy, Ernst Stender was no hero of the German Empire.

7

'Bli! I can just see that tram conductor's face when you give him that!' Their mother was looking at Will's call-up papers, waving the travel warrant for a laugh. 'The king wouldn't know a ha'penny from a hole in his trousers but he's paying your tuppence tram fare up the road to the Artillery! That won't break the bank, will it?'

'It's for people who really have to travel – on trains.' Will put out his hand for it. 'I won't bother with that, I'll pay the fare.'

Instead, the warrant went into their mother's apron pocket. 'I'll keep it in case I get a puncture on my bike.'

But Freddie pulled it out again. 'I'll stick it on my wall.' He was proud of his brother now, and so was his dad, who'd come downstairs to be with them for this special Saturday morning breakfast.

Will was reading his instructions. 'I've got to report to the Royal Artillery Barracks at eight o'clock Monday morning...'

'An' what's your young lady...going to think of that?' Their dad wasn't coughing so badly today but he was still alarmingly short of breath.

They hadn't seen so much of Amy lately, she'd said she didn't want to go out of doors until her face got better

– but would Will going off to the war change things?

'Don't tell anyone, any of you—' Will's eyes fixed them one at a time – 'but she's thinking of going for a nurse, or something…'

A quick look came and went on their mother's face; she knew what nursing was about, and this didn't tally with the Amy Margerison they'd met.

'She thinks the Germans have taken away her looks, and she's going to do everything she can to get back at them…' Will's face was red and his voice ran out on him.

'Oh, she mustn't think that. A little bit of face powder…'

'She'll be pretty again, Will, like before.'

'Ta, Fred, she will.'

Freddie decided to change the mood. From behind a picture he brought out a small packet he'd wrapped in string and brown paper. 'Here y'are, Will – it's for you. I got it for when your letter came.'

'Fred! What've you been up to?'

'Open it an' find out.'

Will undid the tight reef knot and took off the brown paper, the look on his face saying he was ready to be delighted. It really did seem as if the old Will was back again. 'Splendid! Oh, thanks, Fred.'

Now his mum, dad and Will could see what he'd bought: a field sketch-book from Baker's the Stationers, a cloth cover with cartridge paper inside, just the right size for carrying in a battledress pocket. He'd checked.

'You could do some pictures of what it's like. To show us after…'

'I will. I certainly will.'

'Some still-lives.' His mum was in on the secret.

'An' some lives'll be so ruddy still…you could stand there and draw their pictures…an' frame 'em, an' they won't blink an eye.'

'Stop it, Sam! Keep your soldier jokes to yourself.'

Will opened the sketch-book. 'You've got to write in it, Fred.'

'Write what?'

'"To Will from Fred."'

He found a pencil and did what Will asked; and Will got his mother and father to sign the same page as if it were an autograph book.

God keep you safe. To Will from Mum x
Give the Germans what-for. Dad.

'I'll never be parted from this.' Will put the sketch-book on the table in front of him. 'Thank you, Fred, thank you very much.'

'And let's hope the war's soon over and you never get time to fill it up.' Alice hid her tears by turning to the stove to get going on the breakfast.

But when it came, nobody seemed to have much room for eggs and bacon.

'Pull those shoulders back! Chests out, stomachs in, show some pride! You're in the Royal Artillery not the Baptist Boys' Brigade!'

Wearing their uniforms out of doors for the first time, Will's battery was being drilled in the basics of marching, halting, standing to attention, and 'dressing' – shuffling about until they were lined up by size, tallest on the right, shortest on the left – with Will somewhere in the middle. His serge uniform was rough and his cap was too tight. The day before, the new recruits had moved along the tailor's tables and been kitted out by eye, tunics held up at them, caps pushed on their heads, and no going back with any complaints. At least his boots fitted a treat.

The drill sergeant had them marching up and down the parade ground almost like real soldiers.

''Eft–ah, 'eft-ah, 'eft-ah; 'eft…'eft…'eft…'eft, get them arms swinging, 'eft…'eft…'eft…'eft.' The sergeant's voice hit the front of the Royal Artillery building and bounced back, louder. ''Eft…'eft…'eft…' He stopped shouting to let their heels carry the rhythm, just the crunch of boots until – 'Battery…wait for it, wait for it… Halt!' He almost screamed it. Will came to the halt with a stamp of his right boot, his arms held rigid at his side, no bumping into the man in front. 'To the left – turn!' He turned smartly, brought his right boot down again and stayed at attention. A couple of men didn't know their left from their right and turned the wrong way. It was hard not to laugh. 'You stupid little soldiers! What d'you think you're doing, performing in Fred Karno's Army? Now – staaaand...at ease!' Will stamped his left foot to the side the way he'd been drilled, his hands held behind his back. 'And – staaaand... easy!' He breathed out, slumped slightly, stood like a civilian and shuffled his feet. *Not* easy this, *not* easy.

'That was 'orrible! 'Orrible! If I was that way inclined I would weep!' The drill sergeant pushed his face at one of the men who'd turned right instead of left. 'Weep, I would!' He took a step back. 'When it comes to gunnery, soldier, if you don't know the left end of a muzzle from the right you'll soon be riding a whizz-bang to kingdom come. But I'm gonna lick you lot into shape if it kills you!' He marched along the line, stopping, looking at this one, moving on, setting another's jaunty cap square on his head – 'We're not the Fourth Brigade of the London Trams an' Hokey Pokey Men!' – stopping, staring into someone's face, doing no more than shake his head – 'Your poor mother!'

Will patted his tunic pocket with Fred's sketch-book in it. He would draw a cartoon of this drill sergeant some time – his piggy eyes, his Blackwall Tunnel of a mouth and his twirled, waxed moustache – it would give young Fred a laugh.

The next day he was issued with a rifle – a Lee Enfield .303 – but because he was a gunner of the Royal Field Artillery and not an infantryman it was for drill only. And with the basic slope arms, present arms, and order arms learned, a week later he was out on Woolwich Common with a Battery Sergeant Major teaching him the routines of being in an eighteen-pounder crew.

'Now, your thirteen-pounder's for the gee-gees, the horse artillery, but us field men has its big brother. Longer barrel, and heavier than what the Frenchies and the Hun has got.' The BSM spoke proudly as if he'd designed it himself. 'But the recoil's slow so we give it lots of drinks of oil, and you keep an eye on that in the reservoir. Otherwise, you're on a damned fine weapon, and you'll be trained up to give it respect and get the best out of it. Got me?'

'Sergeant Major!'

And within seven days, even if his own mother had cycled past, Will knew she wouldn't have recognised such a smart and snappy soldier.

And, yes, he and Amy had been wrong and he should have done this sooner. He felt good now. 'You go and make mincemeat of some German, just for me!' Those had been his dad's words as he went – and he would, if he could. Hundreds of them.

He learned a lot in a short time.

'Right, today you're gonna learn getting there an' setting your platform. Then I shall teach you how an eighteen-pounder is fired, but that's for tomorrow.'

He listened hard to the BSM.

'For today, your eighteen-pounder is drawn by six horses, two-by-two, with a driver to each pair. They get you there, pull the gun to its new *platform*,' he emphasised the word, 'which is gunnery for "position".' He looked around the group. 'An' I hope you can count 'cos you'll carry out your duties according to your number. Your number one is your sergeant.' He pointed to a Field Artillery corporal, who was standing in for a sergeant. 'He'll give the order—'

The corporal shouted it on cue. 'Halt. Action – front!'

'Now, gunners two and three, that's you and you, unhook the gun.' Will was suddenly number three and Stan Denyer – a decent lad from Dartford he'd palled up with – was number two. 'Now you pull this ammunition limber forward and you turn the gun anticlockwise in the general direction of the Kaiser's men. And alongside comes the main ammunition wagon to be unhooked by numbers four, five and six.' He pointed to three other men. 'You, you an' you. You set the dust cap of your axle one foot away and one foot to the rear of the dust cap on the gun's axle. Then it's horses and drivers and numbers seven, eight and nine go back to the wagon line in reserve, and the five of you with your sergeant await orders to start popping away. All clear?'

No – he'd speeded up and it wasn't clear. For a start, here on Woolwich Common they didn't have horses or drivers or ammunition wagons, just two rows of eighteen-pounders, and not all of them had gun limbers, just groups of recruits.

'Any questions before I watch you make complete idiots of yourselves…?'

Stan Denyer came smartly to attention. 'Sergeant Major, why do numbers seven, eight and nine go back to the wagon line?' At the moment those three weren't even out on Woolwich Common.

'Because you'll likely be dead in the first half hour of bombardment, gunner. The German guns'll soon get a lay on you, camouflage or not. They spot the flashes, make their calculations, and do their damnedest to give you what-for.' The man looked around the group of recruits. 'In war, my boys, we make allowances for waste. A butcher knows so much of his cut of meat is going to be trimmed away – so when he weighs it he makes an allowance for the fat. In the same way, the Royal Artillery knows men are going to be killed and injured, so we add our fat allowance before we start. And what's gone before tells us that on an eighteen-pounder gun we need nine men to do the job of six.' He looked around at them all. 'Does that answer your question?'

'Sergeant Major.'

'I didn't hear you, gunner!'

'Sergeant Major!'

Will could see the expressions on some of the other faces, and he guessed his must have looked much the same. Wastage. Some of the crew were planned-for wastage, and it was hard not to start wondering which of these men it would be.

'Right, then. I've given you your numbers; let's see you set up your gun on a new platform.' The BSM stood back and signalled to the corporal, who gave them all their starting positions, Will as number three on the left. But in his head he was doing his own mental arithmetic. According to War Office calculations, two of these six men lined up here with him weren't going to see the war through in one piece.

You could laugh if you were in the mood. Old Kitchener didn't put that on his posters, did he?

8

'He'll be...all right. Be a shock at first, being shouted at...told he's the lowest creature on God's earth.'

Freddie was sitting on the edge of his dad's bed. His mum had cycled off to Wood Street, and he'd carried up a glass of cold water from the kitchen because his dad didn't trust that bathroom stuff.

'Was it like that when you were in the army?' He'd heard some of his dad's stories of the terrible war, but none of them were really about him.

'Armies don't change, mate. If you can't take a mouthful of abuse...how you gonna take a stream of fire from a machine gun?'

'Like you did?'

'Sort of.'

There was a picture of his dad downstairs all dressed up in his best uniform; but in the last few weeks he'd said a few things about being in the army which he'd never said before. Never anything about the actual fighting, though, like the sorts of things he'd had to do. He'd never made himself sound big and brave, like Wally Quinnell's brother. So what had he really been like as a soldier? Was he a bit like him, not the sort to get into a fight if there was a better way out?

His dad was taking a drink of the water. And before

he knew, he'd asked it – the question came out.

'Did you ever kill anyone?'

His dad's water went up his nose. '*What?*'

'People. Those Boers an' that.'

Straight away he wished he'd kept his mouth shut. His dad was looking at him as if he'd said a swearword. He was wiping his chin and he put his glass down and leant forward.

'What would you say…your job was, son?'

'Don't go out to work, do I?'

'You do – you go to school, that's your work. So what d'you go to school *for?*'

'Because I've got to.'

'Don't be funny.'

Hell-'n'-hailstones! This was getting serious.

'Learning. To learn.' Crikey, why had he got himself into this? When his dad went all serious it was worse than standing in front of the headmaster.

'An' do you learn?'

'Yes. A bit. You know…'

'Right. Your job is to learn…an' you try to do it. Is that fair to say?'

Freddie nodded. But he didn't learn because it was his job, he did it so he didn't get the stick.

'Well, a soldier's job…is to win the battle he's in. Which usually means…by killing the enemy.'

He'd really irritated his dad's dusty lungs, it was

costing him; his breathing was getting quicker and quicker, all up in his mouth.

'And I…' His voice had gone very quiet. 'I did my job. Understand?'

He was just going to nod.

'*Enough said?*' – a sudden over-the-river shout.

Now he did nod, and he got up off the bed.

'An' I expect our Will to do the same.'

'Yeah. So do I. Course he will.' And Freddie did his best to slink from the bedroom as if that wasn't what he was doing.

'This is a QF eighteen-pounder.' The Battery Sergeant Major pointed at the gun. 'An' what does "QF" stand for? *Eh?*'

'"Quick Fire", Sergeant Major.'

'Correct. Thirty rounds a minute. So you've gotta be slick, lads, or this beauty will have your fingers off – or worse, it'll ruin your dingly-danglies. Who's the number three today?'

Will came to attention. 'Sergeant Major.'

'Gunner three, you set the line and the elevation.'

'Sergeant Major.'

'And you fire the gun.'

'Sergeant Major.'

'So you watch the recoil, laddie. I've known number threes come home in six different sections.'

Will stayed at attention until the BSM had finished. Being in the army was a rum old business, no mistake. That morning he'd been shouted at on parade because one of his puttees had slipped down over his boot, so when this eighteen-pounder killed him the BSM would probably be more worried about his puttees being down round his ankle than he would about his leg being twenty yards from his cock-a-doodle-do.

They practised and they practised. Out there on Woolwich Common their intake learned how to fire smoke shells, gas shells, incendiary shells, high explosive shells, and the shell they'd be firing more than all the others and that was meant to kill men in the open – shrapnel shells crammed with nearly four hundred lead balls to rip into their bodies and make mincemeat of them.

But, 'They've got 'em, too,' their corporal told them. 'If we can scrape up enough of you to put in two sandbags you'll get a burial. Less than that an' you're "missing presumed dead", whistling in the wind till kingdom come.'

Hearing those sorts of things Will knew he was changing into a different person. Already he was getting used to the idea of being a casualty of war: he just hoped it wouldn't hurt. But since Fred had given him that sketch-book he'd made up his mind not to let go of his artist's eye, his little bit of talent at drawing and painting what he saw. When it was quiet in the barrack room he'd lie on his bunk, close his eyes and see the pictures that he'd paint one day. Or he'd riffle through the roughs he'd done in a stand-down, sketches of the sunset over the Royal Artillery building, the hawthorns in flower on Woolwich Common, the rearing-up of horses' heads as they took the strain of the gun. And he'd tell himself that if he did come out of this war alive, he'd make damned sure he never closed his seeing eye again.

'Doctor says he's a bit better, Freddie. He had half the Arsenal in his lungs, now he's only got a quarter.' His mother was cutting a loaf in the kitchen, holding it against her apron and sawing inwards. He always worried she'd go too far one day and cut herself in half. 'He can't wait to get back.'

And Freddie knew why. It was probably a secret, but everyone in Woolwich knew his dad's shop in the Arsenal was working on new explosive bullets that could be fired from machine guns in aeroplanes.

'"Pomeroys",' he'd told him. 'We haven't quite got 'em right yet, the mix of nitro-glycerine and Fuller's earth. But when they're right you won't get any ruddy Zeppelins coming over an' lording our skies.' Freddie was proud his dad had been working on killer bullets to fire at the Zepps – and Wally Quinnell ought to know that. There were tons of different ways of fighting the Germans.

His mother had nearly finished the sandwiches she was making before going off to Wood Street.

'Can Dad come out for a walk if it doesn't rain?' He could talk to him about getting back to work one day, finishing off those new bullets, cheer him up.

'He's a long way off that, Freddie.'

'Shame.'

'If I wasn't getting most of my sleep daytimes on your bed, I'd never get a wink, not along of your dad. It's still cough, cough, cough, cough, cough – never mind what the doctor says.'

And Freddie almost said it, but he kept quiet. Instead of having his bed while he was at school, why didn't she sleep in Will's bedroom? Will wasn't here, he was up at the Royal Artillery. He couldn't sleep in two beds at once, could he? But Will's room was Will's room, and the minute someone else moved into it – his mum or a lodger – then it would seem like Will was never coming back. So he kept his mouth shut and went out to play football with Don.

Amy Margerison suddenly turned up, not wearing one of her silly hats; she'd grown her hair long, like two curtains to her face. She sat in the parlour and pulled an envelope from her handbag. It was small and buff, and Freddie immediately recognised Will's handwriting.

'I expect you've got yours, and I thought we could share them.'

His mother's face looked as if she'd just bitten into a sour apple. 'No, we haven't had one here, have we, Freddie?'

'No. Not yet, Mum.'

Amy coughed. 'Well, he says he's all right, and he's getting used to army life.' She was running her eyes over the letter, definitely not letting go of it for anyone else to read. 'He says I won't know him with his hair cut short. The food's not bad, and there are a couple of decent chaps in his group, one especially. He's learning how to fire a big gun, and he might be going to France quite soon.'

'Ah.' Freddie's mum was leaning forward. 'Any mention of…anyone else?' She came out with it. '*Us?*'

'No, that's why I thought he must've written to you. It'll come tomorrow, bound to.' Amy folded the letter and put it back into her handbag. 'And how are you, Mrs Castle?'

'Not so dusty, thanks.'

'And Mr Castle?'

'Up one day and down the next. A long way off better…'

'That's a shame. And how's school, Fred? Settled into the new term, have you?'

'Yes, thanks.' School was rotten. Whatever was said, whatever was done, Wally Quinnell was making his life a misery. Quinnell's brother was a foot soldier in the West Kents, so when Quinnell had been told about Will being in the Royal Field Artillery, he just had to make something of it.

'Oh, 'e's one of the softies way at the back. My brother says they sometimes shell our own men. No one likes 'em over there.'

'Well, that can't be Will because he's not there yet.'

'No, it can't. Only just volunteered, 'asn't he?'

There was no winning with Quinnell, and the one way he dreamed of getting his own back was giving him a good walloping, really laying into him one day. The trouble was, Quinnell was tougher than he was, a better fighter, scared everyone in the school with what he could do with his fists and his boots.

'And you, Amy, are you back at work yet?' Freddie's mother was getting fidgety.

'Monday, Mrs Castle. I'm going back on Monday. But I don't think I'll be at the emporium much longer.'

'No?'

'I wasn't sure about nursing, but I'm going to volunteer for work in the Arsenal.'

'*The Arsenal?*'

That sat him up. 'What you gonna do?' Amy wasn't the sort to work in the Arsenal, unless it was in the offices. His dad always said women's work in the shell shops was really hard graft. Amy had definitely changed her tune.

'I'll do whatever they ask me. I'm not afraid of a bit of hard work.'

'Of course you're not, dear – but try to stay clear of the Danger Building. Another canary died last week…'

Canaries were the women who worked in the TNT shop. The explosive turned their skin bright yellow. Everyone could see who they were.

'Well done, then, Amy. Will's going to be very proud of you, I'm sure.' Freddie's mother was staring at Amy's handbag as if she might see through it and read Will's letter for herself. 'He's only up the road, but till he gets leave there's no seeing him. You'll write back, will you? I wasn't aware about letters, not so soon. I'll drop a line to him myself.'

'You won't say anything about my plans, Mrs Castle – please?'

'Of course I shan't. That's between you and him.' She stood up. 'Now, I was just going to put a kettle on the stove before I go off to work. Would you like a cup of tea? I'm expecting two or three births tonight; two full term, and one lazy little bounder who's keeping us all waiting…'

'I won't, thanks. I'm going home to tell my mother and father what I've just told you – and I fully expect a big fuss…'

'I'm sure you'll find the right words…'

'Oh, I shan't need words, Mrs Castle. I only have to remind them of this.' Amy suddenly lifted the long hair from the left side of her face – to show a violent burst of scar tissue like a livid burn, spread from her cheekbone to beyond her ear. 'I'll tell them I'm going to pay the Kaiser back for what he's done to my face, thank you very much!'

9

'If this is Champagne country it could do with a heck of a lot more sparkle!'

Will's battery of No. 9 Division Royal Field Artillery had moved in over the chalky land, and the men were covered from their boots to their helmets in white dust, which would take some cleaning off, as would the chalk on the eighteen-pounders, which had to be kept inspection-clean at all times. Muck like that in the muzzle or the breech could explode a gun when it was fired and send them all to kingdom come. Will and the other new boys who'd been sent out to join the First Army had been sifted down from the Field Artillery Depot to the division, to the brigade, and now here was their battery under the command of Major Hamilton-Jones, with Captain Clarke and Lieutenant Frossage serving under him, and Battery Sergeant Major Belchman ranting and rallying, the fiery snorts from his huge nostrils enough to light a charge.

The sergeant number one gave the order. 'Halt. Action – front.' The horses were unhitched and the gun pulled round to face the enemy lines, way across towards the town of Auchy, landmarked by its huge slag heap. As the limber was being put into position a platoon of French foot-soldiers heading for the Front passed through, all chalked-up themselves and looking exhausted.

'Go to it, Frenchies – give 'em hell!'

'Cup...of...tea!' A young French soldier raised his free hand with his little finger in the air and laughed as if he'd made the joke of the century.

'We'd rather be Champagne Charlies!'

This was going to be Will's first taste of real war: a joint attack with the French to break through the German lines. It would be started at dawn some time in the next four days with a huge barrage of artillery from the whole length of the sector. Men would die going forward – shot, bayoneted, gassed – and the enemy would do their damnedest to put the British guns out of action. Will could picture only too well what would happen if a high explosive hit their own ammo dump. Sandbags of body bits wouldn't come into it.

With the battery's guns in position, BSM Belchman assembled the men so the major could make a speech standing on an ammunition wagon. Will did a secret sketch of the officer in his mind: smallish, sprightly, neat moustache, jabbing his polished briar pipe like a pistol.

'Remember, men, we're up against a stoic enemy. Erich von Falkenheyn wants to stay. He's in France to make the country German for good and all. Well, we're not going to let him stay, and we don't want to stay ourselves, thank you very much. We're here to do a job and go home – with him and his tribe beaten back to where he belongs. He sees permanent occupation as their destiny. Well, we're going to have something to say about that, aren't we?'

In the Shakespeare scene Will had once been in at his school play everyone would have cheered and thrown their caps into the air. As it was, they mostly nodded, a couple said, 'Hear, hear!' and they all shifted their feet to get back to cleaning the guns.

With their eighteen-pounder clean and covered, he and Stan Denyer sat on ammunition crates and ate rissoles, drinking mugs of something tasting faintly of tea.

'Here's to us!' Will raised his mug.

'Cheers – but I wish it was a pint of Whitbread's.'

Will threw out his dregs. 'Where d'you drink in Dartford? Got some good pubs down your way?'

'Don't drink a lot, really – not now I'm walking out...'

'You've got a regular girl, then?'

'I have.' Stan smiled, modestly. 'Her name's Florence – she's Flo, of course – an' the prettiest little thing you ever could see – make a dandy fashion plate if she wanted to...' Dartford was only twenty miles from Woolwich but Stan's talk was different, more countrified.

'Have you got a picture?'

Stan put his hand to a tunic pocket. 'In my pay-book.'

He brought it out and showed Will a small studio portrait on thick card, cut down to fit. But the picture wouldn't have lifted Will going into battle; Florence looked starey and serious, and her lips were one thin line as if she could give a few sharp answers.

'She's nice, Stan.'

'She had to sit a long while, and she got fed up – but you should just see her when she brightens up and comes to life…'

'I'm sure.' Although Will wasn't, not a bit.

'How about you? Who's this Amy you keep talking about, going to your shows and your flicks?'

Will pulled out Freddie's sketch-book. 'I didn't bring a photograph; she's changed a bit since she had the last picture taken…'

'All that glass in her face?'

'Yes, but it's getting better. Anyhow, I've drawn her how I picture her when I get back home.' He opened the sketch-book. 'That's her.' He'd used a soft pencil with finger-rubbed shading, showing Amy in half-profile, the scarred side of her face turned away with her hair curling down over her cheek.

'She looks a dream. You haven't made her up, have you?'

'On my honour.'

'Well, I'll tell you something, Will. We've both got lovely loving girls. Now, I've written something on the back of Flo's picture, private. So if I should cop it an' you don't, I want you to give it to her, an' tell her I wasn't a bad bloke to fight alongside. An' if you write something on yours I'll do the same for you.'

'All right. Fair do's. But we're not going to cop it, Stan. One sniff from Belchman and anything heading for us'll shoot straight up his nose – barrel to barrel.'

And Will left it there; but after cleaning his messing kit and a rub round his mouth with cherry toothpaste he settled down in the battery bell-tent. The light faded through the canvas, the sounds filtering through of neighs and jingles of the horses up the line, and he thought of this quiet place and how in a couple of days it was going to turn into hell-on-earth, with men lying under their blankets tonight who'd never again have the need to argue over a foot of groundsheet space.

They all knew the only surprise to the Germans about the next big offensive would be the timing. It would start with four days of heavy bombardment to soften them up along the twenty-mile Front – killing men, cutting barbed wire, destroying lines of supply – then a final four-hour crescendo of artillery would lead up to the attack. From early morning they all sweated at red-hot guns in their slick routine, twenty missiles to the minute, thousands of shells from limber after limber, wagon after wagon, stack after stack, heaved across to the breech, loaded, and fired. Will's gun jumped, recoiled, and he sighted and re-sighted, his targets changing according to reconnaissance reports. Sleep was something civilians did. Food was whatever the mobile cookers could pour into mess tins. The air they breathed was smoke and cordite. Conversation was left behind in some far-off life – here it was all shout and not much hear, and the language of it was all grunts.

From the start the Germans hit back with their own guns, explosions of chalk bursting up like flour. The earth never stopped shaking, but Will swore only when it jumped his sight dial and he had to do a serious recalibration; and in the heat of the bombardment he suddenly realised he was more annoyed than scared. Well, who'd have thought that?

The third day went into the fourth and now the horses were kept closer, poor frightened creatures with bared teeth and flashing eyes. Observers from their sector came back with reports that the German barbed wire was fifteen yards deep in front of their second line and it couldn't be cut by anything the Ninth Scottish infantry carried, so their battery was to be ready to move forward to enable their shrapnel shells and high explosives to do the job.

Will sweated on with Stan Denyer beside him, and at four o'clock on the Saturday morning BSM Belchman came snorting along the artillery line calling for even faster firing. 'Crescendo! Crescendo!' he yelled, nostrils like pipes.

'Now we're a ruddy dance band!' Stan Denyer didn't break his breech-loading rhythm.

Captain Clarke commanded Will to traverse to a more westerly point, where the allied troops would make their main frontal assault – to hit the German front line at ten-to-six, timed to explode with the chlorine gas released from canisters in no man's land when the breeze was expected to drift into the enemy ahead of the attack. A further forty minutes and he was told to 'Raise elevation five degrees.' This meant the infantry was going in. Will lifted the trajectory to concentrate fire on the German second line, precision work so as to hit the enemy wire and not the advancing allied troops.

His battery kept on pounding until the British infantry got into the German communication trenches between the lines. Word came back fast about the slaughter there. Those poor devils with their Lee-Enfields carrying sixty pounds of kit on their backs, fighting against the Jerries waiting in dug-outs with Lugers, rifles, machine guns and grenades; having to resort to hand-to-hand fighting with knives and bayonets, boots, teeth, and garrotting wire. It had to be hell on earth. Will was ordered to lift his trajectories again. Gunsmoke and mist clung to the ground almost to head-height, and his eardrums felt so shattered that he feared he'd never hear a voice again. He knew territory was taken along the whole sector, to be lost then re-taken; with word coming back that allied deaths from German machine-gun fire were heavy – nearly a thousand men in one assault they said – and Tommies without gas masks were dying from British chlorine gas blowing back on the wind. But everyone cheered when great earth-moving charges of high explosive suddenly went sky-high, thanks to the Royal Engineer tunnellers who'd mined beneath the German trenches.

And on went the offensive to capture German ground.

The Red Cross set up a field dressing station near Will's battery, stretcher-men bringing the wounded back from the front line, sights that etched his mind with pictures he knew he could never draw. There was no camouflaging gruesome sights like these – men without arms or legs, faces skinned to the jawbone, soldiers' futile attempts on stretchers to hold in their ripped-out organs. And all the while Will knew he was creating his own gruesome sights for the Germans four thousand yards away.

The order came for the field batteries to move forward, to get closer in to pound the enemy if they tried to wheel. They pulled down their camouflage and stowed it, limbers and guns were hitched-up, ammunition wagons were re-loaded and made ready to follow; and within forty-five minutes the move forward began. They took a narrow track in the right direction, the first part of it between two fields of corn with cover from trees, before it went into twists that followed a drainage ditch. But everyone could see that in this last section their move forward was going to be along a straight open stretch, very exposed.

This was a mining area and Captain Clarke was up front on his horse, pointing out two tall pithead winches behind the German lines. Stan pointed at them, too. 'They can get a darned good lay on us from up there.'

Will grunted. It meant German observers with field glasses and decent maps could plot some pretty accurate co-ordinates to target them.

Leaning over the neck of his horse, waving his whip in the air, Major Hamilton-Jones shouted at the leading drivers. 'We're like bally ducks at a shoot. Take it as near a gallop as you can.' But with the weight of the guns and the twists of the road a gallop was out of the question: an eighteen-pounder in the ditch or a horse going down would halt everything and lay the whole battery open to the shrapnel.

Will's gun was second in line, the crew sitting on top of an ammunition wagon holding enough high explosive to blow them all to dust. He started to sweat, and he felt his heart racing. They'd better get off this stretch of track pretty darned soon.

The first shot suddenly came screeching in at them and exploded in the cornfield to their right.

'Blimey! They have got a good lay!'

'Ever 'eard of sitting ducks?'

Phew! That was close – so close it seemed as if 'Will Castle' had been chalked on the shell casing. He could see the horses losing their footing as the ground moved under their hooves. But the first gun went forward, and his gun and the wagon followed. Another searing screech and an explosion rocked the whole corner of the field, even closer this time – sending stripped and burning corn choking into all their lungs.

Will was coughing up like his dad. What should he do: jump off the wagon of explosives and run, or stay on it in case it moved away faster than he could go on foot? He couldn't decide. He stayed where he was for the moment – but at the first slowing of the wagon as it took the tight bend before the open straight, Stan Denyer jumped off it and ran alongside.

'Will – get off that powder keg!'

And those were Stan's last ever words. As he put on a spurt and ran ahead another high explosive came shrieking down – and in the blast of it a large flint hit him in the face. God! Suddenly he wasn't Stan Denyer any more, his face was half gone, his neck broken, his body crumpling into the ditch.

Will turned, shouted up at heaven, looked back at

Stan's body on its back, legs splayed, arms flung out, his tunic and its pockets facing up. And he knew he had time to do it: he could jump off the wagon, the same as lots of others who were running through the corn. He had time to get to Stan. Every yard was taking the wagon in under the German howitzer's arch, soon more and more shells would overshoot: the closer the wagon got to the enemy artillery, the safer he would be, but he still just had time to run back, to grab into Stan's pocket for his pay-book and his picture of Flo – so that one day he could find her with his dead friend's special message.

But he stayed where he was. He rode on towards relative safety, looked after number one, clung onto the wagon, starting to make some excuse for not doing what he'd promised. Well, he tried to tell himself – that was war, wasn't it? He wasn't convinced, though. He could tell himself what he liked but he was pretty sure Stan Denyer would have done better for him. Whatever he tried to put into his head, that feeling of guilt wouldn't leave his insides – a message from his stomach of Will Castle's lack of guts.

10

Amy's job at the Royal Arsenal was filling shell cases. She had her medical first, and then they probed her schooling, her family situation and her current job. The supervisors said some girls were the rough and ready factory-floor sort; while others – shop assistants like her – might suit the offices. But she was very clear what she wanted to do. 'I'm no weakling; I want to do real war work.'

They gave her what she wanted, and sent her to the Danger Building where she was checked for matches and cigarettes, and her purse, hair slides, brooch and rings all went into a locker with her shoes, frock and coat. Going through onto the shell-filling floor she was in overalls, mask and gloves, with her hair up under a cap, and wearing wooden-soled clogs so as not to make sparks.

The other girls' questions were as blunt as if they were sisters.

'Done a bunk from home? What hostel you in?'

'Who's done that to your fizzog? I'd give him what-for, the devil.'

But once the shift started it was too busy and noisy for much talk. She was shown how to position the shell case, push a tap in, and pour the hot dry amatol inside, shell after shell after shell after shell, all filled with high explosive ammonium nitrate and TNT. There was time to talk in the canteen, though, and she found out something about Will's father. It started with bawdy remarks about boys and what they got up to if you weren't careful – and Amy told them that her boyfriend was with the Royal Artillery out in France, and one of them asked his name.

'William. William Castle. Will.'

'We've got a Castle here. Did have, anyhow.'

'Yeah, ours was a Sam…'

Amy put down her sandwich. 'That's the same as Will's dad. He works here; at least, he used to.'

'Our Sam got hurt bad, if he's the same one.'

'He's ill in bed, I can tell you that. There must be more than one Sam Castle, though…'

But the atmosphere at the table had suddenly changed, as if there was something special between these girls and Will's father.

'You do know what he did?'

'No. What did he do?'

'If he's the same one…'

'Yes?'

'He's only a bloomin' hero, that man.'

Now they were all talking at once.

'This train, see…'

'We was on cartridges, they're working on some new

101

sort of bullets, an' he was supervising filling 'em…'

'An' this train, along by the cartridge shop, it runs off its rails and, wallop, it comes smack into where we was – buffers and steam, and wall and partitions all over the place…'

'It was shocking! I can still see it.'

'The roof come in – you've seen them beams…'

'An' it's real danger, we're inches from being flattened to pancakes.'

'But instead of leaving us to be crushed to death, Sam Castle gets us all out through that hole in the wall and over the engine, every one. He's there lifting an' pushing till we're all out – and then it's crash, bang and down it all comes, brick-dust and plaster and asbestos, choking everything like a thick pea-souper…'

'With Sam trapped in it till they could dig him out.'

'Good God!' Amy looked along the faces. The girls were genuine, they weren't spinning her any tale – this was no trick on the new girl.

'So when you see him, Ame, you tell him he's a bloomin' hero.'

'Who ought to have a medal – except they don't want to let out what happened.'

'That's if he's the same one…'

Amy looked down at her empty plate, back at the girls as the hooter went. 'He's the same one. He's the same one, all right.'

They took their plates to the clearing table and headed for the door.

'So you've got a brave one there with your Will – if he's a chip off his father's block.'

And with that running in her head Amy went back to the Danger Building to carry on filling the explosive shells that men like her Will would fire.

Freddie's tram fare to Beresford Square Market was a penny-ha'penny return. The trouble with living where they did was that no shops had been built on the new estate – no greengrocer, no butcher, no baker, no fishmonger; as well as no schools, no churches and definitely no pubs. His mum said the place was like a big village with nice houses but no heart. 'Good job we've got trams or I'd never be off my bike.'

But Freddie never minded going on an errand to Woolwich because the tram bucked at the front upstairs and made his stomach turn somersaults almost as much as swingboats at the fair.

Everyone's mum had a favourite stall in the market. Don's went to different places from his. There were half-a-dozen fruit and veg men, but Jimmy Jobling's was the one he had to go to. 'He's up to Covent Garden before all the rest – gets the pick of what there is.' Freddie thought one man's potatoes looked much the same as the next man's, especially after queueing for half an hour, but he always went to the stalls she said. 'Tell Jobling I want apples off the front, and to keep his elbow off the scales – and don't forget to say they're for Mrs Castle.'

Today he had to go to Ron Palmer's the butcher, whose shop on the High Pavement had the longest queue of all. *Hell-'n'-hailstones!* Because of the war, a bit of meat was the sort of thing his mum made last a week so he'd have to wait. While he was there he wanted six ounces of streaky bacon for his dad's breakfasts. But first it was Jimmy Jobling's.

'That caulie, please, an' cut the leaves off 'fore you weigh it. Please.'

'You're lucky to get a caulie at all, boy. The Garden's half empty wi' what's bein' sent over to France.'

Coming here on an errand was a good chance to mooch around the toys, look at the birds in their cages, and then – if it was a Friday or a Saturday – stand and watch Cheap Jack Pratt pretending to get in a mood and smash all the plates and saucers the people wouldn't buy. But best of all was to see Powell the Dentist pulling someone's tooth out. *Aaaah!* No long queues there.

It wasn't so much fun on a weekday, though; and some of the pasted signs on the walls were deadly serious:

POLICE WARNING
WHAT TO DO WHEN THE
ZEPPELINS COME
In all probability if an air raid is made
it will take place at a time when most
people are in bed. The only intimation
the public are likely to get will be the
reports of the anti-aircraft guns or the
noise of falling bombs…

And when he got back he'd tell his mum and dad what they were supposed to do if the warning maroons went up for a Zepp coming over.

> **Inside lights must be shaded or reduced;**
> **windows so screened by shutters or dark**
> **blinds or curtains so that no more than**
> **a subdued light is visible from outside…**

He read the serious notices and then cheered himself up by trying to teach a parrot to say 'Hello Freddie', and he was just heading for Ron Palmer's when a hand suddenly clapped him on the shoulder.

'Get off!' He hadn't said anything rude to the bird, had he?

'Fred!'

It was Amy Margerison – although it didn't look like

her. She was in a short coat, not very smart, and a small black hat that was nothing fancy, with her hair tucked up under it.

'I've just come out of the Arsenal. My first day.'

It looked as if she had, too; and her voice was dry and croaky, like his mum's when she was too whacked to bother finishing what she was saying. And the scar on her cheek was all swollen and red, crying out for a powder puff.

'What's your game, Fred?'

'Shopping. For Mum.'

'Finished?'

'Not yet.'

Amy took his string bag off him. 'Better get going – then we can go home on the tram together.'

Blow! That wasn't what he wanted. Now he'd be stuck with talking to her all the way.

'I've got something special to tell you. Something really good. I'll tell you on the tram.'

'About Will? Have you had another letter from Will an' he's coming home on leave?' Amy always got her letters two or three days before they got theirs.

'No. Wait and see. Finish your shopping. What are you after?'

'Meat and bacon.'

They queued and did the shopping together, and at last, after waiting to get on a tram for a quarter of an hour, the conductress squeezed them in downstairs in front of a couple of boys who'd been to the Woolwich Baths, lucky devils.

'What is it you was going to tell me?' He always hated hanging on to be told something.

Amy leant towards him, her swollen scar a half-inch from his cheek. 'Your mum might know, but I didn't, so I don't think Will does. Your dad's such a quiet, nice, man, he'd never have made anything of it...'

'What?' Crikey, she was really drawing this out...

'He was a hero. In the accident. All the girls say so.'

He listened hard as she told him what the girls had said. It was definitely news to him. Yes, he knew about the Arsenal railway engine coming off its rails and smashing into where his dad was working, and him breathing in all that muck, but he didn't know how he'd got all the girls out before the roof caved in.

'They thought he was bound to cop it, but he saw every last one of them to safety. They really went on about him; took to me straight off because I know him. He should have had a medal, they said, but the Ministry of Munitions wanted it all hushed up.'

'He coughs up a lot of horrible stuff. A broken arm would have done him better.' He'd thought his dad was a hero ever since finding out he'd killed some Boers. But this had been different. It hadn't been, *There's a Boer, quick, shoot him!* Getting those girls out one at a time meant he'd had ages to think about what he was doing, all the danger he was in. And then carrying on doing it. 'He was a good soldier, an' all.'

'I'm sure he was, Fred.'

But now they were coming to his stop. 'Ta-ta, Amy. I'll see you when I see you.'

'Ta-ta, Fred. Give your dad a kiss from me.'

He got out from the seat and went towards the platform at the back, passing the two boys who'd been swimming – where to his disgust they were pointing at Amy's bad cheek and making 'yuk!' faces. Those skunks! Making faces at Amy's scars, something the rotten Germans had done to her. Well, he was going to give them a mouthful of what he thought of them.

But the tram stopped.

Now!

And he got off it, walked towards his house, heard the conductress ding the bell to go. He didn't look back; but he knew in his heart he could and should have stayed on one more stop and told those boys what he thought of them. But he hadn't.

And when he went upstairs to tell his dad what the Arsenal girls had told Amy, a sort of knot in his throat made his voice sound different as it came out, and he knew why. It wasn't just that he was more grown-up these days. He was ashamed of himself for not being the same sort of man as his dad.

11

In the changing seasons since Stan Denyer's death —
the French countryside wreathed in mist, then buried
under snow, and latterly turned red with brave poppies —
Fred's sketch-book was filled, and could have been filled
twenty times over. Stationed west of the River Somme,
Will had sketched men and places, army life, bunkers
and craters and sunsets. He'd done drawings on the
back of advice on lice, and on both sides of War
Department writing paper, a collection stowed away in
his equipment pack. But the sketch-book was always
kept next to his heart.

They were coming towards the end of June 1916 and
all the battery knew they were keying up for a massive
infantry attack. BSM Belchman had been told snippets
by Captain Clarke, who'd been told a tit-bit by Major
Hamilton-Jones, who'd been briefed by Brigade. The big
attack — to be carried out in their sector by the Tyneside
Irish Brigade — was to be on 'Z' Day, which was common
knowledge. The big secret was what day they were on
now. To soften up the enemy they always bombarded
heavily for several days before an attack. Even their
routine firing to keep the Germans' heads down ran
their gun barrels hot with overwork, and he'd never felt
so tired in his life. There weren't enough guns available

so the battery missed out on a lot of the rest periods the infantry was given, and any moment off his feet had Will's head slumping forward, sitting or lying there snoring, hearing himself snort when someone shook him awake.

Now, back at the wagon lines south of La Boisselle, which was held by the Germans, they were waiting for word. The guns and horses were in a farmer's field, and they were in the farmhouse, a real treat. He was slumped at the kitchen table over a sketch of his house – the country-style timbers, the rustic gate, and the 'village green' grass in front.

BSM Belchman elbowed him awake. ''Ere – don't you start dreaming of Blighty an' get all homesick or you'll be no ruddy use to me tomorrow.'

Will sat up, tried to cover his picture. 'It's just where I live, Sergeant Major.'

'*Live?* You mean where you *lived*. We've all got a *lived,* an' a *then* an' a *now*. What none of us poor buggers 'as got is much chance of a next week…'

Will folded the picture into his pocket.

'We start moving to our platform early, so stop your doodling an' get to your bed…'

Ah. What everyone had been waiting for wasn't very far off.

'… Get some shut-eye, gunner, 'cos you've got a few thousand shells to bang off tomorrow.'

'Right you are, Sergeant Major.' He got up. 'Goodnight.'

''Night, Rembrandt. An' don't dream of 'ome!'

The Germans had the high ground, which Will knew meant the upper hand. On the steepest slopes they'd even set their latrines to run down towards them, worse in heavy rain for the French boys in direct line who had to live with the stink and swarms of flies. The Observation Corps put up their tethered balloons, wild sights, which looked like grey whales in the sky, dangling their baskets underneath, with men suddenly dropping down on parachutes when the Fokkers attacked. But on what he guessed had to be 'U' Day or 'V' Day the weather was just good enough for the RFC to put up an observation plane over the German bluff, presumably photographing what was invisible from the ground. But as Will watched, German machine-gun fire quickly sent it disappearing into cloud.

If he'd tried to guess the battery's next order he'd have been wrong. The horses and the drivers brought the battery forward to their platforms but instead of a stand-down and a dawn start, once they were set they were ordered to stay all night, and he was told to take a lay not on the German front-line trenches but on the enemy rear. Next day his gun reverted to shrapnel, aimed at cutting the German wire. Things were definitely hotting up.

'Gunner Castle!' Belchman came strutting over.

'Sergeant Major.' He'd just taken a fresh lay. Was he in for a rollicking because they weren't seeing explosive smoke at the right height? Setting the fuses was difficult: they'd been told if they were too short the shrapnel hit the empty air, and if too long the shells ploughed into the ground and just lifted the wire to fall back again, more entangling than ever.

'Don' know how we've done,' Belchman reported. 'Weather's too vile for the planes to fly, and the balloon's gone pouf. Hit an' hope's what we're doing. So you come with me.'

God, he wasn't that bad, was he? Were they taking him off his number three duties?

'Bray – take over from Castle.'

Will swung round off his seat and the gun fired on, hardly missing a beat.

'Now look smart and look lively, lad, and when I put you up before the Colonel watch your Ps an' Qs.'

The Colonel! What was this all about? Will couldn't for the life of him think what he'd done wrong beyond normal gunnery errors. His head filled with every worst thought as he was marched back to the farmhouse and into the dining room, to be wheeled in before a colonel he hadn't seen before, a tall, youngish, man sitting at the table.

'Gunner, halt!'

Will halted smartly. He was hot and dirty from the gun, a contrast to this cool-looking colonel with his back to a nice draft from the window.

'Gunner Castle, sir.'

'Thank you, Sergeant Major.'

Will looked down at the table – and just stopped himself from toppling forward.

'Stand at ease, Castle.'

Spread there on the table were all his drawings, which had been taken from his backpack. Then what about Fred's sketch-book? Had that been taken in the night as well? He wanted to go to his tunic pocket to check, but he daren't move a hand. In it there was his house, some mates, a toppled French church, Amy, BSM Belchman himself – and a detailed study of his laying-sight. *Was that it?* Did they think he was drawing his gunnery device for getting across to the Germans? Was it special? If they were thinking that, he'd be court-martialled, convicted, tied to a post and shot. *As a spy!*

'You've got a nice way with a pencil, gunner.'

'Thank you, sir.' What was this?

'A talent, I'd say. You've got an eye, soldier. These panoramas here...' The colonel had separated out half a dozen views of villages and copses, and a distinctive windmill with three sails. 'Well, I won't beat about the bush—' he waved a hand at the window, 'the Flying Corps boys can't fly, cloud base too low – and we lost a balloon OP Ack last week. In addition, what we've got—' he slid the drawings aside and skewed an aerial photograph in front of him, 'is this.'

'Yes, sir.' Will leant forward to see a photograph of a stretch of long, straight road running from top to bottom of the picture, showing roofs of scattered farms that had been encircled in ink, and a cross marking a village built around a church.

'Now, good as the aerial boys are, on a cloudy day with no shadows the light's flat as a map from above – and what we're after is the relief of the terrain around here…' The colonel came to Will's side of the table, took hold of a corner of the photograph, and pointed out the road and some circled buildings. 'Roman road, straight as a die, Albert to Bapaume – but this hamlet under the cross is on the far side of a hill, we can't see over it from here, and we're not entirely trusting our maps.' He went back to his seat. 'Now, have you ever clapped eyes on one of these?' From a chair beside him he picked up a wooden frame, which looked about the size of a mantelpiece picture. He handed it over. It wasn't very heavy. At the top in the centre there was a compass, and on both of the long sides rollers held a stretch of paper, with little knobs to move it – a scroll that could be wound on as the paper was used. 'Know what that is, do you?'

'I can guess, sir.' Will had never seen one of these before but it looked pretty obvious.

'Good man. It's an OP Ack's sketching board.'

'Yes, sir.'

'And an OP Ack is what you're going to be tonight. Assistant to an Observation Officer. You'll take this forward with you under Second Lieutenant Whitaker of the Observer Corps, you'll go with him into no man's land, get to the top of that hillock here—' the colonel tapped the aerial photograph, 'and you'll sketch what you see by the light of dawn. We want the lie of the land, the far gradient, their hidden wires, and the purpose of these buildings, which may house machine gun nests, or the entrance to a mining system under our lines. Draw what you see – there might be information for us that you won't understand…'

Oh, my God! Will wanted to put a hand to the table to keep his balance.

'Yes, sir.' He couldn't believe what he was hearing: him being sent forward of the front line into no man's land!

'Mr Whitaker will synchronise his watch, and when you've made your sketches, at "D" Hour we'll give covering fire to help get you back.'

'Yes, sir.' *Help?* Only help?

'Meanwhile stay here in the farmhouse and stow your pictures in a cupboard. Mr Whitaker will brief you at seventeen hundred, then it's sharpen your HBs, say your prayers, and get ready to wriggle like a worm.'

'Yes, sir.'

'Good luck, then.' The colonel slapped the pictures and waved a hand for Will to collect them up.

He shuffled them together as the officer turned the generator of his field telephone, holding off speaking until after he'd been marched out: not a number three on an eighteen-pounder, but an OP Ack who was going to have to get nearer to the enemy than any soldier ever wanted.

He sat on a chair in the kitchen and shook his head. Why the heck did he have to be good at drawing...?

12

Up until now the main danger had been taking an unlucky one at the battery. Will had thought himself luckier than those soldiers who had to go over the top and run through machine-gun fire to drop into enemy trenches and fight with bayonets. Now he'd been ordered to do something just as bad as any of that. They'd all heard the tales: forward parties rolling into craters and finding Germans coming the other way; men hanging in strips on the wire like shredded washing; rats as big as cats coming out of the ribcages of corpses. So wriggling on his belly out there among all that was the last thing he wanted to do.

Second Lieutenant Whitaker was three or four inches shorter than he was, broad, and as young as him with a serious face and a mouth that would suddenly smile at nothing funny.

'They say the word, Castle, and we have to do it, and make the best darned job of it we can.' *Smile*. He sounded Welsh, and he creaked in his leather belting when he straightened himself, which he did a lot. 'So here's the plan.' They were in an upstairs room of the farmhouse with two trestle tables pushed together, covered with charts. Spread out in front of them was the battlefield situation as the Observation Corps saw it – the south-west to north-east road from Albert to Bapaume, with the allied front line drawn in red ink and the German in blue.

'I need to be in position by dawn so we leave the trench *here* at 02:00 hours.' *Smile*. 'Our wire will be cut ready by the sappers, and a helmet hung on a post to guide us through the gap for coming home. We keep our heads and our bottoms down and we get to *here* or hereabouts—' He did a little twiddle with his finger. 'We find some cover – aerial photographs show this as lightly wooded – and when we're there I'll tell you what I want sketched.' *Smile*.

'Yes, sir.' Nothing too difficult, then!

'I want to know the function of these buildings here, if any.' *Smile*. And I want the rise and fall of the ground over here—' another twiddle of his finger – 'and what range of fire Fritz has got for when our infantry arrives.'

'Yes, sir.' Will had never thought there was anything special about being able to draw things that looked like things. It hadn't helped him at school, it had been taken for granted at Pryce's, and his cartoons made Fred laugh, that was all. Now he cursed the fact of it. What rotten luck! Who'd ever have thought your pencil could get you killed? Being number three on an eighteen-pounder was risky enough for him, thank you very much.

'Wear your cape over your uniform or you'll never get the mud out of your buttons.'

'Yes, sir.' Just like the army! Get back alive and they'd be inspecting him on parade next morning.

'Report to me here at zero-zero hours. Meanwhile, man, familiarise yourself with the gadgetry.' Whitaker handed him the Observer Corps sketching board. 'This used to be in the hands of a damned good fellow.' *Smile*.

'Sir.' He took the board, which was set ready with a full roll of paper. He worked the knurl on the right to see how easily the paper moved.

'In your own time, OP Ack.'

'Yes, sir.' Being addressed like that sounded strange, but Will supposed the officer was right – he wasn't Gunner Castle any more, not for the next few hours; he was detached to the Observer Corps. And with a little squirt of pain in his stomach a horrible question came into his head: who did the Germans hate more: the artillery who pounded them from way behind the front line, or the Observer Corps who didn't fight them man-to-man but snooped and spied? Well, he thought he knew the answer to that – and he was going to do his damnedest not to get captured. He'd rather be dead than caught as a spy. Everyone knew what happened to them.

The front-line trench was quiet. Lookouts along the short stretches of shored-up chalk leaned with their periscopes above the parapet and yawned. He could hear men in the bunkers snoring, or groaning, or cursing and turning as they scratched at their lice. An occasional burst of machine-gun fire kept his head down, but as an artillery-man he knew the guns were aimed at their ears not at their hearts. Word was that reinforcing troops for 'Z' Day would be coming in under cover of darkness the next night, and an early morning bombardment would aim shrapnel shells to cut the German wires while howitzer high explosives held back their second line. Between his smiles Second Lieutenant Owen Whitaker briefed him very efficiently.

'To put you in the picture, we're going up and over the parapet from those steps there. You start off as flat as you can to the ground, burrowing like, and if we don't draw any fire we come up to the crawl and put on a bit more speed. We'll round that hillock at ten o'clock – that's direction ten o'clock, not time ten o'clock – and get into position by the time the sun shows its face.' *Smile.* But it had started raining, and the chance of the sun turning up to shine for them was pretty remote.

The officer in charge of the trench came along. In a low voice – both sides had listening devices – the man confirmed to Owen Whitaker that the British wire had been cut for them, not by the sappers but by German shrapnel; and it would stay cut until they were back.

Looking along, Will could see the dented helmet showing their route through – and, Lord, it did look glaringly obvious. But it wasn't for him to question; it was all he could do to keep his stomach quiet from rolling with the old fright: was he going to get hurt, was he going to get killed? Might he freeze with fear, or turn and run in a funk? He just didn't know how brave he was going to be. Could a man who stamped on spiders ever be a hero?

'You up for this, Castle?' Both officers were looking at him. 'You seem a bit distant.'

He lied. 'I'm just working out how to sling my sketching board on my back so I can wriggle and crawl. I've made sure I've got plenty of sharpened pencils.'

'Good man. At the ready, and thinking about it.' And the two officers lit cigarettes without offering one to him.

They went over the top; not in a battle charge but in stealth. Owen Whitaker led the way, swathed in his cape and grunting forwards; but for a short, square man he gained good ground pretty fast. Will came behind, but wasn't pleased when he got no warning of puddles or strands of blown-off wire. The earth was churned up by old advances and retreats, and after a dry spell the ground had hardened so the new rain lay on the surface like a brown wash, Will's cape getting caught under his knees, pulling him down and covering him in mud and vile-smelling muck. There was an eerie silence over no man's land, but at least there were no sounds of shooting – although a man coughing was a man within hearing, and the action of a rifle bolt might not be for cleaning purposes.

But Will was too busy to feel afraid, keeping his backside down and following Whitaker's boots. He was where he was, doing what he was doing. What would Amy or Fred think if they could see him now? The new moon and the low cloud gave a darkness that seemed ideal for this wriggling and crawling, but the vague outline of their target hillock still seemed to be miles away. Whitaker started to raise himself higher, went from a crawl to a bent scuttle, and Will untangled his cape and followed.

Whoosh! A sudden flare shot up from the German lines. The sound held him still for a split second before it burst into life and came floating down over them, flooding no man's land in a shadowless glare. Will threw himself flat, digging his fingers and the toes of his boots into the mud, waiting to be seen and machine-gunned: rigid, tense. But, nothing. When the flare was down it burnt in a ghostly glow across the ground and a German voice shouted something; another replied – were they close, being guided towards him? He dug himself even deeper in, tasting the acrid mud.

Scuttle – a rat with a body fat enough to be heard crawling came over Whitaker's leg and towards him, face to face. He couldn't move; he daren't twitch. He wanted to jump up and run, but if the Germans were close they'd see him even swiping at it. Big body, small head, it came close enough for his eyes to go out of focus. It was going to bite his nose – and could he lie still and take that? Would life be worth living with a gnawed-off nose? No! If this rat went to bite him he'd be on his feet and running, and take his chances. But which way would he go? Back to the British trench and be shot for a coward or on to the German and be shot as a spy?

The rat hadn't moved; it was still breathing in his breath. He put his head down – let it have a go at the top of his head, or at an ear. Suddenly the flare went out with a loud pop, and he swiped at the creature, which ran off down his side.

'Ye Gods!'

Whitaker moved, and he followed. No guns fired, the Germans had probably been doing a routine check. They ran towards the hillock and what looked like a small knot of trees. They reached cover and he drew breath, found a body position something like normal and whispered, 'Did you see that rat? I thought—'

'One of thousands. But the rats I worry about, see, are man-sized and speak German.' *Smile*. 'Now, we're going west of that bluff so we'll be in position for dawn. You'll note and draw what I want until the bombardment starts, then it's us getting back with the information.'

'Yes, sir.' He could smell a night-scent coming off the beechnuts on the trees – a freakish sensation.

'Come on, then.' Whitaker was moving off. Will followed, flanking the bluff on the north-western edge of the sector. With the superior height of their ground perhaps the Germans felt they were safe from attack. But this was exactly what he and Whitaker were probing: getting some better idea of the rise and fall of the land up here, and what those scattered buildings were all about. He understood very well – to hit Fritz where he felt safest could give the British a real advantage, even if it only created a diversion.

By the light of the pre-dawn sky he could see Whitaker's broad back moving forward while he picked his own path up the scrubby slope. They came to a near-summit and Whitaker stopped, looked about. A few more yards and they'd be where the roofs of the buildings could be seen. Stooping, Whitaker went on. This was it, then, the crucial part; this was what they'd come for, getting into the prone positions Whitaker wanted for observation and sketching.

They crept the final yards of slope as more and more of those buildings came into view. Will had seen such places all over this part of France, in fields, clustered at crossroads – rough, cobwebbed, dilapidated stores for grain, potatoes and suchlike. But he knew the British also used them for entrances to tunnels and ventilation shafts, and an alert about that sort of German use would be vital back at HQ.

A brighter, flatter morning light began to seep across them, filling in the detail of where they were. Whitaker turned, nodded, smiled and crept on, his body lower and lower until he lay himself flat on a mound that war hadn't touched – a plateau of wild grasses.

'We're in luck, man. Winter fodder. Ideal cover.' *Smile*.

The man was right; lying here they wouldn't be seen, and when they'd finished their work they could stay until the bombardment began – when it would be double-back, head down and run like hell for that helmet.

Whitaker was up on his elbows, his binoculars trained on the nearest of the buildings. It was more a hut, derelict and ordinary. He was focused on it, then on the other, then the near one again. He lay down, rolled on his side. 'Inch forward till you get a decent view. But don't show yourself – in fact, take your helmet off and put grasses in your hair. Draw for me what you see, with notes, from the right of the far building, across through, and make an estimate of the fall of the land into that dip towards that road. Can you see that road?'

'Yes, sir.'

'That's the Albert to Mametz road. Good for their reinforcements, see, and for ours when we've taken this ground. We've got it covered from the west, but it runs beneath high banks. Plot that exposed section and set it in context with reference to the three buildings.'

'Yes, sir.' Will obeyed Whitaker's orders. He took off his helmet, roughed up his hair and tugged at wild grasses to weave them in. He pulled the sketching board round to his front and tapped his tunic pocket to check that he hadn't lost his pencils in the crawling, and moved forward to get a good vantage point for sketching.

It wasn't too difficult. Sporadic gunfire of all sorts was starting from both sides, nothing heavy and serious. But as it gained force he suddenly heard a horse whinnying and kicking against wood. It was coming from one of those buildings.

Whitaker rolled off his elbows as they both watched an old man harnessing a horse about thirty yards away.

'*En avant!*' His croaky voice shouted above the jingling of traces.

Will parted the grasses – to be shattered by the sight of an old sack of a horse coming towards them pulling something – a reaper that was cutting into the grass.

'*Avance, vieux cheval, ou je te donne un coup sur la tete!*' And now a German soldier was standing behind the farmer, pushing him in the back with his rifle butt to get the horse and the reaper moving faster.

'Lie still!'

'*Vite! Vite!*' the German shouted.

'We'll see which way he's working, how long before we're mincemeat.' *Smile.*

But Will knew they were out of luck and that they'd have to move pretty damned quickly. They were lying at the leading edge of the grasses – and where does a farmer start his reaping? At the edge. The old man was leading his horse straight towards them, followed by the big German with the rifle. Twenty, thirty more paces and the horse would be on top of them, followed by the blades of that reaper.

'It's a rifle,' Whitaker hissed, 'not a machine gun. We've got a chance if we run.' He stuck his head up, bolder – and quickly down again. 'On the count of three, it's up and run for the beeches. Zigzag! Keep apart!'

Will got to his knees. The jingle and clank was coming closer, the horse neighing as if it sensed there was more than lumps of flints in its path.

'*En avant!*'

'One, two – *three!*' Whitaker suddenly leapt up and started racing for the beeches, his knees high like someone hurdling.

'*Halt! Halt!*'

Will heard the rifle bolt. He pushed himself up, too, but the cord to his sketching board got caught under his foot and he stumbled and fell forward.

Crack! The rifle fired – and he saw Whitaker run on for a second, arms windmilling, then pitch forward into the grass and somersault over. He jumped to his feet and threw his hands above his head.

'Surrender!' he shouted. '*Nicht* shoot!'

The soldier swung his rifle round at him, aimed it at his head, drew back the bolt again.

So this was it! He couldn't breathe as he stared at the German making up his mind. Slowly, the man advanced on him. He didn't dare to hope. Would this enemy worry about a French farmer seeing him shoot an English spy? On he came; looking along the alignment of the rifle sights.

'*Hoch! Hände hoch!* Up!' The German gestured 'hands up' with the weapon.

Will reached for the clouds, and a great spasm shook him as the German went round behind him.

'*Geh los!* March!'

He took a sharp jab in the spine. He walked the way he was facing, towards where Whitaker lay. It was only a few steps – Owen hadn't got far – and there he was in an awkward crumple, nothing graceful about his death. His eyes were open as if he might still give some last instruction; and his mouth was fixed in one of his smiles. Forever now.

'*Weiter!*'

He was prodded on, the barrel pressure easing as the German took off Whitaker's identity tag – probably his watch as well. The sound of the reaper started again; he guessed there'd be a kink in the line of cut as it went round poor old Whitaker. He was pushed towards the road, expecting to be dropped by a change of mind and a bullet in the back at any second. But if it didn't come, he knew he'd soon be a hated artillery man, or, worse, an enemy spy. And what could he expect then?

13

Freddie's mum had changed. Normally she was the last person he noticed on account of her mood or her talk. His dad, yes – he always had to be on his toes with his dad, knew when to ask him about something and when not, and if ever the man came out with '*Ye Gods!*' he'd run off out. But his mum was always the same, cooking their meals and doing her job at Wood Street – day shift now that Will wasn't home at night. Mums were mums. But she'd changed. She'd started snapping at him when most times she'd just shove him out of her way or give him a kick up the backside. She'd got crabby – even looking after his dad.

The reason for it came out one evening in July; the lack of news; his dad down in the kitchen behind his newspaper, eating cheese on toast.

'They say here that our...artillery bombardment could be heard across the Channel...in the south of England. Well, that'll be our Will. Giving Fritz a pasting.'

'I bloomin' hope so. Bli, I hope he's all right.'

'No news is...good news, Alice.'

'How long since we had a letter, then?'

'The army don't run a normal postal service. At busy times...they give first shout to the generals and their despatches.'

'They were coming a bit regular before.'

Freddie's dad gave her a look. *Not in front of the boy!* But Freddie was worried already. He'd stopped asking if there was a letter from Will; he'd see it on their faces if there was one, and he knew it upset her to say 'Nope!' to him as if the postman was to blame for not bringing anything. They'd lived on Will's last cheerful words for far too long, folded ever since in the pocket of his mother's apron. She read the words and reread them, and he'd read them himself when she was out at work.

Dear Mum, Dad and Fred

All's well here, still got a good bunch of pals on the gun. We're giving Old Fritz what-for. Food not so dusty, weather so-so. Look forward to seeing you some time, (████████████████ ████████) I'm getting used to the life, wouldn't want to be a soldier for ever, though, and hope Pryce keeps my job open. But don't worry about me, I'm doing all right, and for good old England. I got your last letter, thanks. Hope you're on the mend, Dad, lots of new little babies, Mum – and keep your hands off my gramophone records, Fred!

Your son and brother, with love.

Will xxx

'I wonder…'

'What?'

'Well, he might have written a bit more frequent to Amy. She got his first letter ahead of us, didn't she?'

Freddie's dad coughed and sipped at his tea, rattling the cup on its saucer. 'Could be. Why, are you…planning to ask her?'

She pulled a face. 'I don't know where she lives, do I? Do you?'

'No.'

'Do you, Freddie?'

He shook his head. 'Eltham somewhere, I know that.'

'Perhaps it's in his room, in his drawer. There might be an address, a letter – he's had one or two here…'

'*No!*' His dad's chair squealed on the kitchen lino. 'No one…*no one* goes through his bits.'

'No…' But he knew she meant yes, she would if she wanted to.

'That boy's off at the war. Whatever the outcome… even the worst—'

'God help us, Sam! Don't talk like that.'

'—we respect his privacy.'

'Of course we do.'

She was going to cry, so Freddie cut in quickly. 'I met her down Woolwich that time, didn't I? Coming out of the Arsenal. If she does the same shift every day…'

'The girls in her shop always…do the same shift.'

'...Then I can go down and hang about and ask her.'

'Will you, Freddie? Will you?'

'Course I will.'

'Tomorrow, will you, if we haven't heard?'

'I can get you some cherries or something while I'm down there. If Jobling's got 'em.'

His mother stood up, shook her head slowly and sadly. 'I don't want anything from anywhere, Freddie, except for news that our Will's all right.'

'Don't fret, woman.' His dad opened his paper again. 'He will be.'

But Freddie knew that none of them could be very sure about that.

She didn't look like Amy any more; it was as if she was the wrong person altogether – bent over and scurrying with the other women and girls towards the tram stops.

'Amy!'

'Fred!' She stopped, stared at him, her eyes frightened wide. 'Have you heard something?'

'No.'

'You gave me a turn.' It looked it, too, her hands were holding her head as if she was stopping it from falling off.

'No, it was just, we haven't heard anything from... anyone.' He knew what was supposed to happen if the army had bad news for you: a telegram boy in your street was a scary sight to see, until he'd cycled on past your house. 'We've not heard from Will for a bit, just wondered if you'd had anything...?'

'I was on the point of coming to ask your mum the same thing, because you'd hear something official and I wouldn't. I'm not his wife, am I?'

'No. But we've not had anything. Thank God.'

She suddenly showed a bit of the old Amy again: straightening her back. 'There's a lot going on over there. They say you hear pretty quick if it's...'

Freddie had seen the bits in the local paper, a picture of a soldier and a sentence about how brave he'd been. Every dead soldier was a hero.

'No, not old Will. He could dodge a bull in an alley. But you tell us where you live in Eltham, an' if ever...'

She shuddered. 'Thirteen Boleyn Street. But no. No, Fred. My tram passes your house every day. I know Will's window, I never don't look at it if I'm on that side.' She stopped, said it almost matter-of-fact. 'If ever...' She started again. 'If ever you get anything terrible, don't come up to the house, seeing you there will... No, do me a favour and hang a black scarf in his window, will you? Give me time to get hold of myself...'

A shiver took him, too. 'Is that all?'

'What else?' Amy shrugged. 'Then I'll get off the tram, take a walk up and down, and call.' She put her hands on her hips and stood staring at him, chucked her head at the Arsenal. 'There's lots of girls like me in there. Up in the air or down in the dumps, waiting. You just have to get on with it, don't you?'

He supposed you did. Everyone did. People like them weren't in charge of things.

'You going home, Fred?'

He shook his head, told her he had a lot of shopping to do. After that last tram ride with those boys he didn't fancy another.

'Ta-ta, then. Give my best wishes to your mum and dad.'

'I will. Cheerio.'

She put herself on the end of her queue and he mooched around the market, the grim talk about putting a black scarf in Will's bedroom window making him feel small and helpless. What could he do about what happened to his brother, to himself, or to anyone else in this rotten war?

14

The letter came. Ernst had been waiting and waiting for this news and now it had come: the most important letter he'd ever had in his life – Rachel's loving words telling him that his daughter Josefine had arrived safely: overdue and small but doing well. This was wonderful! *Naches!* Breathing was hard as he read it, and when he stood up he had to sit straight down again. He was a father! He would do in his own home all the fatherly things his own father had done when he was a boy. He felt as high as a Zepp ever flew, and he didn't mind that he'd had to miss the benedictions and the official naming on that first Sabbath. *He was a father!*

He knew Karl Klee wouldn't show much interest in his marvellous news – but he couldn't wait to tell Josef. How proud he'd feel himself if a friend like Josef wanted Ernst or Ernestine for a relative's name.

Josef came into the hut worrying at his moustache and full of rotas and instructions, but when Ernst waved his letter and told him his news, he smiled and gripped his arm. 'I congratulate you. And your Rachel…'

'*Josefine*. We've called the baby Josefine…'

'Very fine, very fine. Pretty name.'

'After someone I know…'

Josef suddenly seemed to understand and stood to

attention as if he was being presented with a medal. 'I'm honoured, Erno, honoured.'

The man's attitude, standing tall, a proud look on his face, swelled Ernst's breast. *Erno* again. After this war they might keep in touch – although they lived a long way apart – but whether they did or not, he was proud himself that his daughter would carry the name of someone so special and brave.

Bare-headed and with his arms held high and aching, Will was marched past a platoon of German troops heading towards their front line. Seeing the enemy up close was scary – lean, mean faces under large grey helmets. Their eyes flicked his way, and he thought the men might spit at him, but the officer in charge shouted something and they marched on past with no more than smirks. It was still early morning and noisy, and he could hear the British guns laying on a heavy bombardment. The weather had cleared up, and the infantry could well be on the attack, while his Royal Field Artillery shoulder title was probably shouting out what he was: a hated gunner as well as a spy. So had old Owen Whitaker been the lucky one – everything all over for him with a quick shot?

He was marched for well over an hour, and halted at the gates of a large house. When they saw him the sentries looked surprised about something. Because there was only one of him? The German who'd marched him here said something and they swung the gates open, and with another prod in the back he was marched in, two others falling-in beside him.

Will guessed this was some sort of château – there were plenty around – but it wasn't fancy, just a large house built of white stone slabs and red brick, and there, just off the path, he saw something that turned him inside-out, one of the scariest sights ever; he couldn't drag his eyes off it. It was a post as thick as a telegraph pole, just over head-height and set in a concrete square at the angle of two walls of an outbuilding scarred with bullet holes. And he knew what it was. This was the post where men were executed.

'*Starr nicht so – geh' weiter!*'

Another jab in the back and he was pushed past a guard and into the château, where they stood him against a wall – and he saw again the face of the man who'd brought him here, large and pale with small eyes behind thin wire glasses. He was a sort of sergeant by the look of his uniform. He leant his rifle against the wall, and put the sketching board and Whitaker's identity tag and pay-book on a chair.

But Will couldn't get the sight of that execution post out of his head. He jumped as the sergeant was called into a side room, dreading his return and the march outside. And he jumped again as the door re-opened and at a command from within the room he was pulled forward by the guards.

'*Los – rein mit dir!*'

The room was large with a big desk in it, behind which a German army officer was sitting, Whitaker's items and his own sketching board on the desk.

'Stand at ease,' the officer said in a good English accent. Will did so, trying to control the shaking of his legs.

'So – you were captured on forward observation duty?'

'Yes, sir.' There was no point in lying – where he was captured and the sketching board told their own story. The officer was a large man with small hands that were turning the sketching board over and over. Apart from the smart grey tunic and two gold pips he put Will in mind of his old headmaster Mr Perrit, who could swish a cane hard but only after listening to you and sometimes giving you the benefit of the doubt. He wouldn't mind that right now!

'But you are wearing Royal Field Artillery insignia. This is not Observation Corps.'

The information on his dog tag was all Will was supposed to give to anyone. He stayed silent.

The officer stood up. '*Durchsucht ihn.*'

One of the guards came round in front of him, the other kicked his legs further apart, and suddenly their hands went everywhere; but he had very little on him: his pay-book, a rag of a handkerchief, his dog tag, and—

'*Ah!*'

A guard pulled Fred's sketch-book out of a top pocket. His pay-book and dog tag were put onto the desk, and the officer was handed the sketch-book, which he looked through, slowly, lingering here and there, pursing his lips, smiling, frowning, finally throwing it onto the desk. He picked up the pay-book, looked into it briefly, and threw that down, too.

'They wanted an artist on their forward observation raid?'

Will's heart raced again. *Raid!* That sounded a lot worse than 'duty'.

The officer stood looking at the sketching board, then back at him. 'This is empty, no pictures. So, what were you charged with finding out?'

He said nothing, at first. They'd got his pay-book but he mustn't give them more than dog-tag information. 'I was ordered to draw what the officer told me, sir.'

'And Second Lieutenant Whitaker cannot talk.' The officer let out a sigh, folded his arms. 'Well, his next of kin will be informed of his death.' He stared hard at him. 'And your next of kin…'

Oh, God! He should have taken a bullet, never surrendered.

'…They will be also informed that you are now a prisoner of the German Empire.'

Not death! Will wanted to cry; but somehow he kept his composure, nodded in a soldierly way. The officer wrote down his dog-tag details and threw the disc back to him.

'Stand to attention.'

He did so. But his eyes left the officer's and went to Fred's sketch-book on the desk; the officer's went there, too. He picked it up as if about to hand it to him.

'Identity disc information only for me.' The officer smiled; now more like Mr Perrit when he was reaching for his cane. 'And identity disc only for you.' And he dropped Fred's sketch-book into his waste paper basket.

He was a prisoner of war, out of the fierce action, held on his own at this château. They put him in the 'execution' outbuilding, a large barn-like room where empty bunks and half-full chamber-pots told him of prisoners who'd been here and moved on somewhere else.

But after an hour or so, a huge commotion sat him up, a lot of shouting in German and snatches of talk in English. In a clatter of boots a round-up of a dozen men was brought in, some walking, some stretchered – blood, splints and bandage, shock, fear and anger all over their faces. Will watched, tried to help as the wounded were given first aid and the rest bagged bunks. He soon heard their story. They were from the Eleventh Battalion East Lancashire Regiment, known amongst themselves as the Accrington Pals – lads from Burnley, Chorley, Blackburn and Accrington itself – and that morning their battalion had been massacred in a forward march on the German lines.

'Serre, we were s'posed to tek town of Serre, top of a ruddy hill...'

'Four waves of us. Us first, ran smack into their machine guns an' grenades...'

'Lads cut down like corn at harvest time...'

'We got through their wire an' dropped down into t' front line...'

'But behind us, the poor blighters never reached no man's land...'

'An' we was left high an' dry in their trench, no support, an' here we ruddy are...'

It all poured out, none of them taking a lot of interest in him, until one of the lads saw his badges.

'Royal Field Artillery! Waste o' time, en't you? Dud shells all over t' place an' wire not cut but re-arranged! Sittin' blitherin' ducks, our lads were.'

Will didn't argue. He hadn't made the shrapnel shells that didn't explode, and he wasn't one of the generals who'd sent these lads over the top. 'I'm very sorry about your mates.'

'Gi' yerself up, did ye? How come they got yer,

all that far back wi' the guns?'

No! He wasn't having that. 'Hang on a minute!' He told them what he'd been doing, how he'd crossed no man's land at night, been taken prisoner, how they'd shot Owen Whitaker – although he put it as if he'd just been lucky himself, not tripping over before standing up and surrendering.

'Oh. Right y'are, then.' Which seemed to say a lot.

And after a day and a half of mucking in together, with some new French prisoners brought in, he was taken out with the rest, crowded into a lorry and driven for miles to a railway halt, where he was shoved tight into a railway wagon and shunted off somewhere else.

And that, they all reckoned, would be Germany.

But from the names of the railway stations and some fading signs along the way, this round-up of French and British prisoners was still in France when the train stopped. The heavy doors slid open and Will could breathe again. They were tumbled out onto the platform of the Gare de Laon, and straight away he counted three machine gunners on the roof of the station, with all the other guards carrying rifles and drawn pistols.

'Hey up!' someone said. 'Wha' a welcome. 'Ow'd they know it was me on board?' But a pistol butt knocked out his humour and some of his teeth, and Will kept his mouth shut tight.

They were marched to a cluster of civic buildings

surrounded by barbed wire, manned by guards in sentry boxes. The town was devastated, bullet holes all over, standing walls and the rubble of the rest lying about to tip a boot and twist an ankle. Heads were low, every man aware that there was nothing they could do now to help to win the war.

They were halted and separated, the English from the French, and in the yard behind the buildings they were marshalled and pushed, shouted at in German and pidgin English, and put into stone-walled barns, Will with fifty others – the Accrington Pals and men from the First Newfoundland Regiment, there already. Inside, they redivided the thin straw and made room to sleep; all on the ground without blankets.

And with hardly any food, either. Will was shuffled out before dark into a mess hall in the main building and given a tin mug of something a guard called coffee, with a piece of bran-and-potato bread and a ladle of thin bean soup – a rancid diet that had him running to the latrines before he messed himself, squatting over a stinking pit swarming with flies – and then it was back to the barn, where there was no chance of sleep with the sounds of rats, and his feverish scratching at lice.

He tried to think of Amy and his family, but the awful thing was, there was no way he could picture them as real people any more. They were names without faces. The Accrington lads talked into the night about their dead pals, and about the way they'd been taken themselves – brave boys, all of them, giving a big lie to anyone thinking a prisoner of war was a shameful coward. But the big weight on his own heart was whether he was or he wasn't.

And as some French cockerel told him dawn had come, he fell into a sort of unconsciousness, only to be kicked out of it by a guard and told to get ready to move.

But at least he was alive, wasn't he?

15

Freddie's eyes were sore with staring out for anyone coming up the path in a uniform – the postman, the telegraph boy or a soldier; that's how news of Will would come to their house. And eventually it came, on a Saturday morning. He knew the envelope the postman fished from his bag was important because as he dropped it through he gave the letterbox a rattle.

Freddie's mother rushed from the kitchen and stood staring at the envelope on the doormat; buff-coloured, very official-looking and without a normal stamp. It was addressed to Mr Samuel Castle. She stared at it as if it was a dead rat and her hand went to her mouth.

'Bring it up to your father.' Her voice was shaky, and still she didn't want to touch it. They went up the stairs and Freddie took it into the big bedroom.

His dad must have heard the letterbox go; he was sitting up in bed looking like a sick king.

'Oh my good God, Sam.'

Freddie gave it to his dad, accidentally kicking the chamber pot under the bed and giving it a doomy ring.

His dad opened the envelope with the edge of a teaspoon, his mum staring as he took out the letter and read it. Without a word he handed it for them both to see.

It was a small official form, with a slip of paper clipped to it.

I regret to have to inform you that
a report has been received from the
War Office to the effect that
(No.) 703145 (Rank) Gunner (Name) W. Castle
(Regiment) No. 9 Division Royal Field Artillery
was ~~posted as missing~~
taken prisoner
after the engagement at
.... on ....
Should he subsequently rejoin, or any other
information be received concerning him,
such information will be at once
communicated to you.
I am,
Sir,
Your Obedient Servant,
J.W. Dalrymple
Officer in Charge of Records
Royal Field Artillery

'Posted as missing' had been crossed out, which left 'taken prisoner' as the message, although the where and the when were left blank. Freddie felt numb outside, fizzy inside. Will wasn't dead! He was a prisoner of the Germans – but he was alive.

The other slip of paper was a typed note, signed with the same blue pen.

Details of Gunner Castle's whereabouts may also
be sought from the British branch of the
International Red Cross at 44 Moorfields, London.
Yours sincerely
J.W. Dalrymple

'Thank the Lord!' His dad sank back. And his mum stood shaking and crying, went to pieces, and Freddie helped her to sit on the edge of the bed.

'He's not dead, Mum. He'll be all right, I know he will. We'll get him back when the war's over.'

'I wonder how…he was…taken.'

'I don't care!' She flared at his dad. 'He's alive. Alive.' And she slid off the bed and did something he'd never seen her do; she knelt, leant on the counterpane, and put her hands together like a little girl. 'Thank you, God!' She looked up to heaven. 'Thank you, God!'

But it was Freddie who made them all a cup of tea.

Amy had wanted to be one of the first to know, too, and she came as soon as she saw Will's white silk scarf hanging from his bedroom window – she and Freddie's mum crying and hugging one another like sisters.

'*Forty-four Moorfields. Red Cross.*' Amy read the letter for herself and gave it back. 'I'll be onto them, Mrs Castle, I'll change my Arsenal shifts if need be and get up there and find out where they've got him.' And the look in her eyes told them she'd sit on that Red Cross doorstep until she got an answer.

Freddie left his mum and dad on their own and walked home with Amy to her house in Boleyn Street.

'Thanks, Fred. You've turned out all right.'

Well, he didn't know what she meant by that, but he took it as meaning to be nice, so he ran off while it lasted, taking the short way home – which, bad luck, took him too near to his school. And, although it was the school holidays, who did he have to see in Westmount Road but Wally Quinnell?

And Quinnell had seen him first so there'd be no dodging him. He always looked the same, school-time or holidays, winter or summer, in his tangly jersey and kicking boots.

'Oi!' Quinnell ran across the road. He came close up to him and snorted. 'Castle!'

'Wally.' Freddie didn't want trouble, he wanted home, his dinner, and a game up Jack Woods with Don and his Well Hall mates, tell them about Will. 'How's your brother?' He'd get in first.

'All right. Fightin' Fritz 'ard I 'spect.'

He waited for it.

'An' 'ow about your'n? Still up the back with the guns?'

'No.' He didn't want to let out any more than he had to, but if he lied now it'd be worse when something got printed in the local paper. 'He's been captured. Prisoner of war.' He looked hard into Quinnell's face to see what he'd make of that.

Quinnell smirked. 'Coward! Rotten coward!' He spat on the pavement. 'Knew 'e'd find some way of gettin' out of it.' His top lip had curled up, his nose had gone wide, his eyes were hateful slits. 'I wouldn't wanna be 'is brother any more'n I'd wanna be a dog turd.'

Freddie should have hit him, right then. He wanted to crack his fist into that hateful face, let him know he wasn't taking that.

But he didn't. He didn't have the guts. 'You c'n think what you blooming-well like.' He turned away and ran towards home – followed by a loud shout.

'Coward! Yellow belly! Got no fightin' guts, none o' your lot, Castle!'

And when he got indoors, out of breath, not hungry, not wanting to play up Jack Woods any more, he kept out of his mother's way, and in this room or in that or out in the garden he tried to tell himself all sorts of things about what had happened; except that Wally Quinnell was right. He was a gutless coward.

16

'She's nearly two hundred metres long, Ernst, and she's fat because she's got nineteen gas cells, which'll give us...' Josef seemed to be waiting for some response, adjusting his moustache.

'What?'

'A flying height of five kilometres. Who's ever been that high before?'

Ernst didn't know, but he didn't want to be one of them. He, Josef, and Karl Klee had been transferred to the Nordholz base where the new Zeppelin R class L31 was being fitted out. And just looking up at her sent his head spinning: the thing was awesome; she'd certainly scare the skin off any Londoners who looked up and saw her.

'Six Maybach engines. We can race across the sky at nearly a hundred kilometres an hour, with oxygen to help us cope with the height.'

'I'll try not to be sick.'

'And carry over four thousand kilos of bombs. Think of the damage we can do!'

Ernst blew out his cheeks to show how impressed he was.

'Got to be done,' Josef said, 'got to be done.'

* * *

Thirteen Zeppelins set off, and things started badly. Crossing the North Sea they were fired on by ships off Harwich and their former airship L13 was hit and had to turn for home; and when Mathy climbed the L31 to get out of the guns' range she was buffeted by high altitude winds – a strong southerly that slowed them, as it slowed most of the others, who one by one turned tail.

But not Mathy. 'It's us, then. Again.' The lieutenant's chin was lifted as he ran his eyes around the gondola, and Ernst felt a small lift himself, of some of the fighting spirit he'd thought he'd lost. This was a commander who filled you with confidence. Josef located the seaside town of Margate and guided Ernst's steering up the Thames towards London, with not a shot of ground artillery coming up at them.

'They must be sleeping at their guns! They thought we were never coming back.'

It was as if the English guard was down, and who could moan at that? And there was no sign of enemy aircraft, either; but as they started dropping their bombs near Millwall Docks the south London searchlights started criss-crossing the sky and suddenly hit them – although the beams were struggling to get through the city dust, the cloud, and the mist. But for the L31 there was little chance of pin-pointing military targets.

Soon Josef was calling out a likely route from a large

atlas of London. 'Dept-ford, Green-wich, Ell-tham...'

'I've been here, Eltham Palace,' Mathy said, 'King Henry the Eighth of England. A grand tour with my uncle. So we shall send down our greetings.' And he ordered more bombs to be released. 'Send Royal Eltham a special gift.'

The mist was lifting now and a searchlight got through full beam, quickly followed by anti-aircraft shells.

'*Oy gevalt!*' Ernst looked at his watch. It was 01:40, they'd been dropping bombs for ten minutes, and as Mathy ordered the L31 into a cloud-bank and Josef started plotting her course for home he prayed for a safe passage back to Nordholz. To him tonight had been so easy: very little resistance from the ground, with the Royal Flying Corps seeming not to have an aeroplane to put in the air. But he knew that had been rare – although any trip he survived was another chance to one day hold his little girl in his arms.

Second Lieutenant George Simmonds was alone in his Royal Flying Corps BE12; he'd taken off and was climbing away from Sutton's Farm. He was keen to get up to operational height because this plane was new and could climb faster that the old BE2. Also, it was fitted with a forward-shooting Vickers machine gun that fired through the propeller arc – giving a better aim than the backward-firing Lewis gun of the older plane, and meaning he could fly without the weight of a navigator-cum-gunner. It also gave him a bigger fuel tank and more flying time. But best of all was the ammunition he was carrying. Tonight he was armed with an alternate mix of Buckingham tracers and the new Pomeroy explosive bullets the munitions people had developed. If he could get a stream of ammo among the gas cells in the hull of a Zeppelin, the combination should explode on contact and set the thing ablaze.

He chased the searchlight beams over London. The crews down there could hear the raiders' engines and get across the sky a lot quicker than he could. So just show him his prey and he'd go in for the kill...

And then he saw her: a wavering searchlight caught the Zeppelin through a sudden break in the cloud.

'Oh, my God!'

He'd never seen anything this big in the sky – a huge silvery monster, long, fat, with three gondolas hanging beneath her. She dwarfed him as he banked sharply to get a line on her belly, thumb ready on the trigger, planning where he would dive to avoid the beast when she was hit and burst into flames. But as he came out of his banking she was suddenly gone, lost in cloud, and fly and search as he might he didn't get another sighting. Disappointed, his fuel running dangerously low, he had to set his course for Sutton's Farm. And when his heart had stopped its racing he shook his fist up at the sky and swore an oath. 'Another time, Menace – another time!'

That third Thursday of August Freddie was bored. His mum was on the two-till-eight shift at Wood Street, his dad seemed comfortable, so he took himself off for a day out with Don and went to Woolwich for a few rides on the free ferry, dodging the boat's crew who wanted them off. When they'd had enough of that they walked along Plumstead High Street to Beasley's Brewery for a ride on top of a barrel of beer – because Don's uncle was a drayman and if they timed it right he'd be setting off on his afternoon deliveries. They were lucky, and with a wink from him, they climbed almost to heaven to get up on top of the highest barrel, breathing in the smells of beer and horses. And on the way up there'd been the giggle of seeing one of the horses letting down his long dinky-do to splash Lakedale Road with the loudest widdle he'd ever heard. There was never any excitement like that up at Eltham; nothing much ever seemed to happen where he lived.

Tired out, he got quickly off to sleep that night. It was good having his mum in the house. These days she tucked him into bed, told him something funny about Wood Street, kissed him and put his light out for him.

'Night-night, sleep tight, hope the bugs don't bite.' She always said it.

"Night, Mum.'

'God bless.'

And that was it; dark, quiet, peaceful. The trams stopped, his dad wasn't coughing tonight; and if he did start, his mum was there to see to him. He said his own quiet little prayer for Will, closed his eyes, and in no time at all he was off, too dog-tired even to daydream. He went into a deep, deep, sleep...

...To be woken by a loud noise, something near, a sound telling him this was part of the real world, not some dream. His mother shouted, 'What the devil was that?' and his dad went into a cough and a spit. The sound had come from a couple of streets away. Now he heard something else, a droning getting nearer, and not from the road but from up above him: an aeroplane, or—

He shot up in his bed. This noise was louder than any aeroplane – and he knew what it was. His skin prickled and iced. It was a Zeppelin, and it was coming closer and closer.

Another loud explosion shook the windows from somewhere over the other side of Well Hall Road.

'Freddie! Freddie! Get yourself up! Get downstairs!'

He threw back his sheet, scrambled out of bed and ran for his door – just as everything caved in. There was a loud shrieking sound, a huge cracking above his head, and then there was no more. It was the last he knew.

Where was he? At first he thought he'd fallen off the dray and hit his head. But what was all this thick, bricky fog? He could taste cement, all sour and gritty in his teeth. But he couldn't see anything, he was under something, his eyes prickling as he tried to stare. He could smell burning, like boiling tar, and he heard coughing, but it wasn't his dad, it was him, choking.

But there were voices. Faint. Someone saying, 'There's a boy. There ought to be a boy as well.'

And that was it – he went off into another black silence again.

He knew where he was the next time. He was under his bed. By a dim light filtering through a crack he could just see its wires and springs. He wasn't in his bedroom, though, he was in a tight, small cave – and from outside it he could hear the scrape of something like a shovel, and men shouting. He tried to shout but nothing came out, his mouth was too clogged with brick dust. He started to panic. He was under his bed, yes, but his bed was under something else. His house! He was under his house. That Zeppelin had dropped a bomb and hit his house. He kicked his feet and scrabbled his hands to get out of there – but he couldn't move, there wasn't room. He spat. He tried to shout again but he could only cough.

A whistle blew.

'Quiet! Quiet, all of you! Can you hear me, sonny? Freddie! *Freddie!* Can you hear me?'

Yes, he could, but still he could only cough and spit. And he went berserk. He was trapped. He could hear them but they couldn't hear him. They'd think he'd been blown to bits and go away and leave him. He pitched and struggled to move every bit of his body he could; he shook, he kicked and clawed, but stuff just fell around him and bent the bed lower down. He was going to die. Suffocate. Starve. He threw his head back, cracked it hard, and somehow out came a scream like a fox in the night. He screamed again. And again. He screamed until his throat was raw.

'*Quiet! Quiet!* I can hear him. He's somewhere over here. Do it again, Freddie.'

He screamed until his throat packed up and he went into a choking fit.

His dad! His mum! That voice wasn't theirs – but if he was here, where were they?

'Lie still, sonny. We're gonna get you out.'

He heard the clink of the shovel again, and a chink more light came in, with a waft of fresher air.

'My mum!' he shouted. 'Where's my mum?'

'You lie still as you can. Never you mind about no one else.'

He heard the sunk-in top of his bed being cleared –

until more light came in and he could see the sky, and then these peering faces: police, soldiers and people he knew. They took a piece of iron mantelpiece off his trapped foot, and stopped.

'Careful here, lads. We could have a frac— a bit of a problem.'

He could see a nurse through the gap, who was talking to him with a load of kind words and nonsense as she reached down to bandage his foot and ankle, tight.

'Where's my mum and my dad?'

She held his hand as he was lifted out. 'Probably gone ahead. It took a long time to find you, Freddie.'

Two men carried him to a stretcher and they went towards a Red Cross ambulance in the road.

'Thank God, there's Freddie!' It was Don's mother. But where was his own mum?

'Where are we going?'

'Up to the Cottage Hospital.' The nurse got into the ambulance with him. 'There's a "Casualty" there, and a children's ward.'

'And grown-ups?' Is that where his mum and dad would be?

'And grown-ups, yes.'

Before they shut the ambulance doors he lifted his head to look at his house. But it wasn't there any more. He could see through to the big tree at the back of their garden and the houses in Congreve Road. But never mind his house – what he wanted was to see his mum and dad, and as he came over drowsy he fought to stay awake for them. But it didn't work, and soon he was drifting off again into that old blackness, and the silence.

17

Amy always tried to sit on the side of the tram nearer Will's house, on the look-out for a scarf. She'd been woken by the explosions in the night, some towards Woolwich and a couple from up in the woods, but at the tram stop at Eltham Church no one knew much about what had happened. Yet. But from the tram she saw the devastation in Well Hall Road, and at first sight of it she was down the tram stairs and jumping off, running towards the men who were making the building safe – *Will's house. Bombed.* The bathroom was hanging down, but the rest was rubble with people standing looking at the place as if it was a tram crash.

She dodged the policeman on duty and ran to the nearest workman. 'Excuse me, excuse me – I know the people here. Can you tell me what's happened to them? Please?'

The workman in his dungarees stopped piling bricks and called another man over. Amy looked at the wreckage. There were rags of curtains, charred beams, bits of furniture, broken china and glass everywhere – and thousands of white feathers fluttering about. If there'd been anything worth salvaging it must have been taken away.

'Yes, Miss? Can I help you?' The foreman was an

older man with a jacket over the top of his dungarees.

'I'm Amy Margerison, the friend of a man who lived here, William Castle. He's in France with the Royal Field Artillery. Well, a prisoner of war, actually…'

'Oh, yes.'

The policeman had come up, but he let her stay.

'…and I'm also a friend of the family and I want to know what's happened to… Please…'

The policeman took out his notebook. 'The Castles?'

'That's right.'

'Could you give me their names, Miss?'

'Sam – Samuel – and Alice. I'm their son's fiancée, he's over in France,' she repeated. 'William. And his brother Frederick lived here.'

This seemed to confirm her right to know what had happened to them. 'It's bad news, Miss.'

'What?'

'Mr and Mrs Castle both copped it, I'm afraid.' The policeman checked his notes. 'Taken to the Woolwich mortuary.'

'Oh, Lord! And Frederick? The boy?'

'He's up at the Cottage Hospital.'

'Bad? Do you know how bad he is?'

'No, Miss, 'fraid not – but he was alive when he was took.'

Amy stood there, just looking at the remains of the house.

'But you'll have to back up a little bit now. We'll be pulling that bathroom down in a minute.'

'Yes. Thank you.' She moved away, nearer to some of the neighbours.

'Did they tell you, love?' she was asked.

Amy nodded.

'I think Freddie's all right. By all reports. Someone saw him go into the ambulance, and he was sitting up, looking back at his house.'

'Thank you. Mrs…?'

'Brewster. He's a friend of my Don.' The boy was standing there, but silent, his head slightly bowed.

'Does Fred know about his mum and dad?'

'I doubt it, love. They'll have a way of telling him when the time's right.'

'Yes. Thank you.'

Amy took a last look at the ruins of the house and walked towards the road and the trams, but on the Eltham-going side; off home to get changed out of her Arsenal clothes and into something to wear for a hospital visit.

Freddie sat up in bed. The children's ward wasn't very big, and they were all in together, boys and girls. The night before he'd been cleaned up and a doctor had inspected his right ankle; poked it, squeezed it and tried to twist it – made him yelp – and with a bit of a look as if Freddie was putting it on, he'd said nothing was broken. 'Just a sprain.'

Now, this morning, bandaged up and with his ankle throbbing, he'd hopped to the bathroom to have a wash. But then he wasn't allowed to get dressed and was put back into bed instead. There was only one thing he wanted to know. When could he go through to the grown-ups' wards and see his mum and his dad? In the night he'd thought he'd heard his dad coughing, but he'd been woozy with a spoonful of syrup and he couldn't really concentrate. He asked everyone, from the sister to the nurse to the cleaner.

'My mum and dad. Mr and Mrs Castle. Sam and Alice. How are they? When can I see them?' But every time he asked he got the same reply in some form or other.

'First let's get you properly on your feet, young man.'

'We'll see, Freddie, we'll see.'

And, 'Dunno, love. I'll try an' poke my nose later.'

He looked around the ward. There was a big girl two beds along on the other side who definitely didn't like being in there. She kept staring at him and wrapping her bed jacket around her as if he might be looking at the top of her nightdress; but he couldn't have bothered less. In the bed nearest to the nurses' desk there was a very sick boy who hardly lifted his head, and along from him there was a younger boy who kept crying all the time and didn't want his breakfast. But there didn't seem to be anyone else who'd been bombed, and no one to tell that *he* had.

Like the big girl he reckoned he was too old for here. On the walls were tiled pictures of nursery rhymes: Little Bo Peep, Little Jack Horner, Little Miss Muffet – all *little* – and Simple Simon. There should have been footballers instead, and cricketers, and cars and ships and aeroplanes, something better for people like him to stare at all day. Perhaps this nurse would get him a comic to read. If he had to stay in bed there ought to be something to do other than not look at that girl. He sat up higher to get the nurse's attention – and there standing in the doorway was Amy, looking as if she was on her way to church in a white blouse and black skirt.

She waved to him, as the sister followed her in and had a quiet word with the nurse; and although it wasn't visiting hours, they let her come over and sit on a chair.

'Fred.'

''Lo, Amy.'

She'd brought him a *Boys' Realm* and a bar of Fry's Turkish Delight.

'Thanks very much.'

The nurse drew the curtains around the bed.

'How are you, Fred?'

He was all right, thanks; but he didn't like the look in her eyes, nor the nurse drawing that curtain closed. He'd visited a hospital before when Don had had his tonsils out, and they didn't pull the curtains round except for something special. He knew his house had been bombed, and he knew he was in hospital with a bad ankle, but here he was sitting up feeling fine this morning, and yet anyone would think he was at death's door. Especially the way Amy was looking at him. She'd got something to tell him, he knew she had. She'd got something bad to say.

'I'm ever so sorry to tell you, Fred – and I've been given special permission to do so since you're getting on so well – but…'

Go on, get on with it! Get on with it, Amy!

'I'm sorry to say, Fred – your mum and dad weren't as lucky as you were…'

He knew they weren't, he'd guessed they weren't, but he hadn't let himself think it. So, were they ever so injured? Or, please God not! Were they…?

She held his hand and squeezed it. 'They didn't get out alive, Fred. They died straight off. The bomb went right through their bedroom. They didn't suffer, love, they never felt a thing…'

A weird feeling came over him. He almost wanted to smile, make it all right for Amy telling him her terrible news. He wanted to fold his arms the way some defiant boys did when they were being ticked off at school. But he didn't want to cry; he was as dry as a bone. And the next thing he said seemed so selfish, but he was only being straight.

'What's gonna happen to me?'

'I don't know, Fred. They'll make proper arrangements. They'll know what to do.'

He didn't know who 'they' were. But he did know what he was hoping already: that she'd say, 'You can come and live with me.'

But she didn't – and now he did want to cry. He thought of his mum, his dear old mum doing everything for everybody, doing her job at Wood Street and cooking dinners and cleaning and looking after his dad. And he thought of his dad, not in his sick bed but when it was them together over at Church Manorway giving special cheers for Charlie Lewis. And although he tried to force it down, a sort of sucker inside his throat pulled up a great sob from the depths of his stomach; it came up to choke him, heaving out hiccups and setting him off crying, crying, crying down his pyjamas.

And he wished – he truly wished – that the devil's bomb that had killed his mum and his dad could have done the same to him. He wouldn't have felt a thing – and right now he'd be in heaven, the three of them all together, and happy, like the best of olden times.

But as he got over his crying and hiccups and Amy held his hand, he realised that here he was on his own, the only Castle left in England.

18

Will wasn't transported to Germany. Most were, but some were put into gangs to work on the French roads, the railway and the farms. And he was on the railway, every day the same – hell. On the straw at night, hitting out at rats and scratching at the lice in his head and hair, exhaustion finally taking him off until another reveille in the dark for a measly fifth-of-a-kilo bread ration and a tin-can of coffee. Dog-tired before he started, his gang was marched under guard to work on the railway track for twelve hours, forking and shovelling crushed-stone ballast under the rails to take the weight of German guns going to the Front. The shovel was heavy enough in itself – a handle about two-and-a-half feet long with a large curved, rusted blade at the end, unwieldy to men not used to them.

Three well-placed marksmen stood on the embankment while a pistol-carrying corporal with a bit of English shouted orders.

'Dig, pig!'

'More on!'

'Quick, fast!' – and a kick or a punch would make sure the next shovel-load dug deeper into the ballast, or got thrown faster.

Will hated the corporal. He was a beast of a man; he

looked big and strong enough to carry a horse across his shoulders, or throw a man halfway up the embankment. They all called him Attila the Hun.

Digging and throwing ballast soon brought up blisters that wept all night. And the itching of the lice never stopped. There were no scissors around so he'd started biting his fingernails, but keeping one nail on each hand for scratching. No one was de-loused, and there was no change of clothes; he was still wearing what he was in when he was captured; and apart from his face and hands under the dribble of a tap in the yard there was nowhere to wash until someone produced a 'water cow' – a folding cloth bag whose fibres went watertight when wet. That made life slightly easier, but he knew he stank, although so did all the others, everyone mucking in like farmyard animals.

Every day was life-long. Mid-morning on the track there'd be some cold soup – mostly grass and horsemeat but occasionally beans, beets or bony codfish – and a few minutes' sit-down while Attila the Hun hunkered over them, spitting out tobacco juice. When they got back to the prison camp it was watery soup again, and sawdust bread. He knew he was getting weaker, day by day: the shovel felt heavier, the ballast harder to lift, and he was getting slower to move off the track when the whistle went for a train coming through. Men talked about escape, but only one had tried, a Frenchman from another barn who ran at a sentry at the gate, hitting out at him before being floored himself. What happened next was appalling: he was set upon and given a kicking and a rifle-butting, and thrown into a solitary cellar in the main building. And when he came out weeks later he'd gone mad, ranting, jumping about all over the place like a jerked puppet, rat bites all over him and a head that looked like the skull of death itself. As one of the lads put it, 'It's an officer's duty to escape, but ne'er a Joe Soap's. Ferget it!' It was drudgery, getting beaten, exhaustion, and the only thing he lived for was those short hours of unconsciousness every night. As for thoughts of Amy, or Fred, or his mum and dad – they were part of some other life that he'd never see again. In his head they were almost like characters in a book.

Yes, it was hell. Hell on earth.

At the Zeppelin base at Nordholz a bulletin was put up in the mess with a roster of seventy-two hour leaves during the final fitting-out of L31. They'd begin the following Saturday. Ernst clenched his fist and smiled. At last he could get home to meet his new baby daughter.

Before he left for Berlin that Saturday morning Karl Klee suddenly took an interest in his weekend, and with his eyebrow arched he sat at breakfast and gave him some advice – from who knew where?

'Mother first, Erno. Don't rush for the child, make sure you kiss the mother first and tell her how clever she is to give you such a beautiful daughter.'

'Of course.'

'And don't grab the baby and expect her to love you as much as she loves her mother – unless your titties are different from mine.'

'No.'

'And be sure to hand her back as soon as you smell something "off". I'm an uncle. And that's the nearest I want to be.'

Ernst went carefully into the house that evening. He didn't use his key but knocked quietly at the door, to be hugged and kissed by Rachel in the hallway, as he told her how much he loved her and made sure to admire her figure.

'Come and see her! Come and see her! Your little Josefine!'

He washed his hands before they went into the small nursery – and there she was. His daughter. His Josefine. She was small, and he couldn't say that she was pretty – yet. Rachel bent to the crib and picked her up, coaxing her awake.

'She's beautiful.' But he held off from taking her.

'Don't you want a hold? I won't let you drop her.' Rachel offered the baby and he cradled her in his arms, joyous after the months of waiting, his own child, one of the two most precious people in the world.

And she bawled. He couldn't say she cried, she bawled, and in no time she was back with Rachel, and being given a little mother's milk, and gradually quietening.

'Time. It will take a little time, Erno.'

But there wasn't enough of that this weekend. She was settled with Rachel, but every time he held her she cried, every single time; and, worst of all, when the candles were lit for the family dinner, everyone sitting around the table in the parlour – his parents, and his younger brother Isaac – Rachel brought her down to say goodnight before she served the meal. His mother wouldn't have a hold – 'Too many hands, yet. Let her settle for bed.' And Isaac wouldn't, but he did. And she bawled again. But who stopped her – not Rachel, but Opa Stender who took her from him and held her, swaying her very gently and making comforting noises in his throat. And she quietened – so it was his father who took her upstairs to lay her in her crib, and who sang lullabies until the soup was served.

And Ernst could only sit at the table and think how different it might have been if there hadn't been a war and he'd been here from the day Josefine was born. But then he wasn't the only new father in the world with a distance between him and his child, was he?

*　*　*

The nurse brought second-hand clothes from somewhere: a shirt without a collar, long trousers and a pair of boots. Freddie just hoped they hadn't belonged to a boy who'd died in the hospital. They tried to force a baker boy's cap onto his head, but he wasn't having that.

'Now stand up straight and look smart, or they won't want to take you.' This day-nurse wasn't as nice as the night-nurse. The other one had sat on the bed and read him bits from the Bible, talked about heaven, and told him not to be frightened of having a good cry. So he had. But he wasn't going to let this hard one see him blubbing. Anyway, somehow his mind hadn't got hold of the awfulness of what had happened.

And no one had told him he was being taken off today – or who was going to do the taking. Would it be Amy: was she coming for him after all? Or would it be a 'home'? There was a boy who came to school from somewhere called The Hollies. He seemed all right, not like a workhouse boy; they could be mates, if it was there.

The nurse pulled open his curtains and led him out of the ward, took him to a small room off the hallway.

'You sit there, and don't kick the furniture with those boots.'

He looked down at them; they'd been nicely cleaned, and the big thing was, they fitted. His trousers would tuck in nicely. Around him on the walls were pictures of whiskery old men; one of them with a big gold chain around his neck as if he was a mayor, and the others with watch chains on their waistcoats, which made him think of his dad's watch and fob. Dear old Dad. He used to wear it on a Sunday, and even when he knew what the time was, when the dinner came in he'd take it out and give it a look. But that watch hadn't been gold like these, it had been silver and a bit dented. And gone to kingdom come.

He wasn't going to cry, though, not if these people were coming for him any time now.

They were there before he knew it, Sister saying hello to someone in the hallway. And when he heard the man's voice he groaned, out loud. No, not him! Not them!

'Where is 'e? In 'ere?'

Uncle Len walked in with Grandad behind him, and the sister was saying, 'Go right in, he's all ready for you.'

Was he, heck! He'd never be ready to go with these two. Uncle Len was holding a weedy cigarette in his fingers, staring at him. He'd never liked the man, and he knew his dad had got no time for him. He was weaselly, always hunched over from humping sacks of logs, and in Barth Street Freddie had once seen him kick a cat almost over a house.

'I'm sorry about your dad and mum, boy. Aren't we, Pop?'

'We are,' said Grandad. 'Almighty sorry.' But he said it to the sister.

Freddie hadn't seen Grandad for a long time and he looked smaller than before, but he still seemed tough. Neither of them looked dressed up to come to the hospital; Uncle Len was in a grimy waistcoat with string round the legs of his trousers, and Grandad was much the same but wearing an old jacket over the top.

'You're a big lad, aren't you, boy?'

Freddie shrugged. He supposed he was tallish, like Will was, and his dad.

'Well, we'll give 'im a good 'ome, won't we, Pop?'

'We will. We certainly will.' Grandad shuffled a boot, like a horse pawing to go.

Freddie's eyes were misting over, but he was darned if these two were going to see any tears. This was the worst thing that could happen to him. His Nan and Grandad on his mum's side were both dead, and there weren't any other uncles or aunts that he knew of, so the only family he knew was these two, and someone, probably at the Arsenal, had got their names and address written down. If there'd been another door out of that room he'd have shot through it and run off to live rough over in Bostall Woods.

Their horse and cart was outside, loaded up with logs at the front and sacks of firewood 'splits' at the back. Sister came out with them and stroked the horse's head.

'You get up front wi' me,' Grandad told him; and Uncle Len went to the back where he perched, dangling his legs.

'What's his name?' Sister asked.

'"'Orse".'

'I know that.' She laughed, sort-of merrily. 'But what's his name?'

'I told yer, "'Orse".' Grandad shook the reins. 'Giddup, 'Orse!' And 'Orse started pulling away, towards the High Street.

'Be good!' Sister waved after them. But Freddie wasn't in the mood to wave back.

And as soon as they were round the corner Grandad stopped the cart. 'Get on the back, boy.' He elbowed him off the seat and made him swap places with Uncle Len, and they headed off again, not for their house in Plumstead, but on their Saturday log deliveries to 'Fanny on the Hill' at Welling, and the 'Woodman', the 'Old Mill', and the 'Ship' on Plumstead Common, with a few streets of house deliveries in between, Uncle Len ringing a cracked old handbell and shouting, 'Best logs! Slow-burn ash!' When someone came out they heaved the sacks of logs through to their sculleries. But since he was there – 'Be a bit useful, boy!' – Grandad made him carry sacks of splits through for starting the fires. 'Keep your ankle moving, best way. It might only be August, boy, but boilers gotta be ready fer Monday's wash.' Like

Freddie's mum, most people burned coal in their grates, but wood was cleaner for laundry.

'An' coal's gettin' low, they've started countin' rooms an' allocating accordin'.'

He knew that, his mum had moaned about the rationing.

'Suits us, though, don' it, Len? Wi' all the war fact'ries burning coal, we can shift a tidy few sacks o' logs – so get yourself heavin'.'

Freddie didn't know what to think, couldn't begin. As he carried the sacks through the narrow hallways he couldn't get his brain sorted; not even to feeling sad about his mum and dad. It was as if he'd turned into a different person. Could moths look back to when they were caterpillars? Well, that was how he felt, like some totally different creature from what he'd been before. *Well Hall Road?* Where was that? *Wally Quinnell?* Who was he? In the couple of hours since he'd climbed onto that cart he'd changed. He wasn't Freddie Castle the boy any more. He was Frederick Castle, soon to leave school – taken over by these two because of the law, but on his own in the world. Definitely on his own.

The sheets on his bed in Kashgar Road had never felt the heat of an iron, and instead of a soft pillow he had a hard sausage of a bolster. At home his bed had springs and a thin feather mattress, but here the mattress was in a sort of box and he sank down into the middle of it. The house wasn't very big, but after them shifting out a broken bike and some old lumber, at least he had his own bedroom at the back, with Grandad in the front and Uncle Len in the middle. They still had gas lighting but only downstairs, and when he went up in the dark he had to make do with a candle.

The next day Grandad cooked a Sunday dinner – black-burnt peas and a gristly piece of meat with hard roast potatoes. The other two drank tankards of beer, and he had a cup of water. But there weren't any 'afters' – they just went on drinking – and then it was elbows on tables and Grandad running his tongue round the inside of his mouth.

'Now, tomorrer…'

Freddie knew about Monday. It would be back to school, and Grandad was going to tell him he wouldn't be going back to Grangehill Road but somewhere nearer – probably up to Plumstead High Street at the top of the road.

But, no.

'You left school yet, 'ave yer?'

He shook his head. The date of his birthday meant he couldn't leave before the end of term at Christmas.

'Well, you 'ave now.' Grandad took another swig. 'Big lad like you.'

His old life suddenly came back into focus. 'Mum and

Dad said I was going on to secondary...' He hadn't wanted to stay on, he'd wanted to be grown-up and getting to fight the Germans, but his heart sank at what he knew was coming.

'Waste o' time.' Grandad pulled a pouty face. 'Yer best edication is to get out an' learn the lessons of a bit of honest work.'

'Like me.' Uncle Len drained his tankard and looked to see if Grandad had anything left in his. 'Get a bit o' graft under your belt in a honest trade.'

Here it came, what he was dreading.

'Don't s'pose no one's got yer birth certificate after the bomb.' Grandad polished the top of his head with his hand. 'No one won't know, time you've settled in 'ere, got used, buried your mum an' dad, 'blimey, they wouldn't espect you anywhere afore Christmas. By which time you'd be the age...'

'You'll be well into work.' Uncle Len flicked the ash off his cigarette.

But Freddie wasn't thinking about school or work any more. It was that other thing, that shocking thing Grandad had just said all casual, something he hadn't thought about – burying his mum and dad. And sitting there the cold truth of what had happened really hit him again. They were both dead. Gone. And now their bodies had got to be buried.

As if all that school-leaving talk was done and dusted

the two men started on about going buying off 'ol' Widder Johnson down the Darenth Valley', who had an ash wood on her land. 'Best for fires, boy, best for fires,' and about how he was going to do the firewood splitting at the yard as well as the delivering – but also, when they were both dead and gone, how there'd be a nice little business left to him.

He didn't take in much of that. He couldn't. His Sunday dinner was backing up in his gullet and threatening to sick up his unhappiness all over the table. He'd got this dreadful thing to come – the burying of his mum and dad. *His* mum and dad. Their funeral. *Funeral!* They were going to be buried, down in the ground for ever and ever.

How on God's earth was he going to cope with that?

19

Freddie didn't want to see the bodies beforehand, not after them being bombed on. They'd been taken to Messent's the undertakers and left there because the front parlour was too small for two coffins.

'Best way, boy. Remember 'em as they was.'

Uncle Len said something under his breath about 'Sam as 'e was', but Freddie didn't quite catch it.

The funeral would be a couple of streets away; Grandad had gone to the nearest church and fixed things up at St Nicholas. Freddie wondered who'd be there. Amy, probably, and some of his dad's Arsenal mates, and his mum's people from Wood Street – so he wanted to look smart for them, as well as for his mum and dad.

'I'll sort you out wi' a collar an' a black tie. Or a dark navy, if it comes to it. An' yer boots are black, which is handy.'

He lay awake most of the night before the funeral, dreading the sight of those hearses coming down the road. His mum and his dad would be lying inside them and he couldn't stop thinking about what they'd look like inside their coffins. Grandad said they'd looked peaceful in the funeral parlour, 'Like they'd just nodded off, boy' – but he didn't believe him; how could they, bombed by a Zeppelin?

Grandad had come in with a small bunch of flowers and given him two white roses for laying on top of the coffins, but as he lay in bed his heart thumped with the thought of being inches away from their bodies, just the other side of a bit of wood, and in the end he turned over and tried to smother such thoughts by burying his face in the bolster.

Now, on the day, and spot on eleven o'clock, he heard the horses coming down Kashgar Road. His head felt funny as he stared between the slats of the blinds. The front pair of horses stopped outside the house and his eyes went straight to the glass sides of the hearses. He'd pictured dark wooden coffins in them, covered with funeral flowers, but these coffins looked light and plain – and bare, which meant Grandad's bunch of flowers was all there was going to be.

At least Grandad and Uncle Len dressed properly for the funeral. Grandad had got out a black suit, and Uncle Len had found a dark grey jacket. They both had black shoes, and Freddie had given his boots a good clean and polish. They'd fitted him out with a pair of long flannel trousers and a grey herringbone jacket from somewhere, darned in a couple of places, but with his collar and studs and a black tie and arm band, he felt proud enough to keep his head held high.

'Come on, boy, don' keep the vicar waitin'.'

Nervously, he went out. No one was about in the

street; everyone's wooden blinds were down and closed. The carriage for mourners was behind the second hearse, which meant walking past both of them. He set his face, took no notice of the horses with their black plumes, nor of the men in top hats sitting up on their seats, and he followed the chief undertaker towards the carriage. And now, as the moment of passing close to the first hearse came, his nerves suddenly went away and instead that feeling came again of being alone in the world and very grown-up. He stopped, took his time, and bowed at what he guessed was his father's coffin, then he went to the second hearse and he bowed to his mother's.

'Very nice, boy, very touchin'.'

No, he wasn't afraid of their dead bodies any more. How could he be? They were his mum and his dad, and when they were alive they'd loved him and always given him everything they could. No one could have had nicer, kinder parents. How could he have had those scary thoughts in the night?

'Up 'ere, boy, come on, lively.'

They shut the carriage door, and with a jingle the first hearse moved off, the chief undertaker walking at the front with his top hat in his hand. They turned right, the undertaker climbed up front with the others, and the horses broke into a trot. As they came within sight of the church its bell started tolling: *dong... dong... dong... dong...* a sad sound that seemed to ring inside him. And now he knew that this truly was the end, the big, final goodbye to his mum and dad – and he thought of Will, whom he'd have given anything to see coming running alongside the carriage to catch them up.

There was no one waiting at the church gate but the vicar. Grandad hadn't invited anyone. "Ain't got the money for ham an' such when I'm payin' for two hearses.'

They were helped out of the carriage and ushered along the path and into the cold nave. And still the bell rang and rang: *dong... dong... dong... dong... dong...*

'I paid extra fer that, boy. Sets it off, don' it?' Grandad's voice echoed into the vaulting.

Freddie said nothing. Things were bad enough without being made worse by that sad sound; he never wanted to hear a bell again.

The sight of the first coffin coming in stopped his breath. It was balanced on the shoulders of the four men in black, no hands – until out of the corner of his eye he saw Uncle Len fish a cigarette out of its packet and put it in his top pocket for later.

They brought the coffin down the aisle behind the vicar, and put it on a pair of trestles in front of the altar. The men turned like soldiers, walked back up the aisle and brought the next one. But now he didn't know which coffin was which; who should he think of lying in this one, and who in that? Well, he told himself, the first coffin must have been from the front hearse, but was that his dad's or his mum's? It had been put on the left-hand trestle, but they'd always slept the other way round in bed. He had to know, though, and now he made his move. Holding his white roses he slid out of the pew and walked to the front to put them on the tops of the coffins, and to read the names on the brass plates.

But although Grandad might have paid extra for the bell, he hadn't paid for brass plates; the tops of the coffins were bare, and both were the same length. He wanted to turn around and walk to the church door to ask the man which one was which. But he didn't, he went back to his place and made up his mind for himself. Whether he was right or wrong, given the order they'd come in, the left-hand one was going to be his dad, and the right-hand one was going to be his mum; and he'd keep a careful eye on the order they went out again, and which was first down into the grave. He'd forgotten all about their injuries. To him they were lying there looking the same as they'd always looked, and his dad wouldn't even have been ill. Their eyes would be closed and they'd have the same looks on their faces they had when they weren't going to answer a question, sort of wait-and-see. His dad would be in a collar and tie and jacket, and his mum would be in a Sunday blouse and shawl; and that would be them, for ever.

'"*I am the resurrection and the life,*" *says the Lord. "Those who believe in me, even though they die, will live,* and everyone who lives and believes in me will never die."'

The voice startled him. He took his eyes off the coffins and looked up at the vicar in the pulpit who had raised his hand like a policeman in the traffic.

'We meet in the name of Jesus Christ, who died and was raised to the glory of God the Father. Grace and mercy be with you.'

'Thank you,' said Grandad.

'We have come here today to remember before God our brother Samuel and our sister Alice; to give thanks for their lives; to commend them to God our merciful redeemer and judge; to commit their bodies to be buried, and to comfort one another in our grief.'

That sat him up – hearing his dad's and mum's names being said in the same sentence as God's; but the vicar had looked down at the coffins as he said them, and moved his hand towards this one, then that one. He'd been right; his dad was on the left, and his mum was on the right.

The service went on, no hymn-singing but a lot of praying, Grandad down on his knees on the cushion on the floor, and Uncle Len leaning forward a little bit.

'Brethren,' the vicar said in a down-to-earth voice, 'I knew neither Samuel nor Alice.' He was leaning forward, his face looking chatty. 'But I know from what I'm told that they were both strong family people...' Uncle Len cleared his throat loudly – '...and both gave service to our country. Samuel served in the Boer War, and latterly worked in the Royal Arsenal where his work will be, we hope, instrumental in helping to win this dreadful war; while Alice, a Florence Nightingale within our cherished south London, brought skill and succour to her work as a district midwife at the Wood Street Hospital for Mothers and Babies…'

All this came close to home and he was going to cry; but they'd be tears of pride for his dad and his mum. And leave Uncle Len out of it, Grandad must have been proud of his son, Sam.

'And we pray for Frederick, their younger son, and for William, a prisoner of war of the Germans, and for their wider family.' The vicar opened his arms to the whole church, which was just the three of them.

'*Praise to you, Lord Jesus: dying, you destroyed our death; rising, you restored our life: Lord Jesus, come in glory.*

'*Our Father, which art in heaven, hallowed be thy name…*'

Freddie joined in the words of the Lord's Prayer, which could get you a good slap at school if you didn't know it. And now was the moment he'd been dreading most of all – the time for following the coffins outside to the graveyard.

The four men carried his dad's coffin to the door. The vicar came down from the pulpit and ushered the three of them to follow. It had clouded over and a breeze off the Thames was getting up. At the far side of the graveyard Freddie could see the gravedigger standing to attention next to a mound of earth where they took his dad's coffin and put it on a trestle again. The three of them followed and he could see the sharp-cut sides of the hole in the ground – his mum's and his dad's grave. And in that moment a great breathlessness caught him and his brain really took it in that he would never see them again. Literally. He hadn't even got a photograph of them.

'Nice words the vicar spoke.' Grandad had a croak in his voice.

His mother's coffin came outside, and now the vicar was speaking.

'*We have entrusted our brother Samuel and our sister Alice to God's mercy, and we now commit their bodies to the ground: earth to earth, ashes to ashes, dust to dust: in sure and certain hope of the resurrection to eternal life through our Lord Jesus Christ…*'

Freddie didn't hear the rest of the words. He was outright crying, sobbing loudly, racked with the grief of seeing the four men in black putting a wide sash under his dad's coffin and lowering it down like brewery-men putting a barrel into a cellar. His mum's coffin went after, and the vicar threw two handfuls of earth on top of it. Now the chief undertaker came to him and gave him back his white roses.

'For your own committal.'

He didn't know what he meant.

'Throw 'em in, boy.'

He stepped forward and was shocked to see how far down the coffins were. He'd heard about graves going down six feet but this was a lot more than that. He threw his flowers in, as Grandad came to stand beside him to throw down a handful of earth.

'Gawd, it's deep – but I paid for you and for Will, in due course…'

'…*and the blessing of God Almighty, the Father, the Son, and the Holy Spirit, be among you and remain with you always. Amen.*'

'Amen,' said Grandad.

'Amen,' Freddie got out somehow.

Uncle Len said nothing, just made a noise in his throat.

The breeze off the river picked up into something stronger, but it was clearing the cloud, and the sun suddenly shone on the graveyard. Freddie imagined it lighting the way to heaven for his mum and his dad.

God bless, sleep tight, hope the bugs don't bite.

The vicar, the undertaker and the other men walked back to the church leaving just the three of them.

'Come on, boy, don' dwell.' Grandad looked up at the sky. 'Life goes on, life goes on.' He took his arm and firmly led him away.

Freddie didn't want to go. He wanted to stay and cry his eyes out before the coffins were covered with earth. But as Grandad walked him off he twisted his body to stand and salute them like a soldier, for him and for Will.

To see Uncle Len still there – spitting a great gob down into the grave.

20

The prison camp guards were frightened of paper. Anyone hiding a piece of paper was beaten or thrown into solitary confinement. Charlie Unsworth, one of the Accrington lads told Will, 'You put a mark on a piece o' paper an' it's a document. An' they're scared rotten of a document tellin' o' these manky conditions, an' the treatment, an' the abuse – come the end of the war an' us free again, it'll go 'ard on Fritz.'

Paper had meant something different to Will – he'd sketched and painted on it, but he couldn't have moved a pencil across a sheet of it now, even if he'd been allowed. As day followed day, the appalling conditions in the camp were killing him. Lifting a shovel of ballast had him gasping for breath worse than his dad and he woke each morning cursing that he was still alive. Dog-tired, hungry, itching, hopeless, his spine about to snap like a twig, he'd be lifting that heavy shovel until the sun went down. Attila the Hun was more violent than ever, shouting, pushing, kicking, rifle-butting to get the railway sleepers lifted and the track packed with crushed stone. Why couldn't he die in the night, go to whatever next world was waiting for him?

But, *Red Cross!*

Marching back into the camp one night he heard

those lifting words. The Red Cross were there; a group of French prisoners were already holding that forbidden material – pieces of paper. Letters from home.

'Any English?'

'Any Scottish?'

''Owt fra' Lancashire?'

The answer seemed to be yes, and they were going to be given out before lock-up.

So had anything come for him? Had Amy written? She was the bright sort who'd find out how to get something through. Or had his mum's regular letters caught up with him?

He did his best to wash in the water cow – at least his face and his hands; if he was about to hold a letter from home it was going to be with clean fingers. He forgot his tiredness and his hunger – now there was something to look forward to.

They'd put an extra table at the front of the mess hall, with the camp commandant sitting behind it, and next to him was a tall man in a suit with a Red Cross badge in his buttonhole. Nobody at their table moaned tonight; tonight the bread tasted of bread and the coffee seemed drinkable. And their eyes weren't on a chance of an extra grab of food but on that pile of envelopes stacked in front of the man in the suit.

The man stood and started calling out the names on

the envelopes, his English good, his French sounding about right.

Suddenly their section was ordered to stand and their names started being called. Now the letters could be seen more clearly, the envelopes already opened, probably read and censored.

'Private E. Turnbull.'

Eric Turnbull looked at no one as he marched to the front, took his letter with a click of his heels, and came back to his place. Meanwhile, others were on their way out: George Mottram, Len Barton, Tommy Olleronshaw from the Lancashires, and Jimmy Stuart and Alex McNab from the Scottish boys. The Red Cross man was rattling through them now, and without bothering about being private they stood and read their letters.

Will waited, couldn't take his eyes off the pile as it went down, and down. The names had been called out randomly, not alphabetically nor by regiment. But somehow he knew. His gut told him well before the end that his name wasn't going to be called. A snake of disappointment bit into him. There wasn't going to be anything from Amy or his mum.

He looked about the mess. Some men were crying, some were looking blank, some were sitting staring into their mugs, while others were cracking smiles and lighting up their eyes. And as the table at the front was finally emptied of letters the exhaustion of the day hit him again, and only some streak of pride stopped him from putting his head in his hands on the table and groaning, groaning, groaning.

It was drudgery, Freddie's mum's favourite word for anything she didn't like doing, never mind whether it was hard work or soft. Washing and ironing had always been drudgery, but cleaning the windows of their nice new house never was. And neither was anything to do with being a midwife. But this drudgery was nothing soft. Grandad and Uncle Len ran their log business from the bottom of Church Manorway among the allotments, just this side of the railway line. 'Orse had a fair bit of space for grazing on a patch of land among the old plum trees, but the stable and the log yard were in a small corner against the railway embankment. A tarred roof kept 'Orse mostly dry, and tarpaulin sheets kept the rain off the logs.

Grandad and Uncle Len were having a special time of it, too. With the shortage of coal, more and more people wanted logs, but that meant faster sawing, quicker deliveries, and more chopping down of ash trees. Hard, hot, drudgery.

That early autumn Freddie found out how hot it could be, his shirt off, splitting logs, dunking his head under the stand-pipe; but on another day how miserable it was when the wind blew off the Thames and the rain came stinging in.

He quickly learned how to use his axe. With a firm chopping block he could take the awkward-shaped rejects Uncle Len slung across at him, balance them upright, and chop, chop, chop, chop – with four good swings he'd hack them down to size, then splinter the quarters for the kindling sacks. When a piece of ash Uncle Len was sawing was too dense he'd be whistled over to take the other end of the bow-saw, and then it was hard, fast sawing and a pain in the shoulders that would keep him awake at night. But he did it all because he'd got to. His schooldays were over, and like all men and lads who weren't at the war he'd got to work at something – although if anyone ever had a hateful workmate it was him. Just listening to Len Castle cursing a piece of wood was hard work on its own. Mental drudgery.

He learned, too, how working men had their routines to break up their days. Except on delivery days they'd stop at eleven o'clock for a can of cold tea and a slice of toast, and at one o'clock when the Arsenal gun went off they had a knob of cheese, a pickled onion and water for him and beers for them. Then it would be a sit until half-past, and back at work until five or six when 'Orse was seen to. Most days he ached all over but he could feel his muscles growing to go with his roughening hands, and he found he had to spit a lot more.

The only good part was the one o'clock break when

the others had drunk their beers. He'd take himself up onto the railway embankment and watch the regular London train, enjoy the shaking of the ground under the engine; and now and then there'd be a troop train carrying soldiers to the war, all whistles and cap-waving; and, once, a Red Cross hospital train came the other way with men on stretchers stacked in twos: no waves or whistles this time, just the clackety-clack of the wheels on the line. It had him thinking of brother Will who was God knew where, but he hoped like heck Amy had done what she'd promised and gone to the Red Cross. He'd give it a couple of weeks and one Sunday he'd go up to her house and see how she'd got on.

The worst times were when Grandad had gone off on his own with 'Orse and the cart, drumming up business – new houses were being built over Abbey Wood way, and they'd all need logs for washdays. It meant he was left on his own with Uncle Len, which wasn't so bad at first – he could cope with the looks and the work and the moaning. The trouble was, as time went on the man started getting louder and more open with the things he said about his dad. Nasty stuff. They started off disguised, he could have been talking about some enemy he'd once had; but bit by bit his tongue loosened-up and he put *your father* into what he was swearing about, and always – Freddie waited for it – he'd follow it with a sneery spit, even when his mouth was dry. The man rarely spoke directly to him, and even when he was going on about 'your father' it was more muttering to himself, just about loud enough to be heard. Freddie pretended not to hear at first, went on with his job, but as things got worse he knew he couldn't go on for long without saying something back.

He came close to it one Sunday morning when Grandad had gone to give Nanna Castle's grave a tidy-up. It was rotten being on his own in the house with Uncle Len, and he'd got out of his way by going into the parlour to sit up at the table and draw a picture of a Zeppelin on fire, nose-diving towards the earth. His mouth tasted bitter as his mind acted out what he was drawing: the thing he wanted most in all the world apart from having Will home again – the horrible death of every single Zeppelin airman. He drew fast and hard, gloating at imagined fear and pain.

But Uncle Len came into the parlour, sniffling, looked at the picture over his shoulder.

'Ashes,' he said. 'What about the ruddy ashes?'

'In a minute. When it's on the ground I'll do people dancing round the wreck.' He'd been surprised to hear Uncle Len say something that wasn't about his dad, or how he sawed wood.

'The ashes in the grate, you lazy little turd.'

'Oh, yeah.' Yes, he should have raked it out, it was one of his jobs.

'Course, I'm not surprised. Chip off the ol' block, ain't you? Just like your ol' man – live for yerself. Selfish as a cat with a dead bird.'

Selfish? His dad wouldn't have known the word. He'd do anything for anybody when he was well, fixing a tap, laying someone's lino – and when he helped with the washing-up on a Sunday he'd whistle as he worked, and go round the kitchen with a cloth, even if he did have a look on him as if he was a bit of a saint. *Selfish?* You miserable ape! Something started coming up in Freddie's throat, a choking feeling that made him want to answer back. But Uncle Len was standing over him, and if he told the man to shut his big gob he'd get a smack round the head. So Freddie bottled it up and went to the grate to get busy with the brush and shovel.

'That's more like it! Think of someone except yourself for a change!' The man went out and slammed the door.

Freddie's hand holding the shovel was shaking – with a fierce hatred that could almost have set those ashes alight again. No one would take Uncle Len for being his dad's brother. He only ever had one look: mean and jealous, as if he'd just been beaten to a bargain. His dad had thick black hair that he'd ruffle himself and twinkle his eyes and give you a grin, but Uncle Len had a mouth that puckered up under his nose like a polly parrot's, spouting foul language that even had Grandad blinking. And that was without the rotten stuff he said about his own brother. Whatever had gone on between the two of them must have been very deep – kept quiet about at home in front of a boy like him, but enough to put a sour look on his dear dad's face.

He took it as long as he could, until the following Tuesday when Grandad was out with 'Orse and the cart. And this time hateful Uncle Len went too far. They were both on the bow-saw, him helping to tackle a knotty branch, when the man suddenly stared at him and shouted, 'Put some backbone into it, then! Come on. Like your old man, you are!'

'Good-looking and a gent?' But he could feel something fizzing inside him.

'Two-faced, looking like what you're not. You're a lazy little turd. Put some effort into it, for cris'sake.' The man started pushing harder and faster, working up into a frenzy, until he caught him off balance and sent him flat on his back in a heap of sawdust.

'Oi!'

The man dropped his end of the saw and came bending over him. 'I'll give you "Oi!". You're a lazy little turd, an' the son of a turd, nothin' but another ruddy mouth to feed, forced on us 'cos the ol' man couldn't say no.'

Freddie tried to get up but he was pushed back again, hard.

'D'you think choppin' a bit o' kindling earns you your bed an' board? The ol' man's too soft – the Union Workhouse is the place for the likes of you. Then I shouldn't 'ave to look at your ugly mug every day – the spittin' ruddy image of your rotten father…'

Looking up into this loathsome man's face Freddie felt himself filling with his own anger, and with anger on behalf of his dad. This creature would never have dared speak like that if he'd been here. He scrambled to his feet. This burning spite against his dad had been coming out more and more; but now, with Grandad not around, the man had suddenly gone berserk – and as he stood facing him all at once he was Freddie Castle *and* his dad, and he was not about to take it any more.

'I'll tell you what, you little runt, I'll tell you what—' The man was gulping down air as if they were mouthfuls of beer, spluttering and spitting. 'Biggest traitor on God's earth – that was your father.'

'Shut up! That's not true!'

The man spat again, this time at him. 'An' I'll tell you something – that ruddy Zeppelin done me the biggest favour goin'!'

What?! Freddie tried to breathe but his lungs were sucking at nothing. The hatred on this sneering, evil face was like staring at the devil come to earth. His head felt light; his focus went to mist. The anger and hatred of two men filled him with a strength he didn't know he had.

'Best bleedin' place for 'im, where 'e is! Down that 'ole!'

That was it! From the top of a pile of timber Freddie grabbed a length of thick ash and swung it at Len's head, missed him the first time, but before the man could move he took another mighty swing and caught him square on the left cheek. With a loud sucking sound Len went flying off his feet – his head cracking onto the chopping block, and with a twisting of his neck like a man hanging from a gallows he made one last sound. *Gloop!*

Freddie ran. He knew what he'd done. He'd killed Uncle Len. He'd caught him an unlucky one and broken his neck. He was a killer, a murderer. He ran out of the yard, up Church Manorway and along Plumstead High Street towards the nearest place where he could lose himself – Bostall Woods – where everyone said the old highwayman Dick Turpin used to live in a cave. Well, if Dick Turpin could, he could, too. An outlaw.

But he had enough sense not to pelt along the road like someone getting away with a purse. He made it more of a trot, while still putting distance between himself and the dead body. Already a rough plan was coming into his head: keep out of everyone's way for a couple of days and then make a run for it, head for somewhere a long way off from Plumstead. He fleshed it out as he trotted. He would lie low in the daytime and walk the roads at night, get well out into the country.

He'd steal eggs from chicken coops, milk from farms, apples from orchards, and doss down in haystacks and barns. And when he came to the docks somewhere he'd jump a ship to another country, say he'd run away from a workhouse. He could show people his muscles, and get himself work. But he'd have to be someone else, because this life was over.

Coming near to Bostall Woods, he slowed to a walk and took stock. His brother Will was gone, he was on his own in the world, and what happened to him from then on was going to have to be the best he could do for himself. There was nothing else for it – he was looking after number one. From now on he was going to live by using his own brain and his own brawn. And if anyone like Wally Quinnell ever stood in his way he'd make mincemeat of him.

He kicked off again and ran into the woods, heading in the direction of Dick Turpin's cave. The boy who'd once had a family was well in the past. And, until the day he died, if he ever met anyone out of that Zeppelin who'd turned him into this someone else, he'd brain him ten times over with the nearest thing he could grab, just like he'd done to loathsome Len Castle.

21

It was nothing like the way it was in books. Robin Hood leading his men in the greenwood or Billy the Kid lighting his camp fire or Ned Kelly bush-ranging in Australia; all the outlaws in the *Boy's Own Annual* got through their nights all right. But it wasn't the same in Bostall Woods. It was cold. Freddie shivered his way through until morning. He'd run off from the wood yard in his shirt, a skinny jumper, and his trousers tucked into long socks – but curled up or stretched out, the backs of his legs twitched and his shoulders shook. If only he had a coat, or even a jacket.

Dick Turpin's Cave was nothing more than an overhang of dug-out chalk for mending the roads, and to get to it he'd had to jump over a stream, just missed the bank, and ended up with a boot full of water which sucked at his foot all night. The place was too open and near the road, anyway. But behind the diggings the woods went up thick and high, and there'd be better hiding places for tomorrow. During the day he'd have time to find somewhere deeper and more sheltered. Right now, though, the chalky soil with the dew on it was slippery and hard, and bugs and beetles wanted to get inside his clothes. It was hell. Miserable. Living rough needed proper planning. He didn't close his eyes. He heard trains, trams, ships on the river, the snapping of twigs and the rustling of night creatures – and he was on his feet before a bird flew, his eyes skinned for the sight of a patrolling policeman. He needed people about so he didn't look special, but he didn't need people about who might ask what he was up to. What a fix!

All right, then. He suddenly changed his mind about another hiding place here. What he'd do was, he'd lose himself somewhere local during the day, and start getting to a ship that night. Then when he got to the docks somewhere he'd stow away on a ship like that boy with Captain Cook – it had happened, it was a true story so it could be done; Miss Cape had read it to them. But where to go; which docks would he head for? Where was the best place to sneak onto a ship? That was the question.

And one answer came whistling in on the cold air: the sound of an early-morning train coming up from Kent. Those wounded soldiers he'd seen had come off ships, hadn't they, and the new soldiers going out to France were being taken to ships – which meant those trains went to docks somewhere – so when it was dark all he had to do was follow the railway line.

But for now he was hungry and he was cold, and he was a murderer who'd killed his uncle. He had no mum and no dad, a brother somewhere – but he could be dead, too – so there was no one to help him. Even if he went to Amy, her mother and father might turn him in. It was just him on his own. And today no one was going to give him a breakfast. But plums would help, wouldn't they? The old trees down by the river had plenty of plums on them; they were going mouldy on the branches. He could hang about up here in the woods until children started going to school, pull his jumper up over his face, walk down to the old orchards and then scrump – juicy fruit, both food and drink – before lying low in the long grasses and snoozing off. And later, when the trains had stopped running he'd start his trek along the rails to the docks.

He climbed up and through Bostall Woods, came out in the streets of Abbey Wood and ran down to the railway. A dank old tunnel took him under the line, and sure enough there were enough plums on the trees to fill his jersey and go scuttling for the longer grass down by the river. He kept well away from a group of gypsy horses, but no one came to water them, so he found a small hollow and gorged on his plums, watching the clouds coming in over the Thames and hoping to God it wasn't going to rain. He crossed his ankles, cradled his neck, and tried to get into some sort of a position for dozing – but in no time the plums turned him inside-out down in a ditch, where he cleaned himself up with handfuls of grass and felt better; and as the sun eventually came through the clouds and gave off some warmth he found himself going drowsy – and comfortable in himself. That so-and-so Len had got what he'd been asking for. Will would have done the same if he'd heard him saying he was glad their dad was dead. He'd done it for them both, for their bit of the Castles – and one day, one day, they might meet up again, and go to the churchyard together for a special spit on his hateful grave.

The red light on the rear of the guard's van disappeared down the line and he was itching to get a move on. That had to be the last train – short, mostly empty, the engine seeming to be taking things easy, painted up with 'LCDR' – London, Chatham and Dover Railway – so it was definitely going in the right direction. He heard the signal clatter back to 'stop' and he slipped through the railings and onto the track. Looking along it, the line was dead straight, glinting in the moonlight. He bent himself double and set off, but measuring his steps was hard: the sleepers were awkward distances apart for his strides, so it had to be head-down all the time, watching where he was going. He tried walking on a rail, but he slipped and nearly turned his ankle – and he began wondering if it wouldn't have been better if he'd gone on the Dartford road. But roads were patrolled. Burglars broke into houses in the early hours of the morning and got away through the streets, and the police knew that. Searchlights and guns were stationed in parks, and the police were always around to help in air raids – so he'd have to be pretty nippy on the roads. No, he'd stick with his plan for now and just be dead careful when the railway line took him through stations, or over level crossings and under road bridges. He skulked, he ducked, he laid himself flat between the tracks when he heard voices from down an embankment – a man's, a girl's, laughing like drinkers – and then on he crept. The river was never far off and a breeze came off it and shivered him, but on he went, on and on, wondering what time the first engines would come through in the morning.

When, *help!* Suddenly he heard this low, growling sound, like someone singing to keep himself company. He stopped dead. Was the voice coming from ahead of him, or behind? He crouched to make himself harder to see, picking out the words of the song as it came closer and closer –

> *'Oh, me name it is Sam Hall, chimney sweep*
> *Oh, me name it is Sam Hall, and I've robbed both*
> *great and small*
> *And me neck will pay for all when I die, when I die…'*

It was from behind, coming along the track at a good lick. He twisted round – and he saw him: a short man, limping along between the tracks with something under one arm, carrying a dim light in the other hand. *Who was he?* A rail inspector? A signal-man going on duty? He heard the kick of gravel as the man stopped and peered along at him. Now he could see more clearly. He had an old stovepipe hat on the side of his head, and a violin case under his arm.

The man suddenly ran at him like an ape, twenty yards in no time at all, thrusting the light thing in his face.

'Hold still! Who's there? I got yer. Who is it? Let's see yer!'

The thing in his hand was like a clay ball, hollowed out and showing just enough light but no more; something secret.

'A boy!'

The man smelt of gin, and his face was twisted like those mad people he sometimes saw in Woolwich: this face, then that, different looks all at once.

'What the divil you doin' here, this time o' night?'

If the man put down the violin case to do anything he'd run, he'd risk his ankles.

'I missed the train. Getting home...'

'Home? Where'd that be?'

'Down the line.'

'*Where?*' The shout shot him upright. 'Rosherville? Gravesend?'

'Sort of...'

'Well. Jest you turn yerself around, an' back where

you come from!' The man poked him in the stomach with the violin case. 'I'm workin' down the line. You ain't queerin' my pitch with yer missed train. You're goin' back, an' if I see youse on my walk another night I shall kill yer, 'cos I've got the wherewithal to do it.' He lifted the violin case as if he might bring it crashing down on Freddie's head. 'You hear me?'

'Yes, sir.'

'Go on, then, an' make sharp. I'm comin' back this way in a while, an' if there's a sniff of you around I shall hev you! You understan' that?'

Freddie nodded, hard. Fear like an exploding plum nearly did for him, but he held off, and with a sudden spurt he ran away from the man. But now he was facing towards London again, where he'd come from, and between him and the ships was this monster man, this burglar going for the posh houses down the line.

So it was off the railway and through some fields. He'd be blowed if he was going back to London. He daren't. He'd killed Uncle Len, he was a murdering boy who might not swing, but he'd be locked up for ever. He was still Freddie Castle if they caught him before he could become someone else – but that wouldn't be until he was miles off across the sea on his way to Australia or America or India.

He took his chances, cut back to Erith, followed the Dartford road, walking on through the night, diving into hedges when he thought he heard something coming. But the road soon became all country and he'd be able to hear the clop of a horse from some way off. He slipped through Dartford – more care, his boots the biggest problem, but he wasn't taking them off – and then it was open road again, the signposts saying Gravesend. On he went, up hills, round bends, down dips, and on. If he could keep close to the river he'd come to the sea and docks and ships, so he kept his head up, his nose sniffing in the air. He knew it by its smell, the salty, seaweedy Thames; and it was off to his left, and not all that far, no more than a couple of stiles away – and in the first glimmerings of light in the sky the road brought him to what had to be the edge of Gravesend, where a couple of big houses sat on the top of a sort of cliff. And there it was down below him, the river, with – thank you, God – some trees and bushes where he could lie low for a bit and plan what he was going to do next.

He slept. Well hidden down by the river he curled himself up as tight as a fox in a hole and all at once he wasn't there – or anywhere else. He didn't dream. Whatever creatures might have sniffed at him or crawled over him he felt nothing. It wasn't until he heard someone coughing and it was himself that he felt a faint warmth and he came round.

This was a weird place. It was a sort of riverside park with several buildings dotted about and a few statues, a stage, and a walkway leading to a pier without any boats. And in the light he could see how he'd got here, down a long winding path that led up the overhang to the road.

He crept to the water's edge, managed to splash his face before he headed up the path and onto the road. He needed fields in the daytime – he'd be better off where he could lose himself in woods or ditches, look a bit like a country boy.

He was in luck. He soon had a pointer as to where he was. Up on the road he was just in time to dodge being seen from a double-decker bus coming past – and what did it say on the front board? 'Chatham'. And Chatham meant docks and ships, didn't it? So if he followed in the main direction the bus was going, that's where he'd end up, too.

'Lucky little spadger!' as his mum would have said.

22

The road to Chatham was easy to follow. Every village told him where he was – Chalk, Shorne, Higham – and their signposts pointed to Rochester and Chatham. He was on a country road of long stretches, which gave him plenty of time to see anything coming or going. It was a warmer day but he made good time, although his neck hurt with turning around so often to check he hadn't been seen.

In the late afternoon he came to a junction with a wide road at the top of a steep hill, and half an hour later he was down where he could smell water again, on the London side of Rochester Bridge, looking across at a castle. So, which way did he go to find the ships at Chatham – left or right, or across the bridge?

'Oi! What you lookin' at, boy?'

He jumped. He was getting careless, hadn't heard this girl creeping up on him.

'Them boats, that's all.' Along the river there was a line of boats with tall red sails. He was outside an old white-painted shop and it must have looked as if he was after some of the fruit and vegetables outside because this girl was eyeing him like a market woman, standing there with her arms folded.

'I'm not here pinching stuff.'

'Dead right, you're not.'

She was a bit older than him with a sharp face, and dressed old-fashioned with a shawl wrapped around her shoulders.

'What's in boats for you?'

He could tell she wasn't going to let him just wander off – and the last thing he wanted was a policeman called. 'I'm down from London. Been bombed out by a Zepp.' That made no difference. 'I'm looking for a job.' He pulled himself up as tall as he could, puffed out his cheeks, tried to look like a working man again and not a boy on the run.

'You'll get one along there all right – men away in the army, an' that.'

He leant on the shop's wooden wall. Along the waterfront there was a long stretch of factories. 'All them chimneys an' smoke – what is it they're making?' Best to show an interest while he tried to get away.

'Don't you know?'

'Wouldn't ask, would I…?'

'Cemeng. Chalk an' Medway mud, we got the best cemeng going…'

'Ah.' Cement, she meant.

'Famous. Sent all over, that cemeng.'

'All over the world?'

'Said. *All* over.'

'In them boats?'

'Barges, we call 'em. Go off from here first, take the cemeng to the docks, then it's on ships across to the continong. Gawd, you are soppy, aren't you?'

'No, I'm not.' But he felt it. 'I'll get along there, then. If there's jobs.'

'It's hard graft. "Muddies". Diggin' it out.'

'Don't bother me.'

She wrinkled her nose. 'Tell you what – you come back this way sometime an' I'll give you a cake for your tea.'

Hello! – she'd changed her tune. 'Ta.'

But he knew very well that he'd never come back this way, not for years and years, anyhow.

He counted over twenty barges moored in front of the factories, flat, wide and long, some with their red sails tied up and others with them flapping in the breeze that was coming up-river. He'd seen these barges on the Thames, too; they'd probably been off to ships somewhere. And now he knew what he was going to do – he was going to climb onto one of those barges and hide himself away, and get himself taken to where the ships were. And the first part of doing that would be to hide up until it was dark. His good luck was, it was knocking-off time in the cement works so he could hang about like a lad meeting his dad, all the while working his way down towards the water. He knew he wasn't going to get aboard a barge in the daytime so he'd have to find a secret corner somewhere, get down behind a wall or under a wheelbarrow until the time to make his move. But his spirits were up. He was here and the barges were there, and the cranes had stopped loading them and he could see tarpaulins being pulled across holds and laced down. He just had to bide his time, squeeze himself under a tarpaulin and stay hidden until he was at the docks, then get onto a ship and keep his head down. When they were well out to sea he'd come out and tell them he was someone else whose mum and dad had been killed by a Zepp – and he was blowed if he was going to get sent to the workhouse. Show a bit of spirit, they'd like that. And, anyhow, part of that was true, wasn't it?

And they wouldn't turn around a whole ship of that girl's cemeng just to bring him back, would they?

After that, well, he'd start a new life somewhere else in the world.

And perhaps one day, who knew? When the war was over and the dust had settled and Len Castle was old bones in his grave, he might find Will somewhere, and then there'd be a proper Castle family to carry on again.

Although, what sort of an outside chance was that?

A good opportunity suddenly showed itself. Running down the slope of factory buildings were lines of long pipes as wide as people were tall – each about half the length of a football pitch – which had to be something to do with the cement-making. Under the nearest one there was a space between two short brick-stacks holding it up, just big enough for him to crawl beneath. He watched the men hurrying off, and in a quick flash when there was no one in sight he shot down into the crack. Done it! Got here! Now all he had to do was lie low.

Everything went quiet; the only voices came from the river front, and looking out he could see that the sky had gone dark. He was cold again, but he wasn't hungry; he'd eaten fruit off the trees in the fields, and he'd done all his business, too. The good thing was, the nearest barge was only yards away, and when it was even darker and he couldn't hear voices any more he was going to slink out of here and get onto it.

He dozed a bit, but he looked out from time to time, seeing the sky nicely clouded for his run to the barge. The voices told him the men slept on these barges. A small dog yapped. Someone sang a weird old song and then just stopped. The sky got darker still – but suddenly there were footsteps, near to him, coming down towards the river. Crunch, crunch, crunch, crunch. He drew in his legs, made sure no one could see a boot sticking out. He held his breath.

The footsteps came nearer, then went on past – and

someone shouted from the barge.

'Where you bin, Billy? Get aboard, you little Romeo. Nine o'clock this lot's off to the Pacific. We're on the ebb and we'll hit the flood in the estuary.'

Billy only growled, sounded young, could be the skipper's son.

But, *the Pacific!* That was down Australia way, wasn't it? Well – wouldn't that do him just right? Get on a ship across the sea and start his new life on the other side of the world...

He heard some sort of a hatch opening and then slamming shut, and another one went, too. Had they both gone below on the barge?

What had the man said? *'Off to the Pacific at nine o'clock'*? Would that be tonight or in the morning? Well, he'd better be ready for either. He'd have to keep cavey and pick his moment to make his move, sooner rather than later, and get onto that barge. It was all in his own hands now.

He went sooner. If he failed here, if he couldn't get aboard or squeeze under the tarpaulin on this barge, he'd have time to pick another one. And he might as well be on a barge as under this pipe.

It was going to rain, but that meant the sky was even darker, and with sharp eyes all around he crept out from between the bricks, doubled himself over, and worked his way down the pipe to where it ran into a sort of shed.

Jumpy as a jack-rabbit, he crept round the shed and down to the wharf where, *blow!* – the wooden boards were all creaky. But then everything was all creaky – the ropes, the masts, the flaps of the sails, even his boots. This close, he could see that the barge was moored-up with a foot of space between the wharf and its side, no more than a step when he got to it. He listened hard. All along the line of barges it was quiet, but from somewhere on the mud flats came the bubbling call of a bird, doing its best to stay alive, he thought, like him.

So, *now!* He ran forward and simply stepped onto the barge. On deck it was all masts and winches, hatchways and rope coils, with wrapped-up odds and ends at the front and back that could have been tool boxes or food supplies. So the good thing was, when it came to dodging about getting off in the docks, there'd be a few places to hide.

And then it would be Australia!

He crawled around the hold, checking the edges of the tarpaulin for a way under it; but, rotten luck, it was laced down too tight – all the way back to where he'd started. He definitely wasn't going to get under it, not anywhere. So what was he going to do now? Well, he'd take off his boots for a start; if he started clomping around on the deck looking for somewhere to hide he'd soon get caught. He did the same as he always did when he was paddling in the Thames or walking in mud: he tied his bootlaces together and strung them round his neck. Quietly, on his feet now, he tiptoed to the back of the barge where there was a big tied-down tiller, and a low porch that probably led to where the skipper slept. Near it was a winch and a big mast – but this was the business end of the barge, and it'd be all go when the sailing started; he couldn't hide anywhere here. So what was he going to do? Was he going to have to hop off, quickly, and hope another barge had a looser tarpaulin – or go on to Chatham on the road, or even walk down through Kent until he got to the crossing to Tilbury Docks?

But what was that? Down behind the back of the barge was a small boat, tied up and resting on the mud. And under two oars lying in its bottom was a pile of rags wrapped around odds and ends of some sort. He could get under them, couldn't he?

Carefully, just stopping his boot toecaps from knocking on the barge's hull, he let himself over the side and slid himself down, feeling for the boat with his toes. And he'd got it! Looking down to make sure of his footing, in no time he was in that little boat, and tucked under the rags among spars and fish-hooks even quicker, feeling like a fisherman's catch. He made a quick last check – yes, the rope from the boat was tied to the barge, he wouldn't get left behind – and he settled.

He heard the bird again, and he hoped it had caught

a fish. For himself, he was a heck of a long way from Australia, but tonight could be the first part of his journey which would start on the ebb tide at nine o'clock.

He hugged himself. Well done so far, new man!

23

Men came and went all the time, they were marched in and marched out, but from the day he arrived Will wasn't moved from the corner of the barn he shared with the London, Lancashire and Scottish men working on the gangs. Some died, one went mad, new men were drafted in and the sick were swung out onto carts like sacks of rubbish; but being in this group of comrades helped see him see through the dire days and nights. He was thinner, weaker, forever tired and itchy, morose most of the time – but at least he was alive. He'd lie looking up into the rafters of the barn some nights and think of London and his old life and realise that he wasn't wanting to be a free, peacetime Will Castle any more. What mattered now was being quick enough to get an extra hunk of bread, or a fresh grab of hay to put under his head. He was bullied and beaten by Attila the Hun but at least he wasn't being shot at, or bombed, or blown up. He just accepted what was what and tried to get through one day and then the next.

Until his Red Cross letter came.

It wasn't like before – there was no Swiss official with the Germans on their best behaviour. In the mess near where they ladled the soup sat a scruffy bundle of envelopes that looked as if they'd been left there by accident, a few men around them.

'Hey up – there's one for you. "Castle, William".'
Eric Boundle, the man who'd had his teeth knocked out
by a rifle butt, brought it over.

'Any others for us, Eric?'

'Sweet fanny there, really.'

Will didn't know whether to open the letter
straight away or stuff it in his shirt for when he was
on his own. But when would that ever be? Any sort of
privacy was from a dream world, like home. He
opened it.

He must have pulled a face.

'Wha' is it, man? Ye bin give the VC?'

Will's mouth had frozen; his tongue felt swollen and
he couldn't swallow. He'd taken in the first page in one
huge grab, words in Amy's handwriting that almost slid
him off the bench.

'Let him alone.'

'Pocket it, Will. Tek yer time.'

Will lifted his head and looked around at these men.
'They've bombed our house, the Zepps…'

'Bastards!'

'They've killed my mum and dad…'

'Coward Hun!'

'And my brother…'

'Killed your Fred?'

'…he's been taken to live with my grandad and uncle.

Terrible man, rotten right through, loathed my dad.'

He reread that part of the letter. The words stood out as sharply as Times Roman print.

Poor Fred! With Mum and Dad dead – and living in Grandad's house! There was stuff their mum and dad had let out to him. That boy couldn't be left to live within a mile of Len Castle!

'God knows what he'll do to our Fred.'

'Poor little devil!'

Will closed his eyes, and his hand went to where he'd once carried Fred's sketch-book. He put the letter there instead.

Eric wouldn't leave it alone. 'I 'ated my uncle. But 'e'll be all right. Young blade. 'E'll mek 'is way.'

'Not with Len anywhere near. He'll take out all sorts of grudge on him.'

'What? What sort o' grudge?'

Will rubbed his cheek, didn't know whether to say or not. But these lads were his pals. 'Family feud stuff.' He didn't get to say any more. A great spasm suddenly ran through him and he raised his hand, stood up and shouted across to a guard. 'Latrine! *Dringend!*'

The man waved for him to go. He ran out of the mess and across the yard to the planks and the stink, and just got his trousers down before his insides erupted at the appalling news he'd just received.

* * *

He'd got to get away. He'd got to get out of this prison camp and find his way back behind British lines. He'd got to get back to London and rescue his brother from Len Castle, take him to Amy – or an orphanage, even that would be better. He could tell the council about Len and his own dad, Sam, their hatred for each other and get him moved. But no one else could do it. He was blood.

It was the most important decision of his life. Volunteering for the army had meant risking death, but escaping from a prison camp put that risk higher. Getting killed wasn't random any more; you were in the camp under the thumb of the enemy, who knew your name and your army number. The main job of a prison guard was keeping you doing what they wanted done, and stopping you from escaping; and guards themselves were under harsh discipline, so they wouldn't think twice about gunning down a man on the run. If he ran he'd be a prime target for a twitchy guard – and if he was caught he'd either be killed or left to go mad in a rat-infested lock-up like the Frenchman.

Even so, escape was what he had to do – but how was he going to get away from here? He knew roughly where he'd have to head if he could get out – towards the distant sounds of artillery morning and night, which going by the sun was north-west of here, about thirty or forty miles away, he reckoned. Every day when he was marched to the railway he saw French people going about, under the thumb: shouted at, pushed and kicked around, working for the Germans. So if he could get away and act like some French farm worker he might just stand a chance.

If he could get away.

Even his itching wasn't so bad as he lay on his straw and thought of how he'd do that. And it came fast; it was obvious. *He didn't have to escape from inside this camp.* With the guards and the barbed wire that would be a stupid thing to try – when, unlike the transit prisoners, he had the great advantage of going out through those gates every day. He'd got the best chance of most to make a run for it.

He kept it all inside himself, didn't share a thing. He was quiet – the lads would expect that – and he stayed the Will they knew, swearing at the rotten food and the lice and the hard graft, and saying nothing. Prisoners came and went in the barn, and while he trusted the Scots and the Accrington lads, he couldn't be sure some other person with big ears hadn't been planted by the Germans. But every time he was outside, on the march or at his shovel, he was looking at things through an escaper's eyes – the lie of the land, the position of the guard, the interruptions made by trains coming through – and especially every move of Attila the Hun.

'Sorry about yer mam and dad.' Eric Boundle turned

on his own straw and gave him a hefty punch on the arm. 'An' your bro. But he'll be awright, tough little divils, our kids.'

'Yeah. You're right. Just get this ruddy war over, eh?'

'Might not be so long. Them English guns sound a bit closer to me these days.'

'Or the wind's changed.'

And then some comedian blew off, and got thumped for it.

Will's plan for getting away chased around in his head so much that he dreamt of doing it and then woke up disappointed when he hadn't. It was always the same, based on the daily routine. The gangs were marched along to the next sections of road or railway line further and further away from the camp; but the Germans were more concerned with sorting and shipping prisoners off to Germany, and these days Will's gang of ten was followed by Attila the Hun and just one man with a rifle. It had all got a bit routine. Right now they were working on an embankment set above open fields, but about half a mile away there was a wood, and if he could only make that he might stand a chance.

So he worked out his plan. He'd wait for a train to come through. The guard would blow his whistle and they'd all stand back on the other track. Shovels would be rested, and everyone would hope that the train was a mile long. And this was when he'd do it. At the sound of the whistle he'd manoeuvre himself close to Attila the Hun, and as the train came towards them he'd wind up all that was left of his strength and he'd smash his shovel round the German's head – once, twice, three times if necessary – leaving himself just time to run across the path of the train, jump down the embankment, and sprint as fast as he could across the fields, hoping the guard wasn't a good shot. By the time the train stopped – if it stopped – he could be in the cover of the woods. Then what would the guard do? Chase one man or guard the other nine? If he timed his break for one of the late afternoon trains, by the time word got back to the prison camp and search parties were sent out, he'd have the advantage of dusk and then the night. After that he would head for those sounds of battle and take what chances he could.

Everyone in the barn shaved, and men gave one another 'knife-and-fork scalpings' to deny the lice their hunting grounds. Now he'd grow his hair and his beard so he didn't look like a prisoner of war, and he'd rub manure into them in case it sped things up; well, it helped with plants, didn't it? And he'd steal a farmer's coat and try to look like a Frenchman. Outside the ruins of the town the French were growing food for the German army – so he'd be a farm labourer in a long overcoat and a pull-down cap, laying up by day but moving early in the morning and late at night, asking for food and help from French farmers and always keeping on the look-out for patrols.

These were his waking thoughts, and his dreams. But he'd have to bide his time. One day either way wouldn't make a great difference when he thought of the distant sound of the gunfire; but one bit of luck if it came – like a lift on a farmer's cart – could make up for half a day's walking.

But when Attila the Hun refused to go down after half a dozen shovel hits round the head and he woke up sweating into his straw he knew that the nightmare could be the reality. And that man was like a bull. Would Will Castle have the guts to lift his shovel and attack him? He'd not done what Stan Denyer had asked him to do, he'd saved his own skin instead and been questioning his courage ever since. Would he go into a funk like that again? All he knew was, his mum and dad in heaven would never forgive him if he didn't do everything on earth to help rescue Fred from the hell of living with Len Castle. But would that spur be enough?

When it happened it was almost a stroll. The part of the embankment they were working on crossed a small country road by way of a bridge. They'd just had their midday ration, that day a meagre lump of turnip bread and a can of grass-and-horsemeat soup, without much meat. After weeks on food like this the prospect of him lifting his shovel high enough to smash round the Hun's head seemed less and less possible; his aching arms were just about coping with shovelling at ground level. But it didn't come to that. The same as usual, they were allowed to sit on the embankment to eat, and as the midday sun hit them, eyelids drooped, and after sharing a superior meal from the guard's backpack, the Hun sat chewing his tobacco and spitting out the juice while the guard smoked a stubby pipe. Taking this in, pretending to lie down in the sun, Will started shuffling his bottom nearer and nearer to the edge of the embankment. He waited and waited as the two Germans shared a bottle of water – when, with a last quick look from under his arm, he undug his heels and let himself slide down the grassy bank. It could have been an accident. '*Sorry, Corporal, fell asleep!*' He expected to get a kicking. But nothing happened. His mates looked at one another, said nothing. He'd kept hold of his shovel, could be digging a hole for his bowels. At the bottom of the embankment he listened for the shout but still there was none; so this was it! He bent himself double and skirted along to the bridge and the road. Even now it could have been an accident. If he was shouted at he'd just lower his trousers. But still there was no shout; and – heavens be praised! – right at that moment a long train came through, cutting him off from everyone for a crucial minute. He put down his head and ran, ran, ran on the faster surface of the road, away from the embankment and towards the trees, ears pricked, eyes everywhere for the guard following or a German patrol. But he was dead meat now if they caught him. No one ran half a mile for a privy visit, not even in the country.

Panting, head light, legs like forced rhubarb, he threw himself into the shadows of the trees and ran from the edge of the wood, pushed himself through thickets, up and down hillocks and round ponds, the leaves falling about him like in a Babes in the Wood pantomime. The trees themselves were a reminder of where he was, and what was going on. They were splintered, shafted into two, halved like broken matchsticks, violated by the shelling when the armies had fought for this region. But right now his mind was intent on pressing on while he could. Later without the sun he might lose his sense of where north-west was, although he'd have the dusk and dawn shelling to guide him. Meanwhile he'd have to chance his luck; around noon there was little guidance from the war. Every so often the forest opened out with large lakes to skirt — and at one spot he had to tread carefully around an abandoned gun-site where torn camouflage netting hung like a shroud, the smell of old smoke still lingered, and ruts, cigarette butts and spent shell cases told the story of a gun like his old eighteen-pounder; while the remains of a food kitchen littered with rusting cans said these German gunners had eaten better than the British had.

A rustling suddenly crouched him, fossilised him; but when he saw it – a deer, bounding off – he relaxed a little, a sight of a world that wasn't war; and for the first time since reading Amy's Red Cross letter he relaxed a little. He was a long, long way from home; but although well within their territory he was free from the Germans for now, and instead of obeying their orders he could decide for himself what he was going to do. What he did was in his own hands – while he stayed free. While he lived.

24

All along the quay men were shouting in a barge language Freddie didn't understand, and close by he could hear Billy being told his fortune. The sound of flapping sails had him guessing they weren't long off moving – it was going to be nine in the evening not nine in the morning when they set off – and when he heard ropes being thrown onto the barge and the sails starting to crack he knew they were leaving. He curled himself up like one of his mother's births – and he prayed they wouldn't untie the boat from the barge. But they didn't come near; it was as if it was tied on like the spare nosebag on the back of 'Orse's cart.

They went slowly at first – and he stretched his legs to try to bring them to life: when they got to the docks he'd have to be lively, ready to jump aboard something else pretty quick, or run along a quayside and lose himself again, and he couldn't do that with the cramp.

It was a bumpy ride in the small boat; the thing rocked from side to side behind the barge and he had to hold on as tight as on the waltzer at the fair. At first it was fairly plain sailing. He could see in his head where they were, going down the river that he'd walked beside earlier. But by the time the sun was up they were getting into choppier waters, and as the wind really creaked the sails and they changed direction, the barge suddenly jerked into a new life. From slosh and ripple the water turned to splash and surge, the front of the boat lifting and the bumping beginning. He could only cling on now – he thought he was going to be thrown out any second – and he thanked heaven his dad had taught him to swim. He gave thanks, too, for not feeling sick: perhaps he was a good sailor; well, that'd help in the Pacific Ocean. The barge pulled the boat on and on, up on the left then up on the right, buffeted by sudden freak surges. In all the toss and bump he hadn't a thought of feeling hungry, and when he couldn't put off peeing any longer he did it in a bottle with varnish in the bottom – and spilt most of it. But the boat was half under water anyway, and he needn't have worried.

It had to be early evening when the sounds of the sails changed, the straining became a flapping again, the bumping stopped and he could hear the skipper shouting at Billy – close by, up above him on the back of the barge.

'Keep hold of that mainsheet, boy, an' make fast!'

They'd stopped, so did that mean they'd got to where they were going? If so, they had to be in the docks. Right! He'd got to get ready to make his move – but the first thing was to take a good look around. He needed to know the layout of the docks so he could plan his next move. But he couldn't do it with the skipper so close;

when his voice got more distant he'd risk a move from under these wet smelly rags.

He didn't have to wait long. Billy must have done something wrong again because the skipper swore at him and went on swearing as his voice faded away. Handy.

Now!

He pulled the rags from off his head and lifted himself, held onto the side of the boat and pulled himself up. Even in the evening light his open eyes hurt. He took a first look up at the barge, the *Rose*, and, great, no skipper in sight – he was still shouting at Billy from somewhere. He looked out to left and to right to check on the ship they'd come alongside. Or were they moored up at a quayside?

But there were no ships. On the left the barge was rubbing against a wharf, and on the right was a great width of water, a river across which was a long line of buildings with a name on one of them. *'Metropolitan Wharf'*. Another look left and upwards told him more. The wharf they were alongside had its name painted up, too, smaller than the Metropolitan but very, very, clear.

'Pacific Wharf'.

Hell-'n'-hailstones! The cement in this barge wasn't going to the Pacific Ocean at all, it had come as far as it was going – to Pacific Wharf in what looked like London. He'd been on outings up the river, he knew this sort of place. He'd been fooled – or he'd fooled himself. Behind him he could see sacks of cement being unloaded from another barge, and horses and carts waiting to take them off somewhere.

Damn! He'd got to get off, but he still had to bide his time, he mustn't be caught, not with a dead uncle to his name. He slid back under the rags and waited for his chance to move, out of this boat, round Pacific Wharf and into the back streets. But to go where? That was the question.

The answer was risky, yes – but now it all seemed so obvious that he called himself an idiot every step of the way. It was back to Woolwich. Why hadn't he done this in the first place – because, what was on the other side of the river at Woolwich? Where did the Woolwich Free Ferry go? It went across towards the Royal Albert Dock, that's where. Some afternoons when he and Don were on it, the dockers got on the ferry coming home, so the dock couldn't be far from the north side. Then why the heck had he gone chasing down to Chatham when a dock and ships were just across the river from where he'd lived? Fool, fool, fool!

He didn't blame himself for the barge mistake. Pacific meant Pacific – he'd just got the wrong one! And those sacks and sacks of cement? He soon saw where they were going – for building new houses in London.

Getting onto the quay was easy. The barges were

being unloaded by hoists, their nets bringing up the sacks from the holds. And when the skipper shouted that he was going for a wet at the Bull and Half Moon, leaving only Billy in charge, it was easy to climb out of the boat and mingle in the activity on the wharf. A couple of minutes of that, and he was running down an alley following a wall to a sort of High Street, past the pub, and there was the cement: where houses were being built. A short road was finished on one side – a terrace of houses like in Abbey Wood – but the other side was still open land where a line of new houses was going up. And there they were beside the bricks – sacks of cement covered with tarpaulins.

'*This lot's for the Pacific.*' Why couldn't the skipper have said, 'This lot's for London'?

He knew he looked a state, and he was wet. He needed a good wash and he felt bunged up inside, but he didn't go hungry. Evening or not, on his walk along the Deptford road towards Woolwich he passed plenty of shops still open, so an apple here and a plum there were easy pickings, and he kept himself watered with a half-drained pint of beer left on a pub window-sill.

Lights were lower at night, shutters and blinds were down because of Zeppelin raids, so his eyes were sharp and wide for police, his neck hurting again with twisting around, and once he went dizzy when he turned too fast. But the road through this part of London was all houses, shops, dining rooms, pubs and narrow alleys, and in the dark it wasn't hard to slip out of the way when he saw trouble looming. But there were soldiers, too. They were in a park with a gun, its barrel pointing up into the sky – and as he was creeping past, a beam of light suddenly shot up and started pointing about. Zeppelins? The devils! If he saw one he'd spit up at it, however far short it fell.

And that brought it all back. Those Hun who'd killed his mum and dad – leaving him with Len Castle. And those others over the sea who'd captured his brother Will. So was Will still alive? What sorts of things did they do to English prisoners? And if he was alive, would he ever see him again? It wouldn't be for a long time, anyway – because he was a killer boy himself, and if he didn't want a life locked up he'd still got to do what he was doing. Getting as far away from England as he could.

But now he knew where he was heading to do it. He'd walk this road to Woolwich tonight; once there, he knew plenty of places by the river for hiding-up until next morning when the ferry would be busy enough for him to cross. He'd run to North Woolwich Gardens and lie low through tomorrow, and as soon as it got dark again, he'd head for the docks – and this time he'd sneak onto a boat that was going a long way away. One with a foreign flag – that'd be the ticket.

So it was back to Woolwich where he'd started. But only for one night and one day. Please God.

25

This was more than a wood; it was a forest, because it went on and on, hilly, dippy, all clumps and clearings, with lakes and ponds floating with fallen leaves. This first afternoon and evening were vital; Will had got to put as much distance as he could between himself and anyone chasing him. He kept thinking about his pals, and he hoped they wouldn't be punished for what he'd done; but they hadn't helped him, Attila couldn't say that, and at least they'd know why he'd done it.

As evening came on so did the sounds of bombardment from the distant north-west, and the openings in the forest and a weak moon helped to keep him going. He was hungry – then he was always hungry – but with the ponds that he had to skirt, thirst was no problem.

It had to be about midnight when he saw it. The guns were laying off, the light of the moon was brighter, and he could see a space opening out before him, a broad swath of grass and a cluster of tall buildings, standing in a group. What was this? Was the largest one a château? He dropped down, lay prone like poor old Whitaker with his field glasses. The main building had four turrets, each shaped a bit like eighteen-pounder shells, built in white stone like the walls. And, squinting his eyes in the gloom, he could make out along the side wall a line of ornamental bricked-up arched window shapes, like in a church.

He'd got to be very careful. If this was a château built in church style it could be stuffed with German officers, the way the British commandeered châteaux themselves. On the other hand, it could be a church, and the buildings around it could be the rest of the village – houses, barns, outbuildings, sheds. He'd got to be cautious, he'd got to be double, treble sure he wasn't going to be seen. He'd got to get to these buildings as secretly as he used to as a boy playing last-man-in; but if he could succeed he might do himself some good.

He wriggled towards the buildings, treating the swath of grass like no man's land, belly-flat but hampered by his shovel and having to go round cow flops. The guns had quietened and he could hear his own scraping progress until, as he neared the large main building he heard it: chanting, men's voices, sounding like Sunday mornings at the Woolwich Tabernacle church, but stronger and deeper. Monks, singing in Latin, probably – he didn't know – but sweeter than a hymn in German would have sounded. Bucked up, he stood and made a quick dash for the shadow of the wall. This was definitely no village, but a monk's community like Lesnes Abbey at home, except it had been kept up, it wasn't an old ruin. And the thought hit him – while the monks were at their chanting, who might still be about? Wouldn't they all be there?

Getting away from the church and keeping tight against the walls he came to the smallest building of all, the one most looking like a house. Now he could hardly hear the chanting – which meant he wouldn't hear when it stopped – but he found a back door and took a chance. It wasn't locked. Shovel ready, his imagination seeing a German officer sitting at a desk and pointing a pistol at him as he came round the door. But no – and here he was in an empty kitchen, not a place for feeding an abbey of monks but a small room with a stove and a table and pots and pans on the wall. There was no food he could see, but in the corner was a smaller door that might lead to a larder. He opened it.

Phew! The smell of cheese hit him – rounds of it stacked on the shelves, and straight-off he made a grab, breaking into one using a strength he didn't know he had, biting like a horse. He crammed cheese into his mouth until he choked himself with it, and shoving the rest down his shirt he came out of the larder for a long drink.

'*Qui êtes vous? Qu'est-ce que vous faites ici?*'

A large monk was standing in the outer doorway, filling it with his bulk. Will would need his shovel to get past him, and that was leaning against the table. But the man had spoken French, so they should be on the same side unless all monks' Gods were neutral.

'I'm English. *Anglais! Soldat.*'

'*Soldat? D'où venez-vous? Il n'y a pas de soldats anglais ici. Ils sont tous Allemands.*'

'*Soldat.* Prisoner. Free. *Libre.*' He made a gesture of throwing off ropes, escaping.

'*Evadé?*'

'*Oui.*'

'*Ah.*'

What would the man do? They might all be peaceful monks here – but the chanting had stopped and fifty monks could come running and easily sit on one weak soldier. Would they be frightened of German reprisals and hand him over? Was their peace and their worship of God more important than their being French and him English?

'*Asseyez-vous.*' The monk waved his hand at a chair at the table.

Should he sit, or should he hit him now and make a run for it? More monks could come at any moment and keep him here while the nearest patrol was called. His hand itched towards the shovel. He would use it if he had to.

But the monk came further into the kitchen and turned his back on him to pour water from a pitcher into a mug. He went to a basket in the corner and pulled out a rustic loaf, which he put on the table and started to break.

'*Asseyez-vous, s'il vous plaît.*'

Will sat.

'*Du fromage?*' The monk went into the larder and brought out a cheese, which he cut with a kitchen knife and slid onto a wooden trencher. '*Mangez, c'est du Brie.*'

And Will did his best to eat, but he was already gorged with cheese, and it was hard to get anything more inside his shrunken gullet. Who'd ever have thought he'd have this problem?

The monk watched him as he tried to eat, said no more for a while, asked no more questions – probably wouldn't want to know any answers that could be forced out by the Germans.

Some tomatoes came, they were easier, and wine was offered but milk was sweeter.

'Thank you very much. *Merci.*'

'*De rien.*'

Now, finally, the big question came: the question that would help save his life if this monk was as genuine as he seemed.

'*Alors, qu'est-ce que vous voulez, soldat?*' And, in English: 'What need?'

And in two English words and a simple mime Will told him.

26

October the first. Ernst would be twenty-two tomorrow, and he had a birthday card from Rachel tucked in his locker ready to open when they got back from the raid on London. Another year and there might be a scrawly kiss from Josefine as well – and he might be opening it in Berlin, in peacetime. Who knows?

There was no secret about where they were going that night, no need for Josef to put his fingers to his lips or to wink his eye. There would be eleven Zeppelins in the air, some heading for the English Midlands, but the L31 crew knew from Josef that they were targeting London, Mathy's favourite bombing ground. 'London docks. Destroy their imports, impoverish their people: basins and quays all along the Thames from the City to Woolwich, with a few "love gifts" from Mathy to give them joy.'

Ernst was content with that. Now that he had a daughter, bombing houses wasn't what he wanted to do to help win the war. Imagine Josefine in an air raid: even Opa Stender wouldn't be able to rock her off to sleep; and as for a direct hit! Ernst shut that thought out of his mind.

He felt the tension of the big sortie, everyone did. Even Karl Klee's raised eyebrow seemed droopier today.

And always in his own head was that question, the never-buried crewman's decision that might have to be made: *jump or burn?* He thought he knew the answer, but could he tell what he might do if the moment came? Which made him angry. Jump or burn was a choice in every flying man's head, and it was unfair. If Mathy's 'love gifts' and their other bombs were just a few kilos lighter they could all have had parachutes. So were men's lives so cheap? What would a roll of silk and a few metres of harness cost to make up eighteen of them? More than eighteen men were worth? And what was the cost of a man's eternal soul who made the wrong decision? It was diabolical.

But it was reality. As Josef would say, 'You've just got to live with it.'

It was a cold night on the ground, and colder in the air. Even as they rose from the base, Ernst was shivering, everyone was shivering in their extra-thick clothing, and soon the first gusts of a squally south-westerly started to hit them. Worse, when they were well over the North Sea and near to the English coast, it looked as if he was steering them into a wall of cloud as solid as a castle rampart – and it was no surprise when radio messages told Mathy that four Zepps had already turned back.

The wind suddenly veered and Ernst's steering wheel twisted, needing a strong grip. 'Wind nor'-nor' west,'

Josef announced – and at their altitude rain, snow and hail began hitting the mica all around the front of the gondola.

At 20:00 Josef announced that they were flying in over the Suffolk coast, and looking around the sky they seemed to be alone. So why did Mathy have to be so stubborn? Why couldn't they turn back like most of the others?

And was Mathy actually making a mistake? As he ordered Karl to take them down from the thickest of the cloud so he could see the ground, Josef's compass bearings told them they were over the Great Eastern Railway line near Chelmsford. There it was below them, glimmering along its length of track.

'Follow the railway, Lieutenant.' Josef sounded certain. 'I suggest. The line will take us direct to the east of London.'

But, 'Throttle back engines,' Mathy commanded. 'Wireless bearing. I must be certain where we are.'

Everyone knew what this meant. Wireless bearings took time to take, and here they were hovering in the sky with time to be seen, time to be attacked, where a straight run for London down the railway line would have them in and away much quicker.

Which was when it hit them. Mathy had dithered. A searchlight shot up and flooded the gondola with white light.

'Nor'-west!'

Ernst twisted the wheel fast.

'West three-twenty north.'

'Lieutenant!'

More wireless bearings came in, and they raced out of reach of the searchlight. Josef reported them over Hertford. Now Mathy could set a new course for the London docks. But with the wireless bearing delay the English defences were up, light was scrawling all over the sky, and flashes from the ground signalled the shells that were exploding just below them.

'Hold course for the Thames. Full speed all engines!' Mathy wanted a fast run in to the docks, but suddenly other dangers were up there, threatening.

Aeroplanes!

Ernst saw the flash of tracer bullets from three planes. The Royal Flying Corps was at them.

'Climb! Climb!'

Scheiße! The wireless delay meant the planes had had time to get to their height – leaving them open now to this deadly danger. Tracers! Fiery tracers – and who knew what other fresh ammunition these planes were carrying, and what those bullets could do…?

From the first reported sighting of a Zeppelin over the Suffolk coast, George Simmonds had been climbing ready to engage as soon as he could see something. And what he was carrying tonight gave extra zest to his patrol. Once again his BE2's machine gun had been loaded with a belt of mixed ammunition: nitro-glycerine Pomeroy and phosphorous Buckingham explosive bullets – the new sorts that wouldn't go clean through the Zeppelin skin and pass out the other side. When one of these bullets hit any resistance it would explode inside an airship's envelope among all that hydrogen. And, boom! Well, he'd see, he'd see…

And there she was in the Thames searchlights now – a great beast of a thing hovering way above the docks, pinned by the cross-beams. As the guns opened up below he estimated he was about two miles from his target and some hundreds of feet above her, but at what he reckoned to be about twelve and a half thousand feet she started rapidly climbing away from him and he'd got to be quick. He couldn't follow her at her speed of ascent, he'd have to spiral up as fast as he could, or she'd be away by the time he got there.

Blast! As he raced for her and was closing-in, his petrol pressure pump packed up and he had to start hand-pumping to get enough rich fuel for speed. But at least up here he was out of range of the ground guns – so he dived to get beneath the beast, firing off a short burst of mixed ammo through his propeller timing. But the Zepp was firing back at him, forcing him to bank tightly and come in under her tail where her guns couldn't reach him. Attacking upwards again he pumped lead at her for all he was worth. He held his course. This was madness, she'd get him any second; but he was so near, so near. He kept his thumb pressed hard on the button and went on in. *Rat-a-tat-a-tat-a-tat*.

And suddenly, whoosh! A flame shot out of the fore of her envelope and its inside went red with fire, all in a second. She shot up about two hundred feet, hung there for a few seconds, and came roaring back towards him. He was going to be engulfed. He threw his plane into the steepest nose-dive ever, the blazing mass still searing down after him as, desperate, life or death, he jerked the plane into a spin – and just corkscrewed out of the way as the furnace plummeted past him.

'*Alleluia!*'

He righted himself, straightened out – and looked over the side to see what was happening. The Zeppelin hit open ground north of the Royal Albert Dock in a great shower of sparks and fire and smoke.

He looked at his watch. It was 23:50. He felt sick, giddy and exhausted; the risk he'd run would hit him later, but the truth of it was, he'd only just escaped dying with those German airmen.

By the time he found Sutton's field it was covered by a low-lying fog, and when he made his final approach he misjudged his height and crashed, cutting his head on – of all things – his machine gun. His lethal weapon.

But he'd done it. He'd downed a Zepp – with grateful thanks to the ordnance factories that had developed these new deadly bullets.

27

Freddie couldn't believe his eyes. He saw it all from the high ground above the Woolwich Ferry in Woolwich Gardens up by St Mary's Church, a perfect view. After riding the ferry he and Don sometimes came up here to sunbathe on nice days; but there were good hide-and-seek places behind the tombstones around the edge, and shelter from the rain in the church porch. Both might be handy tonight.

He'd walked along the Woolwich road and come straight up here, legs ready for a rest and his insides ready for a privy crouch – well dogs did it, didn't they, it was all in nature. But dark as it was around the church the sky was alight with searchlights, air raid warning maroons were shooting up over the river and his ears were dinned by the guns from the Royal Artillery. They were chasing something up there in the sky. And as he watched, a searchlight suddenly got it. He shivered from head to toe and he lost his breath. It was a Zeppelin, a nightmare of a thing, bigger than he'd seen before. He could hear the engines like a droning from hell. A coward airship – one of the murdering devils that had killed his mum and dad.

Mouth open, Freddie watched it all happen. The guns on the ground were firing but the explosions were bursting too low and it looked as if the Zeppelin was going to be able to do whatever it wanted, cock of the sky – then something went flashing like a dart through the searchlight beam. It was an aeroplane. British airmen were up there after it. The Zepp must have seen it at the same time he did because her engines suddenly changed their sound and she turned nose-up and shot towards the clouds. But the aeroplane wasn't finished. In the glare of several searchlights he could see it coming up underneath the beast, banking and coming back again, not giving up. The artillery had stopped firing and he could hear it now, the rattling sounds of machine guns fighting it out. He was yelling, standing there bellowing any animal sound his throat could make.

And – *hell-'n'-hailstones!* – the plane flew upwards almost into the belly of the Zepp, on and on, long after it should have pulled out. The pilot had had it; he'd collide and come down too. But there was a long, fierce, final rat-a-tat-a-tat, and a great flame suddenly shot from the Zepp's nose, and in that instant the whole great thing turned bright red, front to back. She gave a mighty lurch upwards – hung there for a few seconds – then did a crazy tilt and nose-dived down in flames, with a great hellish roar going crashing to earth somewhere over North Woolwich way.

He jumped into the air, waved his arms. The Zepp was down! The airman's bullets had blown it up – Royal

Arsenal bullets, he bet! His dad's Pomeroys! And now those killers were dead themselves.

He stood rigid as a churchyard statue while he took it in, his mind making sense of what he'd seen. The end of a Zepp and the deaths of the devils in it. And as if his mum and dad were buried up here he ran to the nearest gravestone, knelt down and put his hands together the way his mum had done beside his dad's bed.

'They're done for, Mum, they're done for, Dad.' And, 'Thank you, God. Thank you very much.'

Flesh and blood again, he sank back, rolled himself up like a hedgehog and he cried, and cried, and cried.

And he told himself that if there was a God in heaven those German airmen had been those same sons-of-devils who'd bombed his house and killed off his family.

It was frenzy in the gondola. The first rattle of machine guns told them the RFC were up at their height, and lethal. Even if their bullets didn't strike, one mistake from a pilot and a collision could burst their skin and send them crashing to the earth. Machine gunners were leaning out of the gondola firing down, and Mathy gave the order to climb – climb fast. There was no question of Ernst compass steering, they must gain height and make the enemy take its own time climbing.

'He's beneath us somewhere!'

Through the front mica he saw the plane come shooting out from below and bank to the right.

'He's turning for another attack.'

The gondola was at a crazy angle in the sudden climb; men were tumbling, hands gripping whatever they could.

'He's coming at two o'clock, beneath us!'

One machine gunner was on his back, the other desperately trying to angle his gun where it wouldn't go.

It was machine gun fire from side and below – and another sudden glimpse of the plane coming out from under their belly.

'He's out again! Lost him!'

'Steer west, Helm!'

'Lieutenant!' Ernst twisted the wheel one-handed, holding grimly onto a stanchion. And with his brain and body hard on their tasks that dreaded catastrophe hit them. What he'd feared. There was the sustained rattle of machine gun fire rising to a crescendo, and at its peak a sudden explosion filled the sky like the end of the world. They were hit. A huge flame shot from the front of the envelope and in seconds all hell broke loose, the sky turned blood-red and the gondola went luminous with the inferno above it. The heat hit instantly and Ernst knew there was no chance for any of them – the whole ship was alight, and from up in the envelope men were jumping as the gondola tipped for a fall. Too high!

The ship was over three thousand metres from the ground.

This was it, the end, and it had come like an arrow and too soon.

'Jump!' Mathy commanded. 'Jump!'

Karl Klee turned, stared terrified, shouted, 'Hell! I'm not going to burn!' and followed a machine-gunner out of the half-hatch.

Josef went for the space, spun round. 'Get out! Don't burn! Nothing worse. Got to be done, got to be done!' He stared hard at Ernst. 'Jump, Erno! Jump to Heaven!' And he went, too.

Erno, at the end. Silent officers went, all within seconds, new faces staring down at death.

Mathy went – and only Ernst was left in the spiralling gondola, his body twisting, his head reeling, sick with vertigo and with fear.

What to do? To follow all the others or to stay? *Jump or burn?* Jump was certain death. Stay and burn was certain death – in terrible, terrible pain. Whichever way, he was dead. So how important was his religion in the end?

He went to the open hatch, clung there, his gloves singeing. The world was spinning out of control. *Jump!* That would be quicker, he'd be dead in seconds. Already the heat was scorching his head, face, hands; his uniform was steaming. Burning to death would be the most terrible way to go, and it would be slow. He held on tight, not to be thrown out against his will while he made this last decision of his life.

And he stayed. He was Ernst Stender, a Jewish man married to a Jewish girl with a Jewish daughter. He had decided. Rachel and Josefine would never be told that he had jumped, that he had killed himself. It was the English plane that killed him, he was not a suicide and he would not be buried separately from them, because no one was going to find his unburnt body on the ground. He'd be black, unidentified bones, but whether anyone else ever knew why or not, he did, and so did his God.

And as the flames broke through and his hair started to burn he gripped harder on the stanchion, and mouthed through his agony the words of a childhood bedtime prayer: 'May it be Your will my God and the God of my ancestors, to lie me down in peace and then to raise me up in peace.'

And the rest was the sound of his screaming.

28

The Prior of Saint-Nicolas-au-Bois rested Will on a
truckle bed and sent him off at first light with a full belly,
a clean thick shirt, field-workers' black trousers, and
a heavy cowman's overcoat that came down to his
ankles. Wearing a gardener's ear-flapped cap he looked
French enough, and with directions from a monk who
spoke English he was ready to set off towards the
sounds of the morning artillery, which seemed to be
about fifteen miles away.

'Problem for you, the river. The Oise. The bridges.
Take direction Chauny north side, small crossings, not
so big army…'

He wouldn't take a map, not even the sketch-map the
monk had drawn. He wanted nothing to be found on
him that said he was on his way anywhere. If he was
stopped and questioned, he was a labourer digging a
ditch, or burying a dead dog; he was not a traveller. To
add to the look of the peasant and the slow growth of his
beard he rubbed his face with earth, and dirtied the backs
of his hands. Now he had to put his best foot forward.

It could have been Chauny that he kept at a distance
or it could have been some other town. On the skyline
was a single spire, which might have been a church or a
town hall, a built-up area anyway, so he kept north of

that and made good progress along a small road. Signs of war were all around him – buildings teetering between standing and collapsing, roofs ripped open, piles of rubble, shell holes in the fields, at one point a line of abandoned trenches that had him on his knees in case a machine-gun nest was lurking. All around, the trees had suffered most – splintered, split, burned along an avenue like a line of lightning strikes. All the while he shouldered his shovel and kept marching on. The area was so open that he'd see or hear anything other than a small patrol or a camouflaged sentry post. Across wide fields he saw horses and men ploughing and planting – all to feed the German army – and he held himself ready with a moment's warning to start working at the side of the road: head down, digging hard, keeping his back turned. He was some way behind the front line, further than the artillery and the supply depots, but an occasional military lorry could be seen across the fields, and now on this road a clopping old horse came pulling a cart with milk churns. He took no chances. He hid in a shell hole and listened to it rattling past.

He came to the river. He heard it first; there must have been rain in the north because it sounded swollen, and already threatening clouds had been gathering, sending dark shadows across the fields like ghosts of the dead. But as he approached the river his chest tightened, his breathing came harder. He could be about to have his first face-to-face meeting with a German soldier since he'd escaped.

With its straight banks the river was more like a canal. Cautiously, between shelled and scattered houses he reached the bridge, which looked army-reinforced for heavy transport — but with no sign of soldiers. Coming across it was an old woman carrying a bundle over her shoulder. He lurked, stood back against a wall and cupped a hand to his face to mime smoking. This was the test. He crossed his ankles and waited for her to pass.

She looked at him. '*Monsieur.*'

'*Madame.*' But it was more a grunt; grunts don't have bad French accents.

The old woman walked on, muttering something, he was a lazy so-and-so, but he'd passed muster, didn't look out of place. Pulling himself off the wall he shouldered his shovel again, pulled his cap down and headed for the bridge. A barge passed beneath him, laden with stencilled crates. Ammo? Food for Fritz? Who knew? Trying to look like a man late for the fields, he walked quickly across the bridge, deliberately keeping his steps irregular and not like marching. This was going all right. Ahead he could see the road winding off into countryside and a distant avenue. He'd soon be across the river and heading for the front line.

'*Halt!*' A German soldier suddenly stepped out from behind the bridge parapet. He unslung his rifle and levelled it. He was tall and youngish, his helmet not glinting but camouflaged, more warlike even than the front line. He chucked his head at Will as if expecting papers to be handed over.

Will shrugged. He opened his hands to show how stupid and forgetful he was.

'*Ausweis!*'

Will shrugged again. He'd better say something, try to explain himself. But he was a French farm labourer. What to say in French?

'*Papiere!*' The soldier was scowling.

'*Sur le pont d'Avignon, l'on y danse, l'on y danse.*'

It was the only French that came into his head, thanks to Miss Cape at school.

The soldier jabbed his rifle six inches and back. '*Papiere!*'

Will opened his hands in apology, smiled, winked.

'*Les belles dames font comme ça, et puis encore comme ça.*' He put his hands to where his fly-buttons would be under his long coat, pulled a rude face as if he'd been robbed while doing something naughty with a girl. '*Honi soit qui mal-y-pense.*' A bit of half-remembered business from Mark Sheridan at the Holborn Empire.

The German soldier stared. Then he laughed, shook his head at the stupidity of French country people, grounded his rifle and waved him on. '*Weitergehen.*'

With his back to the German it was the longest walk

of his life. Had he fooled him? Was the German fooling him? Would he get a bullet in his spine any second? And would he ever know if he did?

He walked on until the distance he'd gone told him he wasn't going to be shot; at least, not right now by the sentry at the bridge. But to be totally sure, he had to make that bend in the road. Twenty yards to go, ten yards, five yards – and as he walked out of sight he ducked into a field and headed across the furrows for a copse, thanking God for dear old Miss Cape and her singing lessons, even if she had conducted them with a ruler, rapping the knuckles of the groaners.

The weather broke. From the darkened sky a deluge fell all over the fields; it started to fill shell holes, to bend already broken trees, and to take down the last of their clinging leaves, while roads ran like streams and tracks turned into sucking mud. Will's cowman's coat was made from a heavy wool that seemed to repel the rain at first, but then absorbed it; and when he lifted his boots to make faster progress they started to fill with water. The downpour was so hard that looking up was painful, but even a glance told him this was no flash flood but a relentless storm. He'd got to push on. This was for Fred. This was to get home and take him away from their hateful Uncle Len. Fred wouldn't have known, but their mother had once told him how Len had threatened spiteful revenge on their dad for stealing her off him. She'd met Len at a wedding and walked out with him for a bit. *'Don't know what I ever saw in him.'* But it was his brother Sam she fell in love with. *'And he said, "All's fair in love and war".'* And Len had never forgiven either of them. He'd threatened that one day their side of the Castles was going to pay for Sam's treachery. *'Don't you ever trust him an inch, Will!'*

He had to stick to the road, which was broken and ashy. There were no wooded clumps here where he could stand under the trunk of a leaning tree, and no sheds, barns or outbuildings in sight – not even an abandoned pillbox. The drenching was cold and he started to shiver and sneeze. The food he'd been given for the past weeks had nothing nutritious in it, there wouldn't be much in his system that could stop a heavy cold from turning into something worse; already his throat was closing up like mumps, and his head was aching. He slogged on, his body bent over, trying to angle the end of his shovel to cover the back of his neck, but his arms couldn't hold that position for long and rain was running down into him. He had to get under something, he had to get into a building. Until the worst of this passed over he'd share a pig sty if he had to.

Dusk fell and he slowed at every sloshing step; at least the weather was keeping the world and his wife inside; the road was his. But now he was at the point of coming off it into a field and lying down on any slight slope that would run the rain off him – when just as he thought he'd crumple down where he was, he picked out through the slant of the rain another spire in the distance, tall, disappearing up into the cloud. That meant he was coming to a town or a village. He'd have to be careful. And if it was a city it would be filled with German officers and men. But there might be shelter there…

He couldn't skirt round this place; he'd do Fred no good at all if he was dead in the fields. What was another day either way? He'd got to lie up. He kept to the road, could no more trudge across open sodden land than he could fly. He must shake his head awake and push on for a last chance to lie down and dry out.

The road took him from the open fields into the narrow street of a town. There had to be a doorway where he could empty his boots, run off some of this rain, or an alley leading to a shed or an outhouse. The buildings were two and three storeys high, but the doors were flush with the street, and there was no alley or side road he could slip down. Until, step by step, stifling a sneeze, smothering a cough, he came to what had to be the town square – where the spire he'd seen was on top of the town hall. And now there was life. He pulled back beneath a large statue, across from which he saw the murky lights of a bar: the *Bar de la Poste*. He listened. Against the drum of the rain he heard the sounds of

German soldiers singing inside – and saw a girl come running towards the bar holding a shawl across her head. He couldn't tell her age but she ran like someone young. She reached the door of the bar, took a pitcher from under her shawl and, seeming to brace herself, went inside. Buying wine for her father, probably, or she'd been sent to fetch beer by a soldier on duty.

He hadn't been seen. He hurried across the square, which ran into a road again, and skirted past a long building that seemed to lead out of the town on the other side. Surely there was somewhere to take shelter? It was still drenching down and he'd got to rest, he'd die otherwise. But what was this building he was coming to, yards from the sound of a swollen torrent? It was a church, large, reaching up almost like a cathedral, really big for a small town. Was there shelter here, even under one of the buttresses? He came to an ancient porch that was supported by columns on either side. He could huddle here if he made himself small. Well, he'd have to because he didn't have another footstep in him. Fatigue pulled his shoulders down. It was dark all around, no one would want to be out in this weather, he could lie here and see if he ever woke up again. If he didn't, he'd tried. Perhaps Fred would know one day that he'd tried.

He reached the top step of the porch, then he saw it. The door of the church was open, just an inch, a piece of slate was under the door, holding it ajar. Quickly he ducked inside and replaced the slate.

It was hard to see anything at first; if there was a moon it had dissolved in the rain, but with patience his eyes got used to the gloom.

The church was very old, columns down the sides and vaulting above, the ceiling disappearing into a vast space that could have been the next world. He was suddenly racked with a great shudder and a sneeze and cough that seared his throat and turned him inside out. Water ran off him, out of the drenched coat, through the laceholes of his boots. He leant against a column and emptied them. Where to go now? Lie along a pew, or sit leaning against a column? But what if someone came in: the priest, who could be under the thumb of the Germans? He made himself walk the length of the church and came to the chancel end; and there beneath a curve of arched windows were three steps leading up to an altar table covered by a white cloth. Under there! He'd wring out his coat as best he could, and lie there huddling, pray for a couple of hours' sleep, then hope he could recover enough to get on his way at first light. Already the guns were promising that he wasn't very far from the front line.

He didn't need a pillow, he didn't need any cover; being under the altar and out of sight meant his mind could relax, and with his hand still grasping his shovel he coughed up his lungs and quickly fell into an exhausted sleep.

What was that? What had he heard first? The screaming, or the slamming of the church door – or both at once? Will uncurled, scrambled to his knees, just keeping his head from hitting the underside of the altar.

'Laissez-moi tranquille, sales allemands! Ne me touchez pas!' The girl's voice was strident, shrieking. She screamed again, like an animal at the violent end of its life.

'Halt den Mund! Reiß dich zusammen! Hör auf dich zu wehren, wenn du am Leben bleiben willst.'

He couldn't understand the words but he knew what was going on. He looked out from under the altar cloth. A girl was being dragged down the aisle by two soldiers, one with a lantern. The men were laughing and half falling over each other, drunk, but gripping the girl with a definite intent as she struggled and screamed. And even by the faint, moving lantern-light he could see who she was: the girl who'd gone into the bar with the pitcher.

'Si vous me touchez, je vous tue!' She screamed again, but the soldiers must know that no one could hear.

'Hör auf dich zu wehren oder wir werden dich töten!'

They threw her into a line of pews, stood the lantern at its end so they could see what they were doing. One of them climbed along the pew to hold the girl down on the floor. The other tore off his greatcoat and went for his trousers.

Will crouched there. What could he do? He could lie here, stay secret, let things happen. This sort of thing went on all over, the girl was one of millions treated like this in the war. And he was on a mission to save his brother from Len Castle. If he showed himself, took action, came out, got caught – probably killed – all that was done for. But for Fred's sake he could cover his head and let the world of war spin on.

The girl screamed again, pleaded in a shrieking voice and called for Papa and Mama. Then she stopped, and gurgled – a hand was over her mouth, or a rag had been stuffed into it.

Had he got the guts to do anything, anyway? He'd been ashamed to let Stan Denyer down, but was that him through and through? Had he got any courage anywhere?

The soldier in the aisle started crawling along the seat of the pew. He spat, wiped his mouth, and made a noise like a neighing horse as he reached the girl.

And out came Will. He hadn't intended to do it, but he did. Gripping hard on his shovel he pulled himself from under the altar and started creeping down its steps. He stifled a cough into the bend of his elbow and got himself behind the first of the line of pillars running along the side of the church. This way he could come up behind the soldier who was holding down the girl.

She was kicking at the pew, gurgling, making strangulated screams, while one soldier laughed and the other made encouraging animal noises. Both were intent on what they were about; it was going to be first one, then the other – but Will was damned if he was going to let either of them do what they wanted. If the Germans had invaded England this girl could have been Amy. This wasn't war, it was human brutality.

Neither of the soldiers seemed to suspect that anyone else was there. Both had their eyes down on what was going to happen, all lip-smacking and obscene grunts.

Moving faster, he came from behind a pillar to the end of the pew. The soldier holding her down was using all his force, his head up, but looking at his mate. The other was ready for what he was going to do.

The shovel almost took off his head. It went into his scalp with the sideways cut Will had dreamed of using on Attila the Hun. Blood spurted everywhere. The man shrieked like a wounded horse, and fell onto the girl, dead or dying. She screamed. The assaulting soldier pulled back and grabbed at his trousers as Will ran along the pew seat and swung the shovel again. The girl was up and scrambling away; but the man was quick, going for his gun holster. Will took one more swing and ran for the church door.

The crack of the pistol shocked the church. A pigeon

flapped somewhere up in the vaulting. And here the man came, running at him down the centre aisle, aiming again.

Will took off, out of the church door and down the steps, away, away, away into the night – find some trees, get round a corner, take cover. A huge building loomed before him, could be a mill, with a line of lorries standing parked. He couldn't risk the lost yard of a look around but ran frantically for the building; dodge, hide, he didn't know what. But he heard the shout – and from not far behind.

'Halt! Halt an, Du Schwein!'

Too close, too close! A bridge ran over the road and a sluiced-off mill race foamed beside the swollen torrent of a river that was gushing, swirling and foaming. He climbed onto the parapet.

'Halt!!'

Will jumped, but his boot slipped and he toppled backwards, cracking his head on the parapet's edge, falling into the swirl, his coat and boots dragging him under, no strength in his limbs, gulping down water, consciousness ebbing. His last sensation was of a weird sort of peace. He had tried. *I tried, Fred. And now I'm done for…*

And his dwindling bubbles told their own story.

29

Freddie curled himself up in the church porch, off the ground on a wooden bench. It was a chilly Sunday night and he shivered through the first hours into Monday morning. Forget what had happened tonight with him dancing and shouting at the Zepp killing, tomorrow he'd got to be pretty clever. His mum had always said she could see right through him, he was as honest as the day was long. He wasn't a thief, but tomorrow he was going to have to do some stealing. Something to eat wouldn't be a problem – market food stalls were easy, and there was a drinking fountain up here for a top-up of water when he wanted. What he needed, though, was something warm to wear over what he'd got on; a thick jumper like Quinnell's would have been ideal. He didn't know where he might find himself when he hid on a ship – it might be in a lifeboat for the first couple of days, and they'd be nowhere near warm waters for a long time. But where would he find a jacket or a coat for the taking?

A shop? Too risky. A stall? He wouldn't get near without them getting suspicious; he wouldn't be out on his own looking for clothes. So, where else? And picturing lines of coats, it suddenly came to him. Union Street School! The pegs. The school was near to where he was right now, in a street behind where Amy had worked. It might mean he'd get a later ferry than he'd planned, but if he hung around outside the school till the children went in he could march in after them and skulk around the boys' cloakroom: choose his moment, pick a warm coat, and leg it away. He'd have to risk being seen, but he doubted if his face was on any 'Wanted' posters around Woolwich.

Planning like this, he drifted off to sleep, dreaming of feeling cold. The bench was hard, his head lolled about, he was a million miles from any comfort – but whenever he woke and turned over, his heart warmed at the memory of that Zeppelin crashing down in flames. It had been true. That hadn't been a dream, had it?

He was woken by the light and by the breeze off the river. He didn't know what time it was, but he couldn't stay in the porch here for long: there would be people walking past, which meant he'd better lose himself in Woolwich until it was time for school. He could go down to Rope Yard Rails among the slum streets behind the Empire Theatre, though he'd need to be wary of the rough people, but you never saw a policeman down there, which suited him fine. His dad had told him it was out of bounds to soldiers, and he and Will were forbidden ever to go there. So of course he had gone, just for a look with Don, and Rope Yard Rails would be just right until school time. He couldn't stay up here for long.

He had a quick wash at the water fountain, hands, face and neck – cold outside, but from first opening his eyes his innards had been warmed by thoughts of the night before – seeing that Zeppelin crash down in flames. That had been marvellous. That would have cheered up his mum and dad if they'd looked down and seen it from heaven. He could still see smoke in the sky from here. With a shrug of his shoulders and a jaunt in his step he walked through the churchyard towards Rope Yard Rails.

Along the main road, cleaners were waiting at shop doors to be let in, and a delivery of ink was outside Pryce's Printers. Along in the market the stalls were being pulled out from under the Arsenal wall, with carts like Jimmy Jobling's standing ready to be unloaded, when his stomach made a noise he'd have had to say sorry for once upon a time. He was hungry. Worst of all, the baker's on the corner was sending out a smell of fresh bread that almost made him dizzy. Before he went across to North Woolwich he was going to have to do some pinching from a food stall; there wasn't anything much like this over the other side, and who knew how long he'd be hiding in a lifeboat or in a cargo hold?

But what was that? He knew that sound! He heard it as he was turning away from the market to go along towards Rope Yard Rails. There was no mistaking it. That bell, he knew it, he'd heard it so often; there couldn't be two the same, that cracked ding-dong as it was swung in the air. His stomach heaved. He pressed himself back against the Arsenal wall and looked along the street – and there, coming up to the market to stop outside the Woolwich Infant pub was a sight he knew only too well: Grandad's cart being pulled by 'Orse.

'Best logs! Slow burn ash!'

It was an early morning delivery to the pub – he remembered it, publicans' wives always did a regular wash of their lodgers' sheets; he'd carried kindling through to the back himself. So that shouldn't be any surprise.

No. But who was shouting the odds? It almost had him jumping up and punching the air. On the cart ringing the bell and doing the shouting like always was Uncle Len. Len Castle! Mean-looking, bent over, and with a thick grey scarf wound round his neck. But Len Castle – alive.

Hell-'n'-hailstones!

The man wasn't dead. He hadn't killed him. His neck had a funny twist to it, but it wasn't stopping him humping a sack of logs off the back of the cart.

Freddie Castle wasn't a murderer! Now even if they caught him he wouldn't go to prison for years and years. But he still wasn't going to get caught. He wasn't going back to live and work with those people, not for all the tea in China; although he wasn't going to Australia,

273

either, not any more. If Will came out alive at the end of the war he didn't want to be somewhere his brother would never find him.

Then, no, he wasn't going to run the risk of stealing a coat right now, although he would need food. What he did need straight away was a good think – and he'd do that where he'd already been heading, down Rope Yard Rails.

He left Grandad and Len sorting out the Woolwich Infant and slunk along Beresford Street. He'd nip back to the market when it got busy and look after his belly; in the meantime he'd got a new future to plan.

30

The two army drivers had brought their horses to the river's edge, a wide tree-lined stretch that looked like a watery avenue. But the trees were as cut, bruised and broken as every other tree around the Somme. The river brought branches and debris from the east towards the sea, but the overnight rain had stopped and the river was quieter now, its bank muddy against the swirls and eddies that choked the inlets where the horses could get to the water: nervous, skinny creatures, chafed by tack and pocked by shrapnel, ears erect, eyes flashing at every sound.

With a frightened whinny one of them suddenly reared up.

'Whoa! Steady! What's eating you?'

The driver saw what it was: a body eddying in the flotsam of the storm.

'He can't hurt you, you've seen enough of them.' But he pulled the horse away to find another spot. 'Hang on!' He took another look. The body was face-up, youngish, arms lying across sticks and muck and uprooted weeds – and he could swear one of the hands had moved.

'Charlie!'

'What?' The other driver was holding two horses

himself, but still trying to smoke the cigarette they were sharing.

'Dead 'un here, but alive…'

'What you talking about? Where?'

'Here.'

They both looked at the half-submerged man. And the hand moved again, it definitely moved.

'Pull him out.'

'Push him under. Could be a Fritz.'

They stared, and dragged on their half Woodbines.

'Could be a Tommy, though. Get him out of it, anyhow. It's a good place to water the nags.'

They finished their fags and pulled him out by the boots, stretched him head-down on the bank, one of them pushing on his chest, the other giving his face a good slap and turning it to one side.

The body gurgled, choked and spewed out bile and bits of debris, which ran back to the inlet.

'Get a burial party.'

'I'll get an MO. Gawd, who'd wanna be found by you? I wouldn't!' He went to find a medical orderly.

The other driver bent down to the head again. And this time an eye opened and after a huge guttural cough the man spewed out his stomach, which had the terrible smell of fermented cheese.

'Phew! Worse'n a gas attack!' And he drew the horses away.

It was going to be either Don's house or Amy's. Mrs Brewster always took him in if he hadn't got a key, or she'd have him in for tea if his mum had to go out somewhere. She liked him, he knew; she'd tell Don how he ought to copy his good manners, and how clean his fingernails were. Huh! They weren't very clean right now!

Or there was Amy – who seemed more family than Mrs Brewster because of Will – if Will ever came back. But those were the only two choices: him going to the council and trying to get into The Hollies wouldn't do any good: they'd have him back with Grandad and Uncle Len before he could say knife.

He walked up and down Rope Yard Rails trying to make up his mind. The doors of most of the houses were open, sending out the smell of dirt, and the pavements by the beer houses were still stained from the night before where dogs – or men – had peed. And he'd been right, no one took much notice of him. He was just another dreg.

It didn't take him long to make a decision. A woman in a doorway did it for him. She was in a dirty shirt that must have been her nightdress; she seemed to have come to the door just to look out. And when she saw him she pouted her mouth and lifted the hem of the shirt. He turned and ran off. She'd be about Amy's age – and what a difference. He'd once thought Amy was flitty and stupid with her wispy hats and bits of feather; but he'd changed his mind about her because she'd changed hers, too, ending up proud that Will had volunteered, swapped being behind a counter in Cuff's for slogging away in the Arsenal. What a really nice person she was. Yes, he'd give her a try. And soon. He didn't belong anywhere around here, that was for certain.

He made sure his walk to Eltham took him through the market, where, in spite of the stomach-squeezing smell of fresh bread he made do with a cucumber, which went down a trouser leg. After that it was follow the tram route up to the Artillery, on to Shooters Hill, and – and this was the hard part – past the bombed-site of his old house: the death place of his mum and dad. It turned him over, looking at it shored up, with an empty space up in the open air where his bedroom had once been. The missing house was just a gap. Yes, that's what it was, a *gap*. A big gap in his life. He swallowed so the lump in his throat didn't hurt so much, and he fought to keep the tears out of his eyes. He didn't want to arrive at Amy's looking a sight.

And only now did it strike him. She wouldn't be at home in the day, would she? She'd be at work in the Arsenal. She wouldn't get back till around half-past six in the evening. So now there were more hours to get through, hiding up somewhere – although not as desperately as before. Now he was just a runaway; they couldn't arrest him for murder.

He lost himself in Harrow Meadow, a favourite place for fun in the Quaggy River – mud fights, jumping from side to side, and skinny frolics. And today, on a school day, no one much was around. There was shelter from the chilly breeze down the bank, with the odd plop of a fish for interest, and when the sun was well up it broke through the cloud and gave off a bit of warmth, just right after a night on a hard bench.

He took his timing from the tram passengers. Back at Eltham Church he waited for the Arsenal workers and late shoppers to be dropped off, looking for a sight of Amy, but no luck – and when he thought it was about right he walked through to Boleyn Street. He'd washed and done a couple of other things in the River Quaggy so he felt as clean and presentable as he could, and holding his breath he knocked at her door. Number thirteen – an easy number to remember.

It was opened by a tall woman who stood back in the hallway. 'Yes?' She looked past him as if he might be delivering logs. She was in a white blouse and a black skirt, not a bit like his mum in her afternoon pinny.

'Excuse me, please, is Amy in?'

'"*Amy*"?' The woman – who had to be Mrs Margerison – repeated the name as if he had no right to say it.

'Yes, please. Amy. She knows my brother, Will.'

'Oh! Will. He's your brother, you say?' She looked him over as if that were impossible.

'Yes, ma'am.'

'Amy!' She turned back and called through to the back. 'It's William's brother. Tell me your name? You'd better come in.'

'Frederick.' He stepped inside. 'Fred.'

'Ah.'

'Or Freddie.'

'Three names to go to bed with.' The woman turned to him and smiled.

Amy came through, still drying her face. 'Fred!' She almost pushed her mother out of the way and gave him a big hug. 'I went looking for you, to see how you were. At your grandad's. But they said you'd gone, and they didn't know where…'

'Grandad wasn't so bad – but Uncle Len was horrible. Horrible!'

'I guessed. Will told me about his father and his uncle. He pointed the man out to me once, he was on his log cart, and I've got to say I didn't like the look of him at all.'

'I couldn't stand it any more. The things he said!'

'About your dad?'

'Mostly. Quiet, like, sometimes, and then coming out with it, hateful as you like – all to get at me. He said he was glad my dad was dead.'

'Poor Fred. So what did you do?'

'Enough!' Amy's mother clapped her hands like a teacher. 'Hallways are for *passage*. Parlours are for talking.' She really looked him over now. 'From the look of you you've had an adventure, Frederick. You tell us about that first, then we'll have dinner. And then we'll see what's to be done.' She led the way into the front parlour, where she took the face towel from Amy and laid it across the seat of an upright chair. 'Sit there and tell us.' She crossed her hands in her lap, but Amy was leaning forward with her elbows on her knees.

Freddie told them. He went back to the insults, the fight, him whacking Uncle Len, although not the murder worry, and his plan to start a new life somewhere a long way away.

'Why didn't you come here and tell us you were being bullied by those people?'

Not wanting to admit to the murder worry he could only say, 'I just thought it wasn't fair on you.'

Amy's mother nodded. 'Well. You can go through to the scullery and wash, and when Mr Margerison comes in from business we'll have dinner. And we shall see what we shall see.' She rose, Amy rose, and Freddie got up.

He was taken through the living room into the kitchen and out to the scullery where the washday boiler stood, and with the luxury of a piece of soap he scrubbed his face, his neck and his hands, and he dried them on another luxury, a roller towel. Burying his face in it he realised he hadn't said anything about why he was there. He'd told them his troubles, but he hadn't asked the question he'd come to ask. *Please could he live with them?* It seemed a big thing to ask; they'd got their own lives, their own ways. Look how Amy's mother got dressed up for just a cup of tea.

He went back to Amy in the living room, and to the loud tick of a mantelpiece clock. Should he ask her? Had she guessed what he wanted? Or would they take him to the council with a complaint against Uncle Len? He told her about the shooting down of the Zeppelin, but she'd heard all about it in the Arsenal.

'Oh, didn't they cheer in there, Fred? It was our Pomeroys that made it catch fire and explode. And that was partly your dad, Fred. Wouldn't he have been pleased?'

That lump came back in his throat.

She smiled. And like that they sat waiting for Mr Margerison to come in from business; and for Freddie to find out what his fate was going to be.

Mr Margerison let himself in, and Mrs Margerison went out to him in the hallway. While Amy sat fidgeting, Freddie could hear the mutterings; until Amy's mother put her head around the door.

'Amy. A moment outside, please.'

Amy smiled at him and went out. He heard them all go into the front parlour and close the door behind them. He could hear the voices but he couldn't pick out the words. He'd never felt so strung up. He measured the distance from his seat to the door, he pictured the hallway and he tried to think where the knob was on the front door. He couldn't be sure if he'd come through a gate at the front, or not. Gates swung inwards and that would hold him up. But one thing he was dead certain about: if they thought they were taking him to the council he was going to make a run for it.

He didn't hear the parlour door open, and they made him jump as they came in. He stood up, put on the look of Mrs Brewster's polite Freddie, but he was really a boy on his toes.

Mr Margerison was a shortish man with a crease on his forehead where he'd been wearing his bowler hat. He came across to shake hands. 'So you're William's brother, then?'

'Yes, sir.'

The man had a big moustache, was stocky, and his voice was quite high. He took out a pair of wiry spectacles and lifted his chin to stare at him. It was like being in front of the headmaster – on a day when Freddie knew he wasn't going to get the cane. *But what would he be getting?*

'Your house was bombed by a damned Zeppelin…'

Mrs Margerison coughed.

'…Tragically, your parents were killed, but you were found alive…'

'Yes, sir. Dug out, sir.' He was going to get all the sympathy he could.

'Oh, please drop the "sir"; we can decide on nomenclature later.'

Freddie didn't know what that meant. 'Yes.' A clear of the throat.

'And you were taken to live with your relatives, your grandfather and your uncle in Plumstead…'

Amy cut in. 'Who hated Fred's father.'

That was waved away without a look in her direction.

'…and you assaulted your uncle after a particularly vitriolic insult aimed at your father…'

'At my *dead* father.' Pile it on. 'Who couldn't answer back.'

There was no change in the look on Mr Margerison's face. '…and you ran away and lived rough for a few days.'

Freddie nodded. It was hard saying 'yes' if he couldn't say 'sir'.

'And you don't wish to return to the care of your grandfather…?'

Amy again. '*Care?*'

'No I don't.'

'So, what to do? What to do?' Mr Margerison turned to his wife, and to Amy. But it seemed as if it had already been decided in the parlour because Amy's mother was smiling.

There was a long pause, like the headmaster holding on to the name of the Victor Ludorum until the very last second.

'Then you shall come here with us. You shall stay here, pending your brother's safe return from France, God willing.'

Dear God! He couldn't believe it. He wanted to put his arms around Mr Margerison's business jacket and hug a million creases into it. 'Thank you, sir.' *He could live here!* They didn't want him to go back to Grandad and Len Castle.

Mrs Margerison ruffled his hair. 'We'll clear out the back bedroom for you. And we'll call you Fred, the way Amy does. And I shall be Aunt Beatrice, and Mr Margerison is Uncle Alfred.'

Freddie bowed.

'But you'll go back to school; I shall take you tomorrow with a letter from…Uncle Alfred…to explain your relationship to us through your brother. We'll put some gloss over that, and the fact that he's being held prisoner of war by the Germans. We shall say nothing about the other family members, the school probably knows nothing about them, and your absence is due to your injuries from the bomb. You were admitted to the Cottage Hospital, that's all the headmaster needs to know.'

'Keep cavey for those two, though.' Amy put her hand on Freddie's shoulder. 'They've got the legal right over us, and they'll have you back working for them as soon as you're the age. I could tell from what they said that they want to find you.'

'The same school, am I going to?' There was a school nearby, Eltham National School known as Roper Street; they won all the sports meetings.

'Long legs like yours?' Amy's mother said. 'It's not far to Grangehill Road. They know you there. We'd have to start from scratch with all sorts of awkward questions at Roper Street.'

'Yes.'

Mr Margerison took off his jacket. 'So I think a jolly good wash all over, my boy, and a shirt I've grown out of, and a pair of my old harrier shorts for tonight...'

'And school on Wednesday, Alfred. He can't go in running shorts, *or* in what he's wearing.' Mrs Margerison's face said it all. 'After I've fitted him out at Cuff's will be soon enough.'

'Splendid.' His new Uncle Alfred rubbed his hands. 'Now, I think we should get our chops around a chop or two, don't you?'

'It's only brisket,' Amy and her mother said together.

The man looked disappointed, but sunshine filled Freddie's belly. Meat of any sort was a feast compared with what he'd been eating for the last two days.

And right then the cucumber burped on him.

'Sorry,' he said. 'All.'

Two back bedrooms, so different. His room at Grandad's hadn't been much different in size from this, but the bed had been like sinking into porridge and they'd left their own bits and pieces in there – two old suitcases on top of the wardrobe and three Wellington boots in a sack. But here his bed had a proper mattress like his bed at home, the sheets smelled of lavender, and the wardrobe and chest-of-drawers had been cleared out especially, with sheets of greaseproof paper at the bottom of everything.

They made no bones about having an extra mouth to feed, unlike the other two who'd kept on about merchant ships being sunk by German submarines and every mouthful having to be earned. Here the food was definitely cut down but no one made a song and dance about it. And, the best thing of all, they talked about Will.

Amy said she'd written to him and told him the bad news, and said the Red Cross people had been pretty confident the letter would get through, sooner or later. Now she'd write again with something a lot better to say.

It all seemed the next best thing to being at home. *Next* best and a long way short, but after that devil's bomb who could ask for more?

It even seemed a little bit as if these people could get to love him…

31

Len Castle was slumped at the kitchen table in Kashgar Road.

'Oi! Are you drunk already?'

'On this?' Len waved his bottle of London Ale at his father. 'Watered-down piddle. Ruddy government! I'm wore out, that's what.' He lifted his head, rubbed at his neck and slumped back again.

'Serves you right, then. Op'ning your big mouth with the boy. Showin' your hate. We could do with 'im more'n ever now it's all go, not much coal around an' people cryin' out for logs. We could make a little fortune with that other pair of hands. Can't saw 'em up an' get 'em out fast enough.'

Len lifted himself and swigged the last of the bottle. 'Should'a tried harder looking for him...'

'Well, I'll tell you. He's still got to be skulking somewhere. He's run off frightened for whacking you, but where's he gonna go? Up the Ritz? He's a bleedin' orphan! An' kith an' kin to us, no good to no one else. We'll 'ave to find him, that's what.'

Len slumped again. 'Gawd, I'll end up sleeping 'cross this table, I swear I won't make them stairs tonight. Ain't got a muscle to call me own.'

'So you can lay off the licrish an' concentrate on gettin'

him back.' The old man sat down and rubbed round and round his bald head. 'Let me put me thinking cap on…'

Len snorted, or it could have been a snore.

'…Where does he know? Eltham. Where they used to live in Woolwich is all pulled down, there's no one to take him in there. But he would've had mates round Well Hall, wouldn't he?'

Snore. A definite snore.

'We're deliverin' to Eltham, Thursday. We'll ask around. Get in a back kitchen with some missus an' ask, all casual. See if someone's took him in an' packed 'im off to school. Them Arsenal boys mostly go to the same schools, don' they?'

A deeper snore, and the empty bottle fell out of Len's hand and rolled away.

'An' he's legally ours till he's twenny-one. Then the way things are going wi' coal, we could start hoping this war don' end too soon.' He got up with a light in his eye. 'I wonder you hadn't thought of that before, Leonard.'

But Len had the last word. He came to just enough to lift a menacing face at his father. 'Yeah, we'll get him somehow…an' he can do us a real good turn.' He burped. 'After I've beat the livin' daylights out of him…'

They gave Freddie a lot of attention at school. The bombing had been reported in the *Kentish Independent*. He was put into his old class, which was smaller now that some of the older ones had left. But Wally Quinnell was still there, wearing the same jumper and with the same sneer on his face, jealous of the boys crowding round him and wanting to know how terrible being bombed had been. The good news was, there was no problem over him coming back. After reading Mrs Margerison's letter Mr Perrit didn't question where he was living, and he didn't want to know anything about his missing weeks from school. She wrote about blood relations as being 'not applicable', which gave the impression that there weren't any, and her letter was vague about how long he'd been in hospital. Only if she were questioned, Mrs Margerison had said, would she tell him about the illegal child labour and abusive treatment meted out by Freddie's uncle and his grandfather. But she doubted if the headmaster would go running to the council for verification.

Freddie could tell he'd grown a bit since he was here before. His knees touched the underside of the desk, and sitting down he could lift it and rock the iron frame.

The bad news was, Wally Quinnell hadn't changed a bit. After a couple of days when things had got back to normal and people were leaving him alone, Quinnell started his old goading again.

'Pris'ner of war? *Pris'ner of war?* Your brother? 'Ands up, was it? "Take me, Fritz, I don' wanna fight."'

'Shut up!'

'"Look, I'm wavin' me white hankie! Get me out of it. Let me come an' live wi' you Germans."'

They were in a corner of the playground where Freddie was eating a piece of cold toast Amy had wrapped up for playtime. He looked at Quinnell. The boy's face was twisted as he spat out his bile.

'My brother's stickin' 'is bayonet in 'em, an' your brother's rollin' over like a yeller belly.'

Freddie would have walked away before; he'd have let the boy shout his insults at his backside. But not today; not after everything that had happened to him. That's what Quinnell expected him to do, but Freddie had changed, and grown. Instead, he placed his feet apart the way he had for bringing down his axe. He leant forward and stared Quinnell in the eyes. 'Why don't you shut your dirty gob, Quinnell? Why don't you run away and finish dribbling down your smelly jumper? Why don't you clear off into that corner over there and piss yourself with fear, because in about three seconds I'm gonna knock your block clear off your neck. Then I'm gonna kick it round the playground, pick it up and shove it up your backside.'

Quinnell just stared back, shook his head as if he couldn't have heard right. He was clenching his fists, getting ready to hit out. Freddie had never seen the boy look so shocked. No one in the school had ever stood up to Wally Quinnell like this, not even the leavers.

'Come on. Have a try. See how big you are, Quinnell. Let's have your best.'

Freddie would get hurt. He knew he'd get hurt – and hurt badly. Quinnell was a tough nut, a street scrapper, a dirty fighter. He'd seen bigger boys bloody and blubbing on the ground begging him to stop kicking them. It was impossible to come out of a fight with Quinnell looking anything like you did before it started. But Quinnell had got to be stood up to, and now was the time. Freddie didn't even take up a fighting stance but stood there with fire in his eyes – while his heart raced like a model steam engine. But he knew. He knew right now that he was going to be a match for this loudmouth. He was bigger than before, he was stronger, he was one hundred per cent sure he could scrap this boy and win hands down. When he went in the army one day he was going to be a brave, fighting soldier, but right now whatever happened to him he was going to make mincemeat of Quinnell.

And Quinnell seemed to know it, too. He stood there with his snarly mouth open. Then, 'Can't take a joke, can yer, Castle? That's your trouble.' His voice was dry and croaky.

'And your trouble's gonna be if you ever try a joke like that again. Anything about my brother. Now piss off and go and play with the girls.'

Quinnell waited a full five seconds, weighing things up for the final time before he turned away, took a step or two, and swung back round. 'Play with the girls yourself. Jus' don' come near me no more.' He walked off, turning his strides into a run and taking a pretend kick at a ball that wasn't there.

Freddie watched him go, dusting his hands, actually dusting his hands like the winner in a cowboy film, while the rush of blood to his head and the joy of victory would have had him off his feet if he hadn't been standing so square.

Now he knew for sure he wasn't the coward he'd been before. And wouldn't old Will be proud of him for that?

32

The Royal Field Artillery officer interviewed Will in the Casualty Clearing Station at Saint-Vaast-en-Chaussée, deliberately set close to the railway. He'd been told he was lucky to be there, west of Amiens behind French and British lines – carried by a swollen Somme which would normally have left him high and dry in German-held territory. The river ran through shallow stretches between St Quentin and Amiens and these had saved his life. The cold water had brought him back from the knock on his head, and he'd bobbed up and gone under, bumped about on the river bed, bobbed up again and been sent sweeping and swirling, bruised and with his lungs half full with muck and water, but just about alive.

But the officer wasn't impressed with his survival, nor with his Observation detachment, nor his escape from imprisonment nor his trek north-west.

'You should have gone south. Got to Rheims.'

The man was tall, thin and fluty-voiced; in a roomful of officers Will would have saluted him last. He had a Medical Corps corporal with him, and a Red Cross nursing sister.

She gave a medical report to the officer. 'Pneumonic lungs, sir; he's inhaled a quantity of foreign substance.'

'But he'll live?'

'It's thought he'll recover in due course, sir, when the lungs are fully aspirated.'

The officer cleared his own throat. 'Well, you're a lucky gunner, Castle. You're alive, and these people seem to think you'll pull through.' He nodded as if that was thanks to him and began to move off. 'And the next...?'

'Sir.' Will pulled himself up off the stretcher. 'I had...' The words were hard to get out, he'd hardly croaked more than a 'yes' and a 'thank you' since he'd been brought here. 'I escaped...for a reason.'

'Of course. Your duty.'

'Yes, sir, and...my brother.'

'A brother gunner?'

'A real brother, sir, in England. A boy.'

The officer pulled a distasteful face. 'You're seeking compassionate repatriation?'

'Sir.'

With great difficulty, in a weak and painful voice, Will told him about Fred, about the Zeppelin bomb that had orphaned his brother in London, and about the danger the boy was in from a violent member of their own family.

The officer hardly seemed to listen. 'What's your right hand like, gunner? Intact?'

He lifted his head and nodded.

'And your left?'

He nodded again.

'How many legs have you got?'

Will held up two fingers – the polite way. He sank back exhausted, and the officer shut his notebook.

'Well, Castle, if you had one leg and you could lie back and kick a breech block shut you'd still be a fighting gunner. Every man in France has got a problem or a tragedy back at home. Yours isn't the only family that's fallen victim to the Zeppelins. Your brother's with his grandfather and his uncle, a darned sight better off than thousands – and there's only your word about bad blood; you could be trying to pull a Blighty one. Won't stand up! It won't stand up! We're at war, man, at war...'

Will closed his eyes.

'...I'm a gunner, you're a gunner, and what do gunners do? They fire guns!' He looked at the corporal and at the sister and made to move off again. 'A bit of clearing out of your inside and a couple of days on recovery rations and you'll be returned to your battery, or one damned like it. And when we've beaten the bally Boche, Castle, we can *all* go home and see to our families. Victorious.'

Will tried not to cough but he had to.

'Excuse me, sir.' The sister turned to the officer.

'Sister?'

'Wouldn't Gunner Castle be due home leave anyway, in the normal course of events?'

'What battery were you in, gunner?'

'"C", sir.'

The officer referred to his notebook again. '"C" battery of Number Nine Division's had its leave. They're back on station, where this man belongs.' He shut the book with a little slap. 'Lead on, Corporal.' And he went on to the next bed.

The sister lingered. She bent to him. 'I had a stepfather like your uncle. A bully. Hateful. I couldn't wait to get away.' She smiled. 'I'm very sorry.'

Will croaked a thank you. But his heart wasn't in it. It wasn't in anything any more. What he'd been doing, the getting away from Attila the Hun, the long trek across country, the killing of the soldier in the church, the near drowning in the Somme – all that and he was left back where he couldn't get to England to sort out his brother.

The sister called two stretcher-bearers over. 'Cover him with a blanket and take him to the station,' she said. 'Platform Two.' She tied a band around his arm with '2' on it.

Will had been told what that meant. The railway took clearing station patients to different base hospitals, one of which would treat him and send him on from there. Back to his battery.

The sister bent to him again. 'Cough a lot,' she prescribed. 'Wheeze it out. Noisily is best, as loud as you can.' And she followed the officer and the corporal to where more decisions were being made.

* * *

Len Castle stood by 'Orse, guarding the cartload of logs. He was outside Grangehill Road School at the boys' entrance in Craigton Road, while his father stood behind a tree around the corner, where the girls came out. It was dinnertime on Thursday, their delivery day for Eltham.

Len was ready. He'd cleared a space on the back of the cart and rolled a tarpaulin ready for smothering a kicking boy. They'd drawn a blank at Well Hall, but if the boy had been taken in by anyone else in the area he'd likely be sent back to his old school. They were giving it a go, anyway. Nothing ventured, nothing gained when it came to making more money.

The boys were coming out. Some ran, some sauntered, some stopped to play glass alleys against the wall of a front garden – dominated by a big boy in a rough jumper and dockers' boots. But there was no sign of Freddie. As the last of the boys came out, Len Castle emerged from behind the tree and checked in the playground. No one was coming across it, nor down the steps from the school building. He walked across the road to the boys playing marbles.

'Freddie Castle – come to school today, did 'e?'

'Nah.'

'You sure?'

'Who wants to know?' The biggest boy stood up.

'Someone with a bit o' good news for a boy called Freddie Castle.'

The boys stopped playing.

''E don' go 'ome to dinner. Some don't. 'E brings sandwiches.'

'Ah.'

'You 'is dad?'

'Uncle.'

The other boys stood up, the game over. They looked at one another as if they knew more about Freddie Castle than they wanted to let on.

'What time d'you come out? 'S afternoon?'

'Quarter past four,' the big boy told him.

Len Castle pulled out his watch. 'Obliged,' he said, and he flipped a silver three-penny bit onto the pavement: 'Scramble!' – before heading off around the corner to tell the news to his father.

Freddie's stomach rolled when they told him Quinnell had given him away. Some of them knew how he'd really got some family but didn't want to live with them, and Don knew all the truth of what had gone on. Now they'd found him! They'd tracked him down, and Len had asked what time school came out – which meant he and Grandad would be in the street waiting. Why couldn't the boys have told him in the playground? He could have made a run for it out of the gate instead of being trapped in the classroom doing English.

Or should he go to Mr Perrit and tell him the truth? The trouble was, the headmaster had already been told another truth by Amy's mother. There wasn't supposed to be a Grandad and an Uncle Len around – so why would he be believed now? No – a hundred-to-one he'd be turned over to his rotten family.

He put up his hand.

'What is it?' Mr Davis had finished chalking up a board-full of grammar questions and was sitting back at his desk as if it had exhausted him.

'Please can I go to the boys', sir?'

'No. You've barely come in.' The teacher rubbed at his grey moustache. 'You should go at the right time, and this isn't it. Carry on with the exercise.'

How could anyone do grammar when their life was going to be turned upside down at a quarter past four? He copied the first sentence.

'The boy stood on the burning deck.'

Single-underline *'boy'* and *'deck'*, they're nouns. Double-underline *'stood'*, that's a verb. Put a wavy line under *'burning'*, that's an adverb – or is it an adjective? And what the heck are the subject and the object? Well, he knew what his object was. Dodge those two outside and somehow get to Amy's.

He worked on until the end of the lesson – a page of rubbish answers – and although English ran straight into

Geography, Mr Davis did give him a few minutes to go to the boys' lavatory. Was this his chance, then, before hometime? But climbing up to look out through the lowest windowpane he nearly came off the radiator. Who was standing outside the girls' gate, waiting there already, across the road with a good view of the playground and the school? Grandad.

He jumped down, ran through a cloakroom to the other side of the building where he could look out on the boys' side. And there, of course, was Len Castle, prowling like a watchman, his neck still done up and twisted; and in his hand was a short log, which didn't look as if it was being held up for sale.

Hell-'n'-hailstones! What could he do? Risk the third gate, the Babies'? But that department was down different stairs, and he'd never get past Mrs Purnell and her cluckers. The terrible truth was, those devils outside were part of the Castle family – the same as him – and the pair of them would be well able to spin a good yarn about him half-killing his uncle.

Which meant that if he couldn't get out of the gates now or at hometime he'd have to wait and find some place to hide in the school – use all the coming and going when the bell went to get down in the basement, or up in a turret room. Then he could stay there till it was dark and break a window to get out.

Yes, that's what he'd do. But he'd got to do it sharp on

the bell – because when he didn't go out at hometime, a hundred to one those two would come in to find him.

He went back to class and sat there, no will to concentrate on Geography or Nature Study. So what was it going to be? Down or up? Basement or turret – and which turret: which one was likely to have an unlocked cubby-hole?

'Are you with us, Castle?'

'Yes, sir.'

'Then answer the question.'

He hadn't heard the question, and for a couple of seconds he wasn't even sure whether it had been about adjectives, Australia or autumn.

'Two hundred lines after school for dreaming. You'll stay behind and write, *"So I awoke, and behold it was a dream." John Bunyan*. And the answer, Lane?'

'Carbon dioxide, sir.'

'Carbon dioxide,' Mr Davis repeated.

It was oxygen Freddie wanted. This was even worse now. Staying behind to write lines meant he'd be supervised, and let out of the building after all the others had gone, and Quinnell would definitely have told Len he'd been kept in. It was going to be all up with him. He wouldn't get to tell Amy, and it was a certain bet the man would make sure he never ran off again. And what would he do to him in revenge for that crack around his neck with the log? His life was going to be worse of a hell than before.

There was a knock at the classroom door. Every move, every sound in the school made his heart beat faster. A large figure loomed through the crinkles of the glass. What was this now? Had those two come in already?

It was the schoolkeeper, Mr Churchway. 'Castle, Mr Davis. The headmaster wants to see Castle.'

'Well I hope he gets more joy from him than I can.' The teacher gestured for Freddie to go with him.

Blast! There'd be no getting away from Mr Churchway; he'd been sent especially and he'd deliver him to the headmaster like a prison guard. And in any case, where could he run? He'd be seen going off whatever direction he took, up or down the school stairs. He'd definitely had it now! Grandad and Len had come into the school, they'd told the headmaster the fact of being his family, they'd have proof with them, and they'd be allowed to take him away – which meant that Amy wouldn't even know what had happened until she came up to the school tomorrow to find out why he hadn't gone home. And by then those two would be sitting on him hard, probably have him locked in the bedroom or the cellar. And what could Amy do, anyway? She wasn't blood. And even her mother wouldn't be able to make anyone believe that someone who'd half-killed his uncle should be given a new home.

Mr Perrit's door was shut, but Freddie could hear an old man's voice. He stared at the varnished woodwork. He'd faced this door a good few times, ready for a ticking off or a swipe of the cane and he knew every knot in it, although the grainy swirls had never looked so scary, they were like little grimacing faces.

Mr Churchway knocked – and for two seconds there was one less hand to grab at him. Could he run, a quick last chance? But with the other hand he was gripped hard by the shoulder. No chance now, no duck out and away, no chase, no chance to put up a fight. This was the end. He was done for.

'Enter.'

He went in. The headmaster was lighting his pipe. But the first thing Freddie took in was the soldier, standing there in his uniform with his head slightly bowed, serious stuff, a man with a sad message. He felt the plummet of his guts. That was why the soldier was here. They'd sent him from the Royal Artillery to give him the bad news. Will was dead. Will had been starved or executed in some prisoner-of-war camp in Germany, and he was about to be told the terrible truth.

The soldier lifted his head as if to do the telling. But he was smiling – first there was the gleam of his teeth and then the sparkle of his eyes.

'Fred!'

A soldier? Yes! But not any soldier! It was Will.

Different. Thinner. Older. Ill. *But it was Will!*

'Crikey Dick!'

'Language, Castle!'

Freddie ran at his brother, threw his arms around his waist. 'How did you...?'

'Escaped, Fred. Nearly drowned in the Somme. Did for my lungs,' Will wheezed it out in an old voice that wasn't his. 'But a Red Cross sister took pity and put me on the railway platform with all the gas victims instead of the "return-to-unit" boys. Platform Two instead of Platform One.' Will was breathing in and out with difficulty, the way their dad had done. 'At base hospital they listened properly...explosives and poisons in the Somme...and sent me for home leave...up the road at the Royal Herbert Hospital.'

'Will...' Freddie didn't know where to put himself; he stood there and cried into Will's tunic, great tears of happiness as he wept his heart out.

'So it's home for you to Amy...'

Freddie had got no words, just more and more choking and tears. And he'd have gladly done it all in front of Wally Quinnell.

'Come on, then, Fred... Let's get off and start being the real Castle family again...'

Mr Perrit patted Freddie on the head, ruffled his hair, for a moment more like a dad than a headmaster. 'Good luck to you, Castle.'

'Thank you, sir.' But as Freddie walked out of the office with Will he was silently thanking God that he'd just had the biggest heap of good luck going.

Ernst's letter arrived a week after Rachel had received official notification of his death on active duty, so when it came it seemed unreal. Had there been a mistake? Was Ernst alive after all? Had they mixed him up with someone else and he was writing to reassure her that High Command had got it wrong and he was alive at the Zeppelin base? The handwriting on the envelope was definitely his, looking just the same as all the other letters he'd written to her – the firm colour of the ink, the cheerful cursive loops and careful commas of the address – all looking strangely alive. Rachel ripped the envelope open, her eyes wide to take in the important news in one look. And any hope immediately evaporated.

Dearest Rachel,
    The fact that you are reading this letter means that I am dead, and by now you will probably know how and when I died.
    I want you to know how much I love you, how happy my life has been since we met at Rosh Hashanah in October 1910, and how much I love our daughter Josefine who will grow to be as beautiful as you and bring you joy throughout your life.

Do not grieve. We will meet again in the paradise of Shamayim and spend eternity together; but until our spirits reunite please know that I will look over you and Josefine, willing peaceful and happy lives for you in the years to come.

Ich liebe dich.

Shalom.

Erno

X

And the signature was strong and firm, the mark of a brave man, the ink running just a little as Rachel's tears fell upon the page.

Will and Freddie walked across the playground together, two soldiers, Freddie with his shoulders back. But there was a worry twisting at his stomach. Those two would still be outside; they'd been watching. Quinnell had told them he was at school today and no one had come out of the building yet; it wasn't hometime for a while.

So what would happen in the street? They couldn't take him away with them, Will was his next-of-kin, but in their hatred they could still do a load of terrible things. Should he warn Will, perhaps go back into school until they'd gone?

'Will...'

'I know. I've seen them. Come on.'

And there sure enough was Len Castle, who'd spotted them and was coming over from the log cart, still gripping that chunk of wood like a weapon, pointing it at them with a look of victory on his face.

'Oi, soldier! Brought bad news for the boy? Oh, what a shame! What a terrible shame!' Len laughed, a sewer sound. 'Well, I don't know where you're off to with him, taking his bad news to wherever he's living, but he's ours, see? I'm his uncle. Me an' my father's his next of kin an' we've got the papers to prove it. So stand aside, I'll have him, if you please.' He was coming on, one hand holding the log, the other ready to grab hold of Freddie.

What was Will going to do? He looked thin enough to be knocked down by a feather. Len could do some real damage before he went off.

Freddie soon found out. Will marched towards Len and met him at the kerb. He halted and put his hand into his tunic. *A gun, a pistol?* – what was he going to pull out? But he went deep inside to his shirt and fished out his dog tag and held it in front of Len's face.

'Gunner Castle.' Will's voice was still weak but somehow it came out sounding full of menace. 'Gunner William Castle, Sam Castle's son. And next of kin to Fred…'

Len's head went back.

'…And if you want a family fight, *Uncle Len*, I'll take you on any time – my fighting strength isn't in my voice.

I'll lick you like a stick of old liquorice – for Fred, for my mum, and for my dad. Understand? Have you got that, you sick old man?' He suddenly shot out a hand and grabbed Len by the throat, a trained soldier's grip.

Freddie went cold. What would Len do now? Would he take this assault – or would he knock Will down, hit him with that chunk of wood? He could see him thinking about it, almost lifting his arm to strike. But Will didn't move – except to lift his chin and stare hard into Len's eyes, before suddenly letting go of the man's throat and rasping at him, 'Now get off out of it!'

Len blinked. He blinked first, and swallowed – as Grandad came along the pavement from the other school entrance.

''Ere, what's this? There's no need for this. Leonard, are you threat'ning one of our brave soldiers? I could hear you round the corner.'

'It's Sam's ruddy boy.' Len rubbed at his throat.

'I know. Freddie.'

'No, the soldier.'

'Ah. Oh, is it?' Grandad looked Will up and down, taking it all in, and Freddie saw on him the face of a loser, and one who knew he'd lost. 'Come on.' Grandad pulled Len away. 'Back on the cart. There's no more to do here.'

Len growled something and went with him, staring his hatred back over his shoulder, and treading in a heap of 'Orse's manure in the middle of the road.

Will put his arm around Freddie's shoulders. 'I didn't stand up to him for me, Fred, or for you… I stood up to him for Dad. He'd have seen off that toe-rag any time.'

'Orse pulled the log cart away, Grandad's and Len's hunched shoulders going off along Grangehill Road; and for a few moments Will and Freddie stood there in silence…until Sam Castle's sons, thinking the same brothers' thoughts, looked up towards the sky. Will saluted, and so did Freddie.

'We'll be all right, Dad,' Freddie said. 'God bless.'

AUTHOR'S NOTE

The German Zeppelin airship L31 dropped its bomb on a house in Well Hall Road, Eltham, south London, in the early hours of 25th August, 1916. The explosion killed a munitions worker, Frederick Allen, his wife Annie and their eleven-year-old daughter Gladys, as well as their lodger Annie Tunnell, whose husband was serving in France. Whilst using the real raid as a basis for that Zeppelin bombing, in the story the Well Hall Road house has the fictitious Castle family living in it.

The book is dedicated to the memory of those who died that night, and to the millions of others who were killed in World War One and those who had to live with injuries and incapacities afterwards.

Shadow of the Zeppelin is fiction based on fact. Incidents occurring on many Zeppelin raids have been condensed into fewer sorties, and I have brought forward the opening of the Royal Flying Corps airfield at Sutton's Farm by a month. Zeppelin L13 and later Super Zeppelin L31 bombed London on many occasions, but while Petty Officer Ernst Stender is an invented character, his airship commander *Kapitänleutnant* Heinrich Mathy really existed, a favourite of Count Zeppelin and fêted in Germany as a wartime hero. In reality the shooting down of the L31 on 1st July, 1916 occurred some miles north of the Royal Albert Dock, at Potters Bar. All members of the crew jumped, and died.

Another condensation is the merging of the real RFC fliers Second Lieutenants Wulstan Tempest, John Slessor, J.I. Mackay and William Leefe Robinson into the RFC's Second Lieutenant George Simmonds. It was Wulstan Tempest who shot down Mathy's L31. He had joined the RFC following his wounding as an officer of the King's Own Yorkshire Light Infantry at the second battle of Ypres in May 1915. Left with a limp and rheumatic gout he retrained as a flyer. For his bravery that night in October 1916 he was awarded the Distinguished Service Order (DSO), but he was later shot down and killed over the Western Front in 1917. He was twenty-seven.

Will Castle's character and story are invented but based on true battle offensives.

Mark Sheridan was a popular music hall comedian, singer and dancer – very big in his day – who starred in his revue 'Winkles' on tour and in London. His famous song 'I Do Like to be Beside the Seaside' is still sung by holidaymakers.

Four hundred women working in munitions factories in World War One died from handling shells containing TNT.

The airship raids on Britain claimed 557 lives and caused injuries to 1,358 men, women, and children.

Casualty statistics for World War One vary, and civilian deaths are difficult to estimate, but rough totals are ten million military and seven million civilian deaths. The allies lost something like six million military, the Axis four million. At least two million servicemen and women died from diseases, and six million were reported missing, presumed dead.

BACKGROUND READING:

The First World War, Paul Dowswell, Usborne 2007
ISBN 9780746088326

Tommy, First World War Soldier, Chris McNab, Pitkin 2012
ISBN 9781841653693

Forgotten Voices of the Great War, Max Arthur, Ebury Press 2002
ISBN 9780091888879

The World War One Source Book, Philip J. Haythornthwaite, Arms & Armour Press 1996
ISBN 9781854093516

Zeppelins: German Airships 1900–40, Charles Stephenson, Osprey Publishing 2004
ISBN 9781841766928

London 1914–17 – The Zeppelin Menace, Ian Castle, Osprey Publishing 2008
ISBN 9781846032455

ACKNOWLEDGEMENTS

I am grateful to many people who assisted with this book: Paul Evans, librarian, Royal Artillery Museum 'Firepower' at Woolwich; the staff of the Greenwich Heritage Centre; Terry Charman, Senior Historian at the Imperial War Museum; Indy Sandhu at the Guildhall Museum, Rochester; the staff of the Local History Library, Southwark; Roger Newlyn of the Society for Sailing Barge Research; D.S. Richards, military historian; and Iris, David and Jonathan Ashley.

I am especially grateful to my Orchard editors Megan Larkin and Rosalind Turner, and to my son, Chris Ashley.

Look out for more books by the award-winning
BERNARD ASHLEY...

PB: 978-1-40831-392-3 / eBook: 978-1-40831-662-7

*Charlie came through a dark mist with his head
pounding and his stomach looping.*

Where was he?

What had happened?

Had a bomb gone off?

www.orchardbooks.co.uk

No Way to Go

Bernard Ashley

*'A tautly written, tough talking
teenage crime story…'*
JACQUELINE WILSON

Amber is shocked when
her brother falls to his
death from a tower block.
She's convinced it wasn't
an accident, and so begins
her journey to discover the
truth and bring some kind
of justice for Connor. With
twists, turns and a fabulous
multi-layered plot, Bernard
Ashley has created a
thrilling and engrossing
tale. Set in south east
London, this is an incredibly
gritty and absorbing novel.

PB: 978-1-40830-239-2 / eBook: 978-1-40831-532-3

www.orchardbooks.co.uk